The Sailor Without a Sweetheart

Katherine Grant

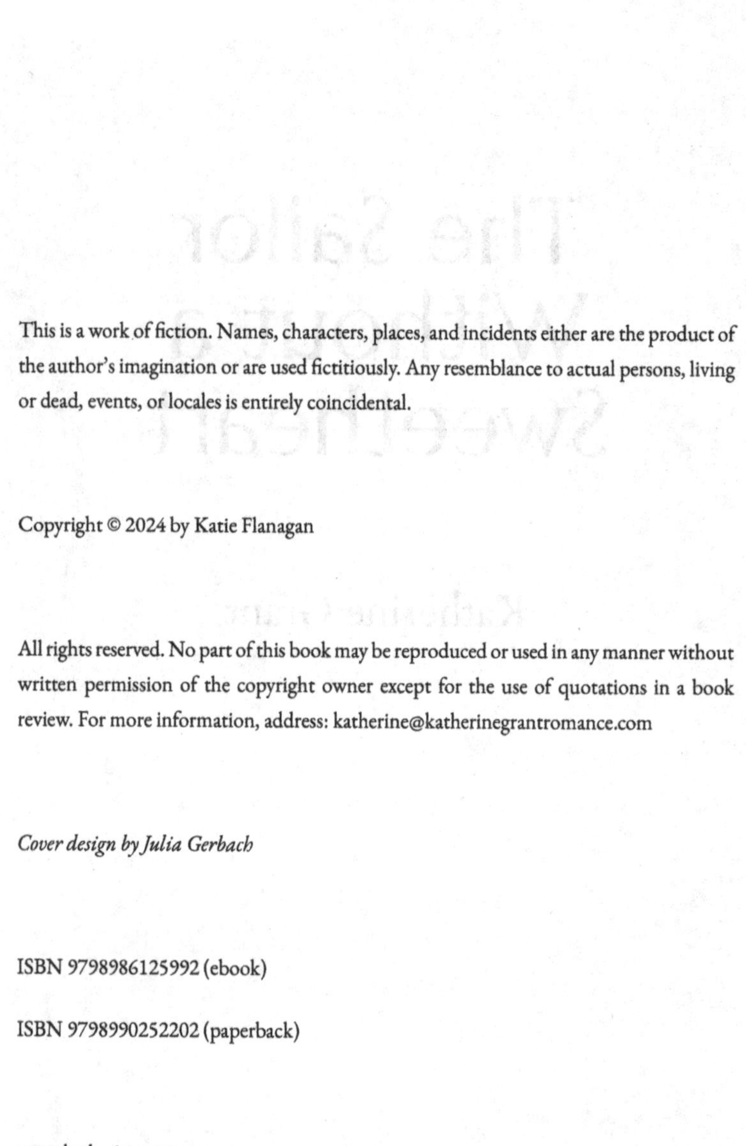

Cover design by Julia Gerbach

ISBN 9798986125992 (ebook)

ISBN 9798990252202 (paperback)

www.katherinegrantromance.com

CONTENTS

ALSO BY KATHERINE GRANT

The Countess Chronicles:

The Ideal Countess
New Year's Masquerade
The Duchess Wager
The Husband Plot

The Prestons:

The Baron Without Blame

The Viscount Without Virtue
The Governess Without Guilt
The Charmer Without a Cause
The Sailor Without a Sweetheart

Northfield Hall Novellas

(an unordered series for the mood reader)
The Hellion of Drury Lane
It's In Her Kiss
Three Nights With Her Husband
Letters to Her Love

Plus, a free short story, The Spinster, available exclusively at www.katherinegrantromance.com

For content advisories, please visit www.katherinegrantromance.com/contentadvisories

PROLOGUE

Swanhill House, 10 miles northeast of
Portsmouth, England

Late summer 1814

The hedges poked Nate Preston in the back as he waited,
but he hardly even noticed.

He was too excited. Anxious. Excited. A little anxious, but
even more excited.

At any moment, the Honorable Amy Lamplugh would emerge from the great house at the end of the drive. He could picture her now: hugging her arms around her chest, sticking to the shadows as she hurried through the dusk, a smile igniting across her lips—no, her whole face!—when she spotted him.

She wouldn't have much. This was to be a proper elopement, done under the cover of darkness and in disguise. They would travel to London by stagecoach as a working couple. They would get themselves a room in an inn, pretending they were already married, until Nate could procure a special license from the archbishop at Lambeth Palace.

And then it wouldn't be a fiction or a wish or a dream at all.

Amy would be his wife, and he her husband, and the rest of their lives would be decided.

First, however, she had to show up.

Nate shifted his weight. He had been waiting for half an hour or so; when he'd first taken his position in the hedge at the edge of Swanhill House's park, the sun had shone long golden rays across the summer fields. Now the sky burned orange in a last gasp of sunset. Before long, they would have only the light of the waxing moon to guide them to the coaching inn.

It didn't concern Nate that Amy hadn't yet emerged. Leaving home was a production even when one was doing it with the support of one's family and servants. Doing so in secret required more time and stealth to pack one's bag, change into travel clothes, and sneak out without a single person in the household noticing.

His only fear was that she would be discovered and locked in a room. Lord Warre, her father, had already refused to give his permission for their marriage. *The gall of you, boy, to even ask. What have you to recommend yourself? You are eighteen, about to disappear on a naval ship to be killed in this war, and you are a Preston.* That last article—Nate's family name—Warre had spit out with a sneer of disgust. His saliva had landed on Nate's cheek.

It turned out that Lord Warre considered Nate's father, the radical Lord Martin Preston, a sworn enemy. Nate could only guess it was because the Prestons had turned their estate into a safe haven for any Briton and shared their profits with all who labored there; or perhaps it was Papa's endless crusade against slavery; Lord Warre's hatred might even stem from the family's insistence on eschewing anything imported from the colonial empire.

Whatever Lord Warre's reasons, it was not the first time anyone had denigrated Nate's family to his face. It was only the first time that such a person had wielded so much power over him.

Nate didn't care, so long as Amy would still marry him. And—when he had found her after that interview and told her its disastrous outcome—she had promised him she loved him no matter who his family was.

As he loved her, despite Lord Warre. There was no end to what Nate loved about Amy. They had met at a musicale at the Greenwood Assembly Hall in Portsmouth, just a week after Nate had first arrived as a new lieutenant in the Royal Navy. Her rosy cheeks and curved body—especially the parts a gentleman didn't mention—had caught his attention first; then they had spoken, and her wit had carried away his heart. She could turn any situation, even the worst, into a moment worth smiling over. She was smart, too, with a natural curiosity that meant she always seemed to ask him just the right questions.

When Nate was with Amy, even if they were on opposite sides of the room, his whole being elevated to another plane. A better plane. She was his soul mate, his helpmeet, the person whose spirit had been cleaved from his, and now they could spend the rest of their lives reunited.

No matter that he was only eighteen. Papa would give his consent for the marriage license, if Nate had to spend a whole night debating him for it. After all, Papa had finally helped procure Nate his commission after years of trying to dissuade him, and Papa believed in love far more than he believed in the Royal Navy.

Nor did it matter that as soon as they married, Nate would be off on a ship for months at a time and Amy would be waiting at port. Their paths would be joined, their hearts complete.

If only she could escape the confines of her father's house.

At last, he spotted a figure hurrying down the gravel drive. Nate's excitement surged. He wiped sweat from his palms onto his trousers. He fixed the perch of his hat atop his brown hair, ensuring it was at that just-right angle that he happened to know best flattered his face. He spit out the mint leaves he had been chewing to freshen his breath.

This was the moment. The start of the rest of his life. And his whole body was ready to meet it.

He stepped out of the hedge to greet Amy. In the same moment, the figure got close enough for him to see. For his heart to stop.

It wasn't Amy at all.

It was her friend, Miss Henriette Curry.

Nate forgot to breathe for the ten steps it took for Miss Curry to draw within speaking distance of him. "Lieutenant Preston."

"Is Miss Lamplugh..." Nate didn't know how to ask what he wanted to know. Was Amy safe? Was she unhurt? Were their plans discovered? "Is she at liberty?"

Miss Curry stretched out her arm, offering a folded letter. Still, she did not step closer, as if afraid to get within reach of him.

As if he were a villain.

So long as he could marry Amy, Nate didn't care if Miss Curry thought him the worst scoundrel in all of England.

He took care not to alarm her as he stepped forward, accepted the letter, and retreated. The orange of sunset had given way to gray dusk; it was almost too dark to read.

"She asked me to say most emphatically that she is sorry, and that she wishes you well," Miss Curry said. "Now, if you will excuse me, I must get back."

Nate didn't believe it. Not as Miss Curry retreated. Not as he waited another half hour, refusing to read the letter, hoping for Amy to appear.

It might not have been until a week later when his ship, HMS *True*, departed from Portsmouth and Amy still did not appear at the docks to beg him to stay that Nate believed it.

Miss Amy Lamplugh had forsaken him for good.

CHAPTER ONE

Selsea Park Dower House, 10 miles northwest of Portsmouth

April 1820 (Six years later)

In a way, it was a relief to be deposited at her sister's house like a crate of wine—aged, creaking, and waiting unendingly for someone to finally open her seal. Amy had spent the last six months with her father and his new wife, Cora, and if she had to remain with them at Swanhill House for even another week, she might find herself committing step-matricide.

Then again, Amy wasn't sure that going from inane gossip about Britain's finest peers to spending day and night tending her sister's two young children was really trading up.

She told herself to feel relief anyhow, especially as Pater and Cora spent the whole half-hour ride from Swanhill to Selsea Park discussing exactly what Cora would wear in London to each ball. The green silk, they agreed, was too pale for a married woman; the dark maroon did not suit her on its own but would make her glow when ornamented with the proper jewels. Pater, of course, had opinions on which jewels would most make her look like a viscountess; diamonds were to be reserved for only the most formal occasions, and pearls were too common, but he would purchase her more amethysts, emeralds, and especially jade to show off her slender, delicate, and perfect neck.

Amy tightened the scarf tied just below her chin, which hid the goiter that seemed to grow larger and more unusual every day. She was glad not to be going to London, where she had no close friends and where she was—at age twenty-eight, her bloom of youth long since lost—of interest to neither the bachelors, the rakes, nor even the matrons of Society with a capital S. She would much prefer to be at Mary's, where she was very much of interest to her nephews. Even if every single moment of her day would be accounted for, at least at Selsea Park Amy felt useful. Sometimes, on a good morning, she could even still have a meaningful conversation with Mary.

And she wouldn't have to see Pater looking at Cora in that particular way, which she did not care to parse for its ratio of lust to love.

They arrived at the dusty court of the dower house—where Mary lived with her husband Fred, four-year-old Charles, and two-year-old Christopher—just in time for the boys to come tumbling out the door in a whirl of fisticuffs. Pater took one look at them, his very own grandchildren, and proclaimed, "My legs feel too weak to leave the carriage. You can see to yourself, Amy?"

She could. Of course she could. In a way, it felt like Amy had been seeing to herself for an entire decade, if not her entire life.

She pressed a kiss to Pater's hand, then to Cora's, then jumped out of the coach—ignoring the step entirely. The coachman, God bless him, was already untying her trunk, so she could go straight to her nephews and tear them apart. "Charles, Kit, give your Aunt Amy a kiss."

The morning disappeared in a blur after that. The boys were delighted to see her; Charles wanted to show her every toy of his in the house, even though she had been there only a week since. Kit clung to her skirts with fingers that were surprisingly hard to pry off. Mary was abed, for she was in the family way again and it always sapped her of the energy to do anything except vomit. The housemaid, Iris, was so happy to let Amy take the boys that she managed to remain invisible; poor Cook was overseeing a luncheon stew and couldn't take her eyes off the fire. And Fred, like any good father and husband, was nowhere to be found.

It wasn't until the grandfather clock chimed two that Amy managed to steal a moment to settle herself in. The boys were napping; Mary was napping; Cook was napping; Iris, by Amy's guess, was probably napping.

Amy didn't take a nap. She wouldn't have been able to sleep even if she wanted to. Her heart palpitations were back. Not at the rapid pace that could overwhelm her and force her to sit down, but fast enough that she couldn't possibly rest. She went to her room instead. Compared to her room at Swanhill House it was embarrassingly modest, with only an armoire instead of a dressing room, a quilt instead of a silk coverlet, and a single window that looked out at the kitchen garden instead of her Swanhill view of an open park and glimmering lake.

Still, it was a room she could call her own, with a door she could shut and lock. Which she took advantage of that very moment. Someone—probably dear John Coachman—had managed to bring up her trunk, so she set about unpacking. Four good day dresses and two evening gowns, for the inevitable supper invitations by Fred's parents to the great house, were hung in the armoire. Her petticoats, scarves, fichus, shawls, stockings, garters, and hair ribbons were tucked away in drawers. A string of pearls, a pair of sapphire earrings, and a ring were placed in their locked case at the bottom of the armoire.

And then there were her medicines. Those went on the stand beside her table: dried seaweed, of which she took a portion every morning; the Cordial Balm of Gilead that she kept on hand for palpitations; and a stomachic essence for tremors. Evidence of her illness, no matter how little notice anyone else took of it. No matter how poorly the physician could define it.

How she wished she could throw the whole lot into the chamber pot for Iris to clear out in the morning.

Moments like these jarred Amy. When she was in transition, defining her life by the things she took with her, it felt like she had suddenly put on a new set of spectacles. Gone was the Amy who was settled as dutiful daughter and invaluable sister; in sharp focus, she saw the life she had chosen. A fading woman, who had never left her father's protection nor traveled beyond Southern England, whose own family didn't have the energy to care that for five years she had been growing thinner and weaker. A woman who, when she inevitably slipped away in the next decade or so, might be mourned only by her two nephews.

Always, she wondered what *he* would make of it, if he saw her.

And always, she cursed herself for still caring.

For she was sure that wherever he was in the world, Nathaniel Preston wasn't still thinking of her.

The boys stirred in their room down the hall, jolting Amy back to her usual self. She retied the scarf around her neck—for Kit had the worst habit of fondling the lump below her chin if she allowed him to see it—and went to see to them. She got there just as Charles prowled towards his brother's bed; she caught the four-year-old in one arm and scooped up Kit in the other and sat them on either side of her for a story.

They were just about to find out what happened to the great big lion who ate a tiny peapod when Lady Olivia Bremridge, their grandmother, called up the stairs, "Miss Lamplugh, are you here?"

At which the boys leapt from the bed and raced down with cries of "Grandmama, grandmama, grandmama!"

Amy followed them without their hurry. She met Mary, who looked rested yet exhausted, at the landing. "I thought I'd try to join you for tea," Mary explained, taking Amy's arm for balance without waiting for it to be offered.

For the most part, Amy couldn't blame Mary for being so out of sorts. Being *enceinte* didn't suit her the way it did some women; she was incessantly sick to the stomach, plagued by headaches and cramping in the back, or otherwise inconvenienced. And yet she and Fred did insist on having marital relations that resulted in the condition. The first two, Amy had understood to be the course of nature.

This third one seemed rather unnecessary, for all the trouble it caused.

Lady Olivia had the boys settled at the formal dining table with plates of tea cake. She had, as usual, brought a footman with her from the great house to assist in serving; he pulled out a seat first for Mary, then for Amy. Mary poured tea, which looked more red than black for how weak it was.

"It is so good to have you with us again, Miss Lamplugh," Lady Olivia said, reaching out to pat Amy's hand. "Has Mary shared our exciting news?"

"I've hardly had a chance," Mary responded. "She has only just arrived."

"Which leaves me with an opportunity to guess. Let me see...has it to do with a trip to the continent?"

Lady Olivia shook her head, a gleam in her eye. "Try again."

Amy took a slice of cake while she considered options that were both plausible and fun to guess. She thought of Fred's sister. "Is Mrs. Crowe expecting again?"

"Not that I know of. No, it's much closer to home than that."

"Ah!" Sensing her nephews losing patience, Amy leaned in and tweaked Charles's nose. "You are having a statue of Charles and Kit erected in the gazebo at the center of the maze!"

The boys laughed. Mary smiled wanly. Lady Olivia hung her head in mock despair. "You do me shame, Miss Lamplugh, for I have never even *thought* of so worthy an idea!"

Then, seeing to it that each grandson had more cake, Lady Olivia explained:

"We have visitors at the house. Of a most exotic kind. A nabob visiting from India, and his nephew, a sea captain."

And just like that, Amy's heart sped up. Not from palpitations, but from the idea of Nate. And it was merely an idea. A suggestion from the words *sea captain*. When she knew from the papers that he was off fighting the slave trade on the coast of West Africa, just as he had always dreamed he would.

Whomever Lady Olivia was discussing, it wasn't Nate. And yet Amy's whole body reacted as if it were.

As if it were Nate, and as if he would be happy to see her. Six years after she turned him away without even having the courage to do so to his face.

"Oh, that *is* exciting," she managed to say, her voice sounding false to her own ears. "Interesting visitors are always in short supply."

"Sir Charles is considering an investment in the nabob's shipping company, so we are keeping them with us as long as we can to ascertain their good character. We are having an informal supper party tonight. I know you have only just arrived, but you must join us. I shall send down Wanda to mind the boys so there is no question about you and Fred and Mary coming to supper." Lady Olivia winked at Amy. "I think you'll find the captain to be quite handsome."

Amy blushed. As if she could fall for any old sea captain when her heart already belonged to another. One who was handsomer than any other man in the empire, and braver and kinder, too.

She was a silly, pining woman to still be thinking of Nate Preston after all these years. She should have put him out of her heart the moment she finished that letter in which she chose to remain loyal to her family instead of running off with him. But if there were a cure for loving Nate, Amy had yet to find it.

Nate had been at Selsea Park for all of three hours, and he already regretted accepting the invitation.

The estate was too massive: a great house with dozens of rooms, a park larger than the fields of Northfield Hall, three separate ornamental gardens, and not a single laborer's cottage to be spotted from the vista of the house's highest room.

Nate was still enough of a Preston for the excessive wealth to make his toes curl.

Worse, the neighborhood felt so very familiar. Without even trying—in fact, in *spite* of his efforts to ignore it—Nate knew almost down to the inch how far he was from Swanhill House: from his bedroom window, it was about five and a half miles and three vertical yards to Amy's second-story bedroom.

Assuming, of course, that she was still there. More likely, she had married some wealthy peer and was in London updating her wardrobe ahead of the Season.

Either alternative made him almost sick to contemplate. Which was why he shouldn't have joined Uncle Graham at Selsea Park. He should have listened to his own good sense and rented rooms in Portsmouth. He still would have been measuring the distance between himself and Amy, but at least he could have distracted himself with pubs and sea shanties and watching boats sail around the harbor.

At Selsea Park, the only company would be polite. And ever since Nate had been ejected from Lord Warre's study, he had harbored a strong distaste for polite society.

If Nate could have his way, he would be back on the quarterdeck of HMS *Vengeance*, surveying the dusty African swells for slave ships.

But a naval officer was confined to his orders, and now Nate was confined further to disciplinary hearings. HMS *Vengeance* had hardly even entered the Channel on her way to Portsmouth when the message arrived that the Admiralty was court-martialing him. Apparently, his capture of a French slaver six months earlier was considered *against orders*. A capture for which his commander, Commodore Collier, hadn't even reprimanded him. The Admiralty, it seemed, wanted to swing its authority around rather than let its officers do their duties.

So Nate was stuck in the neighborhood of Portsmouth at least until his court-martial. Perhaps longer, if the trial ended his naval career.

He had been somewhere in that low sling of thoughts when Uncle Graham had invited him along to Selsea Park. The idea of a feather bed and a hot meal instead of the slops served at the officers' inn had tempted Nate into this folly.

And now he had no choice except to pursue it. A gentleman didn't desert his hosts—not on the first night of his arrival, anyhow—and if Nate wanted to continue his career as an officer of the Royal Navy, he had to be above all things a gentleman.

So he changed into his supper jacket, applied a dash of honey water behind his ears to improve his smell, and brushed his brown hair until it resembled a gentle mid-ocean surf. A dashing naval captain, just as his hostess Lady Olivia Bremridge expected.

He and Uncle Graham walked down the polished wooden staircase together into the parlor where the family was gathering before supper. Uncle Graham, as usual, was dressed as if he were still in Calcutta: a kurta, instead of a jacket, over loose trousers. He had lived in India since before Nate was born, since before even Nate's parents had married, and except for his freckled white skin could probably pass for a native.

Nate had only met his uncle a few years ago, on one of the occasions when his ship was being outfitted in Portsmouth and his uncle was in town on business. In 1813, the East India Company had officially lost its monopoly on trade between Great Britain and territory east of the Cape of Good Hope. Uncle Graham—who had long since made a fortune overseeing a factory for the company—had decided to invest in a ship. Now, he was back in England to expand his trading partners and build a fleet.

The only things Uncle Graham seemed to have in common with Nate's father were his looks—he looked almost exactly like Papa, except for his Indian clothes—and his devotion to his family. Already in the five days that Nate had been keeping company with Uncle Graham, he had heard over and over how eager his uncle was to finish his business so he could return home to his wife and five children in Calcutta.

Nate wasn't sure how Papa would react to knowing that he was visiting with Uncle Graham. For his part, Nate found it comforting to be close to a man who was almost his father, yet without the same expectations. Especially when it came to an evening party, when all the drink and most of the food served would be expensive imports from exotic places and everyone would be wearing Indian cotton or Chinese silks.

In fact, Lady Olivia seemed to be in a gown that combined both textiles, her silver hair ornamented by gold filigree that might well have come from the African Gold Coast. "I hope you don't keep the same habits as your father, Captain Preston, or I'm afraid your diet will be confined to our vegetables," she said as she handed him a glass of Madeira wine.

"And even those are grown in a glass house with seeds from Italy," Sir Charles added.

"Ah." Nate tried to look charmingly rueful. "I assure you, I would have wasted away in the navy had I been determined to follow my family's strictures. I will happily eat whatever you serve me."

He took stock of the party, which so far seemed too small to be called that. Besides the hosts, there was a man of the cloth—currently soliciting Uncle Graham to tell him about Calcutta—and a middle-aged man in a tightly-fitted suit a la Beau Brummell.

No Amy Lamplugh. Not that Nate had any reason to expect her. She probably wasn't still in Portsmouth; even less likely was she still Miss Amy Lamplugh. Nate hated that he was looking for her, that every day in port he found some excuse to dream that they would cross paths. He didn't *want* to cross paths with her. What had a man to say to the woman who had made it so clear he was not worthy?

I apologize for disclosing this news to you by letter, but I regret to say that I cannot marry you.

Nothing. If Nate ever did run into Amy, he would have absolutely nothing to say to her.

"We'll wait just a little bit longer for Mr. and Mrs. Bremridge," Lady Olivia said, referring to her son and his wife. "Poor Mrs. Bremridge is anticipating the great event in a few months, and it makes her slow to leave the house, even to come up for supper."

"Then we must be strong and wait as long as required." With a prickle of apprehension, Nate assured himself that *Amy* wouldn't be Mrs. Bremridge. Surely Lord Warre had held out for a husband with more to recommend him than being the son of a baronet.

Not that it mattered. He slapped a hand against his thigh as a price for thinking of her—*again.* He was a successful naval captain with six years of battles, storms, and captures behind him. He had flirted with beautiful women around the world and bedded more than a few. When he wanted to marry, he would be the catch of whatever assembly hall he entered.

Miss Amy Lamplugh, or whatever her name was now, should mean nothing to him.

Especially when she wasn't even present.

He set himself to speaking to the other guests. The rector told an anecdote about one of his early parishes where he was paid with twenty goats; the Beau Brummell lookalike—a Mr.

Farraday—revealed he had spent a decade in the West Indies by telling a story about the goat disease that had plagued his neighborhood.

"How are the goats in the navy, Captain Preston?" Mr. Farraday asked. "Where were you most recently, anyhow?"

"With the West African Squadron. Patrolling the coast to arrest slave ships."

Nate knew this would dampen Farraday's arrogant smile. A man who had spent a decade in the West Indies and now rubbed elbows with Britain's peers must have made his fortune from profiting off slave labor.

After all, only the kidnapping and transport of slaves was illegal in Britain and her colonies. The actual practice of slavery was still sanctioned by law—and filled the empire's treasury.

"You're not the captain being court-martialed for capturing a French ship, are you?" Farraday retorted.

From the corner of his eye, Nate saw Lady Olivia sweep towards them, her mouth open to save him from the encounter. She and Sir Charles were well aware of Nate's current status but had welcomed him anyhow. Yet he didn't need her to defend him; he was about to put Farraday in his place when Mr. and Mrs. Bremridge finally arrived.

Mr. and Mrs. Bremridge—and a thin, pale, brown-haired woman. A woman Nate would have recognized anywhere, yet who almost didn't look like herself, so faded was she.

A woman whose appearance sent a jolt of unwelcome joy down Nate's spine.

Miss Amy Lamplugh.

CHAPTER TWO

This had to be a dream. Or a nightmare.

Either way, she could not possibly be awake.

For there was Nate Preston, standing in the parlor as if he had been invited to supper.

Looking more divine than that first night they met in Portsmouth. Then, she had thought him the handsomest man in England, with thick brown hair and legs like a stallion's and a chin that could cut glass.

Now she knew better. He was handsomer than any man on earth. He wore gentlemen's clothes instead of a naval uniform, yet by merely standing with his shoulders back, head high, every inch of him ready to pass muster, he exuded an air of command that made Amy want to fall at his feet in submission.

He didn't look at all shocked to see her. His gaze settled on her and his expression, which had previously been a snarl, smoothed into a blank slate. His eyes did not remain connected with hers for longer than a second; almost as soon as their gazes locked—filling Amy with an intense, dizzying shame—he looked away to Mary at her side.

If anything, his lips curled into a bored sneer.

A nightmare, then. Hopefully not reality: Amy must have fallen asleep, and now her mind delivered the fantasy of Nate as Lady Olivia's guest with the twist of a knife through her heart. She had a fever, which was why it felt so vivid. Nate wasn't really here.

Nate wasn't really ignoring her.

Lady Olivia moved to the center of the room, arms extended as if to create a bridge between Nate in one corner and Amy by the door. "Mr. Preston, Captain Preston, may I introduce my son, Mr. Alfred Bremridge; his wife, Mrs. Bremridge; and Mrs. Bremridge's sister, Miss Lamplugh?"

Fred stepped forward to shake Nate's hand and that of the older man at Nate's side, for whom Amy had barely energy to spare notice. For her part, Mary advanced, with a tiny glance at Amy before she laughed her way to taking Nate's hand in hers. "But Mama, you didn't say it was Captain Preston! Why, we are acquainted. How long ago was it that you would call at Swanhill House with those delicious honey oatcakes?"

His eyes darted back to Amy. Almost as if he really was the man who had visited during every one of his free afternoons to spend hours ambling through the garden with her.

Amy fingered the knot of the scarf around her neck to make sure it was still there.

Nate looked away again. His grin—the charming one that had always made Amy feel like the center of the empire—was bestowed upon Mary. "It seems a lifetime ago, Mrs. Bremridge. May I offer you my congratulations and best wishes on your marriage?"

"Thank you, you may." Mary turned now, using the angle of her body to gesture to Amy. "You do remember my sister, Miss Lamplugh, as well, don't you?"

Amy felt herself incapable of doing anything except straightening her spine and smiling—or at least trying to—under his new examination of her.

But even now, he didn't linger. He said only "Yes," and bowed his head by way of greeting.

Surely she would wake from this nightmare now.

The butler interrupted to announce supper. They were uneven in numbers as well as precedent, and so they proceeded informally into the dining room: Sir Charles escorted Lady Olivia, Nate escorted Mary, and Fred offered Amy his arm.

"Steady on," her brother-in-law murmured on that short walk from the front of the great house to the back. "If he's a gentleman, he'll behave."

Good old Fred, who had always been so kind to her—even apologetic, for he had courted Mary while Amy, the older sister, remained unwed. He had been out of Hampshire the summer that Amy fell in love with Nate; all Fred knew was the official story accepted by their neighbors, which was that Amy had been kind to the naval officer and then rejected his advances, in the suitable behavior of a young lady.

Fred thought the unspoken feelings were Nate's. That the heart beating thrice as fast as normal was Nate's, for being spurned. That Amy felt nothing more than residual guilt for turning down a decent young man.

At least—if this wasn't a nightmare—no one but Amy could feel her heart breaking all over again.

She took her seat between Fred and Reverend Platt without replying. Nate was at the other end of the table with Sir Charles and Mary and Mr. Farraday for company; Amy had to lean forward to see past Fred for a glimpse of him. Which she resolved she would not do. Even though she wanted to do nothing *but* look at Nate—look at him, talk to him, throw her arms around him.

Amy could not do any of those things. She should not do any of those things. She would not do any of those things.

"May I say, Miss Lamplugh, how often I bring you up to your fellow parishioners as an example of a woman who knows her duty?" Reverend Platt said by way of conversation as the footmen placed stewed meat in the center of the table. "So often, I must remind a sister or a daughter—or even a wife—that we each earn our glory by doing the duties we are given in life. Take Miss Lamplugh, I always say. An inglorious woman in your position would insist on going to London with Lord and Lady Warre, for that is where young people like to be. But Miss Lamplugh, I say, knows her duty. She is here, tending to her sister and nephews, which will bring her more glory than a dozen silk gowns. You, my dear, are a virtuous pearl in our community."

"Ah." It was what the reverend always said when he found himself in conversation with her, for he knew nothing of Amy *except* that she was always at the beck and call of Pater or Mary or even, for a few years, Great-Aunt Hilaria. "But I am not so young a person anymore, Reverend."

The words escaped before Amy thought them over. She meant them as a jest, she told herself. A little self-deprecating wit that would remove some of the sanctimony from their discourse.

Only it sounded a little like she was hoping someone would contradict her. Amy felt her cheeks blaze at the thought; if Nate had happened to overhear, would he think she was casting out a line for one of the men at the table to flirt with her?

And what *did* he think upon discovering that she was still unmarried, and not even with the promising future ahead of her that he had left her with?

"Even so," the reverend responded.

Amy's heart raced with even more shame that no one had taken up her line than with the fact that she had cast it.

Or—it occurred to her—perhaps her heart was not racing from emotion at all. It had been several minutes since the first time she had noted it. She shifted her fingers to her wrist, where her pulse fairly leapt from her skin.

Palpitations. Not of the romantic heroine variety, but rather of Amy's own particular illness. A heartbeat as fast as if she had raced up a hill, except all she had done was sip some soup.

In a matter of time, her heartbeat would return to normal. Or it would overcome her, and she would feel faint and nauseated and indisposed.

The only way to find out was to wait.

"I object to your compliment on one account, Reverend," said Fred, for apparently the supper remained calm and smooth for everyone else. "You make it sound as if Miss Lamplugh stays with us only because of duty and not because it brings her any joy. I daresay Miss Lamplugh prefers caring for her dear sister and nephews far more than keeping up with London society."

Reverend Platt nodded sagely. "It is a question for the philosophers whether enjoying a duty makes it a less moral choice. Still, Miss Lamplugh makes a choice, and she makes the correct one."

Perhaps it *was* a choice. If she had truly wanted to go to London, she could have mounted an argument to Pater about why he would benefit from her company; she could have thrown a tantrum; she could have appealed to Cora on some feminine level and gotten herself invited to stay in the town house.

It had felt more like a decision someone else made for her. As had the assumption that while staying at Selsea Park she would act as nursemaid, so that Fred and Mary needn't worry about paying one.

If either Fred or the reverend had asked her, Amy might have told them that she had made precisely one choice in her life, and that had been to *not* marry Captain Nate Preston.

But nobody asked. She remained silent, her heartbeat loud in her ears as it rushed ever faster.

And then she caught a line of the conversation down at the other end of the table. "Do they court-martial *every* officer in the Preventive Squadron, Captain Preston, or is it a special privilege reserved for you?"

This from Mr. Farraday, who rather sounded like he had drunk too much wine already. He tried to make it seem like friendly ribbing, but to Amy's ears, it rang out like a taunt. Surely it was some rumor spread to malign Nate's character that Farraday now had the poor manners to repeat.

She held her breath, waiting to hear Nate set the man in his place.

"I suppose you could call it a special privilege. I certainly consider it a privilege to have liberated three hundred ninety-seven Africans who had been kidnapped and held in cruel conditions by an illegal slaver. If I must pay for that in a trial, so be it."

The pride in his voice contradicted the consequence implied by his words. A court-martial could be an inconvenience to an officer—stripping him of some rank, or resulting in a fine—or it could be disastrous. Nate might pretend not to care about it, but fear immediately pressed close against Amy's heart.

Even six years ago, all Nate had ever wanted was to join the Preventive Squadron. The whole reason he joined the navy, he had once confided to her, was to take up arms against slavery.

If the court-martial found him guilty, what would be left to him?

She went cold. As if she were caught in the midwinter snow, chilled through to the bone. From Nate's words, or from her body losing control of itself again?

"A navy cannot run if its men do not follow their commanders' orders," Mr. Farraday countered.

How she wished she could interject to shut the man up. Instead, Amy pulled her shawl tighter around her shoulders and looped her fingers in its folds for warmth. This, like her palpitations, would pass, if she was only patient enough.

"At times, Mr. Farraday, the man within me emerges from the confines of being an officer, and I find I answer to a higher authority than the Admiralty. If you had seen the slave trade as I have seen it, you, too, would be tempted to break the rules to save even one soul."

"Miss Lamplugh watches us," Mr. Farraday said, turning suddenly her way with a smirk. "I suspect you have a discerning mind. What say you: should an officer obey his commanders, trusting they know better than him, or should he let his pride and passion carry the day?"

"That is..." Amy had a rejoinder at her lips, ready to go. Except it was rather humiliating to be called to attention so abruptly; Nate even leaned forward to see her down at the other end of the table. She couldn't meet his eyes, or perhaps she hadn't the energy to lift hers. She was suddenly feeling very dizzy and faint. Her heart, after all, still raced. "...an unfriendly phrasing of the question." There, at least she had managed to say that. Amy swallowed, willing herself to ignore her heart, ignore the icy cold, ignore the nausea swirling up her throat. She forced out: "I put my trust in Captain Preston's judgment."

Now, she really didn't feel quite right. It must be obvious to everyone: Amy knew she often turned pale in moments like these, with a slight feverish sweat to her brow, and she was stumbling over her words like some kind of drunk. She hoped they wouldn't make a fuss over it. She only needed someone—not Nate, of course, that would be impossible—to escort her from the room so she could lie down for a little bit.

But no one noticed a thing. Mr. Farraday said, "A more feminine answer, I'm sure I've never heard."

Mary replied, "You must not think my sister's tongue too sharp, Mr. Farraday."

Even Fred looked away, changing the subject. "Mr. Preston, Captain Preston, I hope you will join me for a ride tomorrow morning."

Would Nate notice?

Amy couldn't wait to find out. She knew she wouldn't vomit, but her heart palpitations had her stomach roiling, and she couldn't stay at the table a minute longer. Hands on the table, feet on the ground, Amy pushed herself to stand. "Please excuse me." She wasn't sure the words actually left her mouth. "I must lie down."

Next thing she knew, she fell into blackness.

Nate leapt to Amy's side before he knew what he was doing.

She lay crumpled on the floor just behind her brother-in-law's chair, most of her face and stomach turned down. Thank God for the imported Arabian carpet lining the room, or else Amy's head might have hit hard wood.

Nate touched her hand to rouse her. "Miss Lamplugh!"

Already, her eyes were blinking open. A good sign. Nate had known many people—women and men—to faint; it was only when they stayed that way for more than a few seconds that one really had to worry.

"You fainted," he told her, since in his experience of sailors collapsing, they never believed what had just happened. "Are you injured?"

She blinked at him again. Hazel eyes—had he ever forgotten? They were that magic color that changed with the light. On summer afternoons, they had always seemed as green as hedgerows. Now they were dark and amber, like seawater in a sandy harbor.

"She's fine," Mrs. Bremridge, the former Miss Mary, replied from her seat. "You mustn't be alarmed, Captain."

Lady Olivia had rounded the table by now and crouched on Amy's other side. "Have you hit your head, my dear?"

"No. I'm sorry. Don't make a fuss." The words came weakly out of her. She was still deathly pale, and her fingers felt like icicles. Nate discovered he was holding onto them like some kind of lovesick husband.

He let her go. "Perhaps the family's physician can be called."

"There is no need," Mrs. Bremridge said, her voice growing shrill. "This is one of her episodes, that is all. By the time Dr. Becket arrives, she will be fresh as a daisy. You really mustn't be concerned, Captain Preston."

Was she scolding him because she did not want to pay a physician's fee, or because she did not want Amy receiving *his* attention?

Miss Mary Lamplugh, after all, must have known about his offer of marriage. Perhaps Amy had even confided in her about their plan to elope.

Was the younger sister playing protector because she was afraid Nate had returned to whisk Amy away once and for all?

Nate schooled himself to keep indignation from steaming out his ears.

"She is right," Amy said, but her voice was still soft and weak. "I need rest, that's all."

She looked like she needed much more than rest. The Amy of six years ago had cherubic cheeks and a generous helping of flesh filling out her shoulders, bosom, and—when she had let him catch her in his arms—waist. Nate wouldn't have recognized this Amy if he hadn't committed so much of her to memory, for now she was all skin and bones, as if she had gone a month without rations. In the parlor, Nate had been stricken by how her eyes sank into their sockets and her cheeks hollowed into her jaw. Pair that with how her lips had no color—and was that a tremble in her hand as she reached forward, trying to rise onto her feet?

This woman needed far more than a few hours in bed.

But—as Mrs. Bremridge made clear—Amy Lamplugh's health was far from Nate's concern.

"I'll ring a maid and have the blue room freshened up for you," Lady Olivia said, wrapping an arm around Amy to help her stand.

"Oh no. I would rather go home." At least her voice was beginning to sound steadier. "To the dower house, I mean."

Nate wondered if that really was what she meant. Would she prefer to be at Swanhill House? Or was there somewhere else—someone else—that she longed for but could not speak of?

It didn't matter. The family had a course of action with regard to Amy, and it did not include him. Nate was about to return to his seat when she took a step on her own—and promptly started crumpling back to the floor.

He caught her, because he was a naval captain and he was standing right next to her and that was what a gentleman did.

Not because he longed to have her in his arms again.

"Oh," Amy cried—softly, for her voice was going weak once more. "Thank you."

She was a rag doll backed into his arms; Nate gripped her from behind with one hand on her left elbow and the other arm wrapped tightly around her waist. Gently, he rearranged the two of them so that her feet were solidly on the ground. "You had better not walk just yet."

"Fred will see her back to the dower house," Mrs. Bremridge said. "Then he'll come back for me."

Mr. Bremridge—who was still in his seat—turned around with a wince. "I should be happy to escort you, of course, Miss Lamplugh, only I did twist my shoulder last week…"

This had to be a farce. A farce of a family, and a farce of a reunion of parted lovers. Nate had no choice but to offer his next words, even though he knew they would make him look overeager. "I shall carry Miss Lamplugh, if you could show me the way, Mr. Bremridge."

There was a pause as everyone in the dining room considered the situation. Nate would welcome an objection, if only there were a better way to see Amy back to the dower house without risking a fall and without requiring her to wait for horses to be hitched to a cart.

Amy's hand landed on his where it sat beneath her rib cage. It was still ice cold, but it was also firm, keeping him there. "Thank you, Captain Preston. I do not deserve your kindness, but I will accept it."

For a moment, Nate was transported back in time to a sunny afternoon at Swanhill House. They had left Amy's great-aunt sitting on a chair by the edge of the lake and set out around its shore. Under a willow tree they had nestled together, Amy between his legs, her back against his chest and his against the trunk. He had felt every word vibrate through her chest into his. Almost as much as he had wanted to steal a kiss, he had felt the magic of that connection and had yearned for the moment to never end.

At the time, he had thought it was the beginning of a lifetime.

Now he knew it was only a memory.

He avoided Amy's eyes as he, with the sanction of the rest of the party, lifted her into his arms. Her arms looped around his neck, her head only inches away from his. Her perfume—lavender?—filled his nostrils. Above his forearms, he could feel the boning of her short stays along her back. If he looked down—

He would not look down. He was a gentleman.

Mr. Bremridge walked ahead of them through the house and onto the gravel drive. The night was young, with enough gray twilight that the lantern Bremridge carried was hardly necessary. "It is a quarter of an hour's walk, perhaps," Bremridge said. "We'll be back before pudding."

As if Nate was concerned about missing a meal.

"Mrs. Bremridge has the right of it, hasn't she, Amy?" the man continued. "These spells come on every now and then, and after a bit of a rest, you're in the best of health again. Overexcitement, the physician supposes, which works differently on each person."

"That is true. The physicians do not have an explanation." Amy adjusted her grip on Nate, her bare fingers brushing against the nape of his neck.

He refused to acknowledge his body's reaction to that.

"A bit of egg on your face, eh?" Bremridge said, turning over his shoulder to smile at his sister-in-law. "Fainting in the middle of the party like that?"

That was too much to be borne. Nate felt Amy shrink in his arms, though she had enough strength to keep her chin held high, even with the angle he carried her at. He spoke before she could: "I've seen men faint at far worse times. Once, when we were in negotiations with the King of Dahomey, my lieutenant collapsed the very moment the king arrived."

Without meaning to, he glanced at Amy. She watched him with wide, solemn eyes. "What a fascinating life you have led."

A life she had chosen not to be a part of. Nate looked straight ahead at the path. He had recovered from her rejection years ago. There was no reason to feel its sting again now.

They turned off the gravel drive onto a path of packed earth and grass. "Just a little bit farther now," Mr. Bremridge promised. "Need you a rest, Captain Preston?"

"No." He had carried heavier things longer distances, but there was no polite way to comment on Amy's weight. Especially when it seemed linked to whatever unexplainable episode she was suffering from. He redirected the question. "Have you need of a rest, Miss Lamplugh?"

"No." She readjusted her arm again so that her elbow clung more tightly around his neck. Her head was that much closer. For just him to hear, she added, "I am quite comfortable."

His body reacted in two halves:

Joy, like sinking into a hot bath after days without a wash. For there was a part of him that had longed these six years to know that he could carry Amy in his arms and she would be comfortable. That she would hold onto him and not demand to be put down.

Pain, like catching the splinters of a broken mast in his back. Because he had wanted this. Had offered this. Had been ready to risk his career and name and wealth for just this. Amy in his arms, for the rest of his life.

And she hadn't even had the decency to explain to his face why she would not marry him. Had, instead, left him with a letter to memorize and twist into a thousand interpretations:

Know that I love you, and if circumstances were different, I would marry you in the very next heartbeat. You must forget me now as you go forth on your destiny. I shall look for your name in the newspapers to hear what a fine, heroic naval officer you become. One day, I hope to read that you are married, too, and raising a family full of boys who will join you in defending goodness from the evils of the world.

A good thing they were within sight of the dower house. It loomed ahead of them in the dark, brightened only by a few windows where lanterns stood in wait. Bremridge led them through the front door. Navigating the stairs with Amy in his arms was a bit of a challenge; Nate angled himself on a diagonal so that neither Amy's head nor her feet would hit the wall or banister. She tried to help by tucking her chin, her ear landing on his shoulder.

Perhaps she didn't consider how much that felt like a lover's embrace.

"This is Miss Lamplugh's chamber," Bremridge said, his words oscillating as they all realized together what an awkward thing it was for Nate to carry her directly to her bed.

In those months that Nate had courted Amy, he had never so much as reached the same corridor as her room. He had never been able to fantasize about her in the specific décor of that Swanhill bedroom, though he had certainly imagined her in his bed plenty of times.

And now he lay her directly on a mattress. He watched her relax against a pillow, her lips spread in a small smile. He saw her legs stretch out, spotted the white silk stockings protecting her ankles from the evening air.

It would be so easy to fall beside her onto the bed. To keep her in his arms. To kiss her once more with that senseless abandon that had so enchanted him six years ago.

But Nate didn't want that. The desire he felt wasn't even real. It was a memory of a younger self that had loved a younger Amy.

He didn't know this Amy—she who was a dutiful sister and obedient daughter—and she certainly didn't know him.

He was just a stranger, straightening from her bed after doing her a kind deed.

"I hope to find you in better health the next time our paths cross, Miss Lamplugh," he said. With a final nod, he took his leave of her.

CHAPTER THREE

Amy woke with the sunrise, not an ounce of fatigue in her bones. The boys were already stirring, so she went into their rooms and helped them dress, then led them outside for a morning adventure before breakfast.

It was a good day. Her body felt settled, with all its parts functioning as they should—except for the goiter beneath her scarf. The skies were clear, the morning air crisp. The boys were at their most adorable: curious, excited, and still sleepy enough to be biddable. Kit tumbled along, looking back at her every so often with such dedication that she felt absolutely revered.

On a day like this, Amy could love her life. What more could a woman want than two nephews who adored her and a family who relied on her? Never mind that she was neither wife nor mother; Amy had the best of being cherished and needed without surrendering her body to husband and child.

She could be content with that. She could sustain herself on that—and her memories of Nate.

Kit fell down as they finished their loop around the little wooded path behind the dower house, and he broke into a wail. Amy scooped him into her arms, much the way Nate had carried her last night.

Oh, she knew she should be ashamed of it. How humiliating to have fainted right there at the dinner table! Amy didn't ordinarily faint, nor did her condition ordinarily get her so agitated. Had it been any other night she would have been in tears this morning, wishing it had never happened.

But last evening after she fell, she'd opened her eyes to see Nate right there. As if he had never left. As if these last six years hadn't happened. He had crouched over her, concern stringing together his eyebrows, his lips murmuring her name. The moment had happened slowly for her, two seconds seeming like two minutes. All she could think was *If Nate is here, I'm safe.*

And then she had been in his arms. A whole eternity nestled against his chest, inhaling his steady honey scent. She had collected the presence of mind to keep herself as distant as possible, not resting her head against his shoulder—or claiming his lips for a kiss—as she longed to do. Still, she had a whole new memory of his touch to feed her soul.

She should be embarrassed, but instead, she was overjoyed.

When they returned to the house, the sun was fully risen and Cook had hot oatmeal waiting in bowls on the table. More surprising, Mary was already about, sitting at the table in her morning robe and sipping a cup of tea.

"You look well for a woman who caused such a fuss last night," she said, after kissing the boys good morning and setting them to their breakfasts.

"As you said, a little rest was all I needed." Amy was able to reply cheerfully because her mood so buoyed her, she didn't even care that Mary never worried about her health. "You look well yourself."

Mary acknowledged this with a mere lift of her shoulders. "I owe you an apology. Mama Olivia never told me our visitors' names, and I should have asked. If I had, I would have known to protect you from seeing him again."

Amy hesitated in replying, pretending a supreme focus on how much sugar to add to her oatmeal. Mary had witnessed all parts of Amy and Nate's courtship, yet she had been so firmly in agreement with Pater about rejecting the marriage proposal that Amy had never confided in her about their plans to elope.

Did Mary want to protect Amy from Nate because she feared Amy was embarrassed, or did she sense Amy's heartbreak after all?

"I am glad to see Captain Preston again," she said at last. "I have always wished him well."

"Oh good. Then you won't mind that he is coming by this morning to go riding with Fred."

"No, I don't mind." Amy stopped her hand from swinging up to her scarf. It didn't matter what she looked like. Her excitement would be fed by soaking in Nate's presence, even if he thought she looked like death itself.

Mary leaned forward to help Kit with his food. "It is surprising that the captain is still unmarried, isn't it? He is perfectly handsome and, until this recent trouble, has had a commendable career. I would have imagined him already married with a child or two."

Surprising, yes. A large part of Amy—one she wasn't proud of—was relieved, too.

She didn't know how she would have reacted if Nate had shown up as a houseguest with a wife at his side.

"Quite."

"Perhaps that is why he decided to come to Selsea Park." For a moment, Mary was interrupted by Charles, who had decided to finish his meal by throwing a spoonful of oatmeal at Kit. Amy helped separate them, her sister's words pounding in her ears.

Did she think Nate had returned to find Amy?

Did he still think of her in his loneliest moments, as Amy did him?

Then Mary clarified: "Mama Olivia is already planning a neighborhood party. Between Miss Howell and the young ladies visiting the Millard family this month, I imagine Captain Preston could find himself a charming bride, if he so chooses."

It was wicked of Amy to hope he didn't so choose. But if he had to marry—and he did, for she wanted him to be happy, and had years ago resigned herself to the fact that he would marry someone else—couldn't he choose someone who was not from *her* neighborhood? Couldn't he save his courtship and wedding and holiday visits for some other English port where Amy wouldn't always have to see him doting on someone else?

"Of course, he is still a *Preston*," Mary mused, "but I'm sure the Millards would be happy to overlook that, as long as he didn't expect his wife to burn all her cotton dresses."

Wasn't that what Pater had said all those years ago? *You can't marry into the Preston family, child. They would throw out your jewels and force you not to drink tea or coffee or wine. You may think you love this boy, but he will be off at sea, and you will be trapped at Northfield Hall, no better than a nun.*

She hadn't believed it then, and she didn't believe it now. Nate himself had drunk Madeira wine last night, imported directly from that Portuguese island that was also a rendezvous spot for so many slave trading ships. He wouldn't expect his wife to take up any habits she didn't subscribe to herself.

Besides, if he really thought that living without cotton and sugar would help stop slavery, then perhaps it was worth doing.

From the courtyard came the thudding of a cantering horse's hooves. Charles took up the cry, "A visitor! A visitor!"

Now Amy's hand really did fly to her scarf. She retied it, just to make sure it covered her goiter. As Mary turned to the boys, Amy pinched her own cheeks to add some color. Even a spinster was allowed some vanity now and then, after all.

As the household erupted in chaos—Fred thundering down the stairs, Iris answering the door, Mary trying to corral Charles as he raced circles around the breakfast table—Nate was shown into the room to say good morning.

The sight of him made Amy's mouth water. He was dressed for riding: brown jacket, buckskin trousers that clung to his thighs, and knee-high leather boots to protect his legs. The picture of masculinity, especially as he clapped a riding crop absent-mindedly against his thigh.

Amy waited for him to look her way. Instead, he looked at Mary, his manner grave. "Pray do not let me interrupt your meal."

Mary smiled brightly, as if she had not just been speculating on his family's behavior. "Would you care for anything? Cook can prepare eggs or toast if you prefer."

"Thank you, I already ate."

Charles came to a stop at Nate's feet, staring up at him as if he had just discovered a giant. "Are you very old?"

"Charles! That is not polite!" Amy scolded, though she did not much worry that Nate would take offense. He was good-natured; it was one of the things she had loved about him.

Nate looked solemnly down at Charles. "I am very old, but not as old as your Aunt Amy."

And then—at last—Nate looked at her. And he winked.

Amy's heart melted. How often he had teased her for being older than him—by four years!—and she him for being nothing more than a babe. They would have batted a few more barbs at each other, then dissolved into smiling at each other, or holding each other's hands, or even stealing a kiss or two, depending on who and where her chaperone was.

She managed not to giggle. "I'm afraid I only grow older every day."

Charles raced over to her side, placing two oatmeal-sticky hands directly on her legs. "You can't be old, Aunt Amy! You must live my whole life!"

She tried to focus on the sweetness of what he said instead of the promise she could not make him. The physicians could not name her illness—could not even dare to say it *was* an illness—but Amy had seen her mother suffer the same symptoms, and she had also watched her mother die young in childbed, when everyone had supposed her healthy enough.

"She shall not live your *whole* life, Charles," Mary interjected. "Aunts must pass before their nephews. Now come here and let me wipe your hands."

Amy looked once more at Nate, who had grown still, as if watching the scene from a remove. "I must thank you again for your assistance last night, Captain Preston. You were very kind."

He shook his head. The riding crop tapped against his boot. "Any gentleman would have behaved the same."

Amy wasn't sure that was true. Any gentleman would have insisted she rest, but neither Fred nor Mr. Farraday nor even Nate's own uncle had offered to carry her home. "Perhaps you are right about the gentlemen in your generation. My elderly cohort would not be so fast to sacrifice a hot roast."

Their eyes connected as Amy smiled, waiting for him to react to her tease. She dared not hope for another wink, but perhaps Nate would grin, or fire back a rejoinder that would make her laugh.

Mary interrupted: "What nonsense you spout, Amy. You are hardly of a different generation than Captain Preston."

"Is she not? Forgive me, Miss Lamplugh, but had I not previously known you, last night I would have mistaken you for a woman of a much more advanced age." Nate turned his whole body away from Amy, angling himself back towards the courtyard. "Excuse me, I will wait for Mr. Bremridge outside."

He hadn't meant it as an insult. Amy was sure of it. He couldn't have. He didn't know that Amy searched the mirror in the mornings in search of assurance she was not yet an old hag; he didn't realize his words would pierce her worse than if he had not recognized her at all.

And yet, he had said them. Without so much as a wink.

And now Amy knew. Haggard, tired, and wretched; everything she felt inside was how she appeared to the world, too.

How ridiculous of her to think she could still flirt with a man when she looked the way she did.

How pathetic that she had hoped Nate would want to steal a moment with her, too.

"Well," Mary said as Nate disappeared down the corridor. "Hell hath no fury like a *sailor* scorned."

He shouldn't have said it.

Nate knew it the moment the words left his lips. He shouldn't have let the whorl of pain leap from his heart to his tongue.

Yet he had. The words were said and Amy insulted. Eyes wide, the smile that had been rounding her cheeks evaporated.

It was that very smile that had forced him to say it. The banter. As if they were still courting.

Amy had rejected him. Sent him away with a letter that declared her allegiance to her family, even though she had promised to start a new one with Nate. It was not fair of her to flirt with him as if they could pick up where they had left off.

And there had been her nephew, rushing to her as if she were his dearest person in the world. The boy had dark curls and wide hazel eyes, just like Amy. Just like a son would have, if Nate and Amy had married.

He hadn't known before that it was possible to be jealous on behalf of a person that didn't exist. And yet apparently he could be, for seeing her with that child instead of one of their own, teasing Nate as if he were her husband and not the man she'd scorned, had sent him straight to cruelty.

It was too fresh to even consider apologizing as he retreated from the breakfast room back to the corridor. He let his emotions disappear into banal conversation with Mr. Bremridge while they mounted their horses and headed towards the riding trails threading the perimeter of Selsea Park. There was far more comfort in hearing about neighborhood feuds than in contemplating how to make things right with Amy.

In fact, by the time their ride ended, Nate decided that perhaps the insult had been just what he needed. He had come to Selsea Park unaware that it would foist Amy upon him; last evening and this morning revealed to him that visiting with her reopened his heartbreak. Perhaps he *should* be able to make polite chitchat with her as if they had never shared anything more than a church pew, but sailors *should* be able to keep their ships clean without needing to be flogged, and yet sometimes a flogging was necessary.

Nate had made the mistake of visiting the same home as Amy. Amy had made the mistake of thinking he had forgiven her.

His barb—no matter how undeserved it may have been—would serve as a barrier to keep things in their natural order.

"Would you like to luncheon with the family?" Mr. Bremridge asked as they cooled their horses with a slow trot down the main drive. "The boys would love to hear your stories of the sea."

If he were being polite, Nate would accept, and he would make a point of pulling Amy aside and apologizing for his earlier words.

Last night, he had been polite. This morning, he had been polite. And all it had done was reveal that when it came to Amy, his wound was still festering.

Better to let his words be, then. If he had to see Amy, then they let her know he was no longer a friend.

And if he could avoid seeing her, all the better.

"I've got correspondence to attend to, I'm afraid," he replied to Bremridge, nudging his horse to stay on the main drive. "I'll have to spin yarns for the boys some other time."

And so he was the villain. Happier was he to be the blackguard who returned to Amy's neighborhood only to spurn her than to be the fool who got his heart broken all over again.

It proved easy to avoid her for the better part of the week. At the great house, there really were letters Nate had to attend to—buckets of letters, it felt like, almost a year's worth of correspondence that had been waiting in Portsmouth for him. He wrote to his father in London, Ellen and Max at their new home, his other sisters at Northfield Hall, and Benjamin in Ireland. He replied to the mothers of his midshipmen and powder monkeys who had sent appeals to their sons' captain to keep their boys safe.

Uncle Graham was eager to speak with Nate, too. He had grand plans for his company, the Oriental Fair Exchange, and wanted Nate's opinion on it all. Would the palm oil factories in West Africa accept Indian cotton as an exchange? Which African kings would be most friendly to a new trading company? What kind of captain was necessary to oversee a fleet of ships, and how many crewmen could they count on to make it from one point of the globe to its opposite?

And then there were all the activities of being a houseguest. Long afternoons in Sir Charles's smoking room swapping opinions on the latest happenings in the newspapers. Accompanying Lady Olivia for walks through the formal gardens, where she inspected the flower beds and hedge maze for signs of imperfection, the whole time prodding Nate about when he would decide to take a bride. Morning rides through the park—now on his own, to avoid the dower house—and quiet evenings filled with more port, more smoking, and more stories.

So long as Nate did not turn down that packed-earth drive to the dower house, he did not need to think of Amy at all.

He devoted most of his energy to preparing for the impending court-martial. They awaited the arrival of Admiral Stratton, who had been appointed a judge in the case upon his ship's return from Lisbon. Once the man landed, the trial might be called within days, or the date might be set several weeks further hence. Either way, Nate could not predict *when* he would face his fate, only that it was fast approaching.

He prepared the only way he knew how: by marshalling men to his side. Nate wrote to Commodore Collier to beg his appearance as a witness; he wrote to the African Institution for a report on the number of people still being purchased as slaves each year; he even wrote to an old pirate he had once arrested to see if, for a price, the fellow would testify to the practice of sailing under false flags.

"Admiral Stratton lives over in Westmore House, only a few miles away," Sir Charles volunteered one afternoon, his words warped by the cigar in his mouth. "Lady Olivia has invited his family to a supper party. She thought it would be useful to you."

Nate bowed his head in thanks. "You and Lady Olivia are gracious in your kindness."

"On the contrary. It brings Lady Olivia great joy when she can use social connections to influence a person's future." Sir Charles offered Uncle Graham another pour of port. "Besides, it is an easy thing to do for decency. I am far from being a man as...principled...as your father Lord Preston, yet even I believe we must do what is within our power to stop the slave trade, or else not call ourselves Christians. At the very least, we must not punish officers such as yourself for erring in the course of duty."

If Sir Charles really wanted to stop the slave trade, he would call for the majority of the British naval fleet to crowd the shores of Africa, Rio de Janeiro, and Cuba, instead of relying on a small squadron of five ships to patrol thousands of miles across the Atlantic Ocean. If the question was really how to stop the misery of slavery, then Britain would learn its lesson from the past decade and realize that stopping the slave *trade* had no impact on the magnitude of slavery within its own colonies.

That wasn't the question. Even Nate couldn't spend more than a quarter of an hour at a time trying to figure out how to end slavery, and he had spent the last year devoting his life to it. He wouldn't ask it of Sir Charles now.

"My question is," Uncle Graham interjected, "after all you have seen, Nate, and now this experience being dragged through the mud because of it, do you still think it worth the fight? Is the Preventive Squad really *doing* anything?"

"It is freeing people." But Nate knew what his uncle was arguing. He had argued it with his fellow officers on endless nights. A squadron of five ships was nothing to the dozens of slavers taking thousands of people from Africa every year, and even though British ships had been patrolling the coast for nearly a decade, the trade flourished just the same.

"Is it worth sacrificing your own health and your good name over?" Uncle Graham persisted. "To pick at the slave trade one ship at a time and never actually bring it to an end?"

Before the court-martial, Nate's answer had been an unequivocal yes. Even if he had only saved a single person from a slave hold, it would be worth it—and in his year on the coast, he had saved several hundred.

He was quite sure his answer hadn't changed. Yet he didn't get a reply out before Sir Charles—a peacekeeper—said, "It should be a problem for the Foreign Secretary. The French must agree not to go to war over actions such as boarding a ship suspected of trading in slaves. Otherwise we all must live with our breath held lest we accidentally blow in their direction and start a war."

Nate responded to them both. "In the absence of a new treaty to absolve me of my sins, perhaps I'll just turn pirate and take my own ship down the coast of Africa to terrorize the slavers."

Sir Charles smiled. "Better to sweet-talk Miss Stratton at our supper party and get her grandfather to cancel the court-martial altogether."

Nate hoped the court-martial wouldn't be a topic of conversation at all. When Mr. Farraday had introduced the topic the other night, Amy had looked startled, which Nate hoped meant she hadn't read about it in the newspapers. He could only pray she stayed in ignorance. Of all people in the world, Amy alone knew how much Nate had wanted to join the Preventive Squadron.

Nate didn't want to see her reaction when she learned how he had jeopardized his command.

The supper party wouldn't be a big crush, Lady Olivia promised him. Just the family and some neighbors who didn't mind traveling after dark.

No need to dress too formally, she told him. His uniform would do, since after all he did look so handsome in it.

There would be no dancing, she swore to him. Why, there were hardly enough people to make up couples, and certainly no orchestra to make it a ball.

And yet, on the evening in question, he ended up in the southern parlor with a belly full of turtle soup, being coaxed into a minuet.

It wasn't that Nate minded dancing. Even on the West Coast of Africa, naval officers were expected to make up parties with governors and merchants, and more often than not that meant dancing with their wives and daughters.

It was that he minded dancing when Amy was in the room. He minded doing *anything* when Amy was in the room.

She had entered the party with quiet solemnity, greeting all her neighbors with nothing more than a familiar "How do you do." Her gown was dark blue silk in the kind of fashion that tried to minimize its wearer, so that she could—and *did*—disappear into the corner of the room. Her only nod towards decoration was a gauzy muslin scarf around her neck and pearl earrings that emphasized her pallor.

Every fiber of Nate's being wanted to go apologize to her. Which would lead to talking to her. Which would lead to feeling his heart twist again. Which was why he absolutely could not do so much as acknowledge her.

He had spent supper focusing on the rest of the group. He sat between two eligible young ladies—Lady Olivia had never claimed to be subtle—one of whom was the promised Miss Isabella Stratton. Miss Stratton seemed happily ignorant of the impending court-martial and flirted with Nate throughout the meal. Now she joined the call for dancing, clapping her hands together and knocking her head this way and that so that the curls ironed into her blond hair bounced against her temples.

"Please, Captain Preston, won't you dance with us?" Her eyes were impossibly round as she turned her appeal to him.

He had no choice except to play along. "But who will make the music if we are all dancing?"

"Amy will," volunteered Mrs. Bremridge, who was seated with her hands on either side of her burgeoning stomach. "I would, only this babe would kick me and I would lose the rhythm."

Nate wished he hadn't asked, since now he had to look at Amy. She was in finer health than at the previous party, pale but otherwise in control of herself; for a moment, her eyes met his, and he saw in them an emotion he didn't want to face.

Then she rose, smiling at Miss Stratton, and walked to the harpsichord. "A minuet, I think you said." Her fingers curved over the keys with more elegance than the finest dancer. She did not even need to look at music to start an opening chord.

No, her eyes were on Nate once more. She still wore that smile—a small one that thinned her lips into a complacent line—yet somehow her expression implied a question.

Will you really not insist that I dance with everyone else?

Will you really dance with Miss Stratton in front of me?

Will you really not apologize?

Nate didn't know what she was asking him. He only knew that in this brief moment before her fingers landed on their ivory keys, Amy was waiting for him to make some sort of choice.

And he knew, as he took Miss Stratton's hand to lead her into the opening figure, that he made the wrong one.

***

Amy didn't know why her heart had leapt at the suggestion of dancing. It had been years since she had joined in at a makeshift party like this one; she was too accomplished at the harpsichord, and too old for Lady Olivia's matchmaking schemes, to be invited to dance. From the moment her younger sister had married—when Amy was twenty-four—Amy had been considered the Unweddable Sister. The spinster, though she didn't wear the cap. Amy was there to make even numbers of the party or to provide entertainment, not to be entertained.

And Nate had made it perfectly clear he was among the rest of the world in seeing her that way. Where she looked at him and beheld the glorious young man she had once loved with all of her heart, he saw her as an old, shriveled version of herself.

So why, when Lady Olivia started cajoling the group to dance, had Amy's heart floated into her throat? Her whole being had turned towards Nate as if he were a magnet, as if she had every reason to expect that he would hold his hand out to her.

It was the same reason she had come tonight, instead of crying off with the excuse of a headache. Even though his words still cut into her skin, even though Nate hadn't so much as visited the dower house since, some part of Amy still believed he hadn't meant it. And that when he saw her again, he would apologize, and they could put things right between them.

Whatever *right* was.

Of course, Nate didn't ask her to dance. He hadn't even *looked* at her all evening. His eyes were on Miss Stratton, that flower of youth who flitted around the room with smiles and titters like some kind of spring tulip. When at last he did glance Amy's way, there was no emotion in his gaze, no remorse twitching at the corners of his lips.

It was almost as if he didn't see her at all.

She played the minuet, as expected. She knew it by heart, which was to say she could play it from memory even while her heart broke all over again. Even as she watched Nate smile at Miss Stratton, that same smile he used to give Amy as he asked her for a walk.

Captain Preston. It would be better if she called him Captain Preston in her head. He had been Nate when he had been hers; he had been Nate in the times when he would have rushed to apologize, rather than ignoring her for a week. This man in front of her twirling Miss Stratton through Lady Olivia's parlor was not Nate. He was Captain Preston.

A man Amy didn't know at all.

She played for nearly an hour, spinning out whatever Miss Stratton or Miss Howell called for: allemandes, gavottes, quadrilles. Only when Miss Stratton asked breathlessly, "Oh, Lady Olivia, mightn't we practice the waltz?" did Amy have the gumption to stand from the harpsichord.

"I beg your pardon, but my fingers will fall off if I play another moment."

"Poor Miss Lamplugh." Lady Olivia wrapped an arm across Amy's shoulders. "We have quite taken advantage of you. Of course, you must sit and enjoy some refreshment."

Amy couldn't fault Lady Olivia for pointing her back towards the corner chair. After all, Amy had swooned at the last supper party; anyone might assume she wasn't well enough to dance.

Still, she wished for some other outcome as she followed the lady's guidance. If Amy could not dance, could she not be excused to go home and sit out the rest of the evening without watching everyone else's merriment?

She had not quite gotten two steps from the harpsichord when Nate—no, Captain Preston—asked, "Do you not dance, Miss Lamplugh?"

He gazed at her with that same blank expression as before. Except, at his sides, his gloved fingers fisted.

Amy reminded herself this was not—could not be—the moment she had been hoping for. He was not hers. He was only being polite. "I do."

"Then you must take your turn." And, opening his palm, he held out a hand to her.

From her seat, Mary added, "Miss Howell, you can play this set, can't you? I heard you play a beautiful waltz this past Christmas."

And so it was arranged by everyone around her. Miss Howell, blushing, took a seat at the harpsichord, murmuring, "Of course, the waltz is meant for an orchestra or pianoforte. It will sound a little strange on the harpsichord." Miss Stratton partnered with Fred. And Amy walked into Nate's—*Captain Preston's*—arms.

She had forgotten how well-matched in height they were. Amy hardly had to reach to settle her left hand on his shoulder; her right hand landed in his opposite without either wrenching her shoulder or lowering his arm too far. Their gazes lined up, so that it was only natural to look into each other's eyes.

Except Captain Preston pinned his gaze on something to the side of her, something that kept him from meeting her glance.

Amy decided to funnel all her attention into the steps, as if she were partnered with a dance instructor and not the man she once had kissed so furiously that she had felt all parts of him press hard against her. Except Miss Howell set a fast tempo for the waltz; Captain Preston's hand on Amy's back grew stronger, pulling her in ever so much closer, so that they could keep up with the steps. And she had forgotten to put her gloves back on after playing for so long, so Amy felt every twitch of his hand against her own bare fingers.

Even with the advanced speed, Captain Preston didn't miss a beat, dancing boxes across the room. Amy's blue silk skirt swirled against their ankles as their steps grew more and more in sync.

And then, he looked at her. Two gazes merged in one; as if he spoke the words out loud, she knew he was asking if she wanted to spin out in a twirl; and he heard her answer. Next thing she knew, his hand disappeared from her waist, propelling her under the arc of his left arm.

For that second, Amy was suspended in time and imagination, nothing more than a beautiful dancer with a beautiful partner.

But what came next was even better: when she landed back in the center of his arms, they laughed at the same time. And he was Nate again, if only for that moment.

The dance ended. Those who had been watching applauded, which Miss Stratton accepted on behalf of everyone with a deep curtsy. "And now you must twirl me like that, Captain Preston," she announced, turning to him without waiting to see if Miss Howell was willing to play again.

Amy was euphoric enough that she could watch him accept the lady's command without feeling it in her own heart. But she had no interest in watching him lead Miss Stratton through the same dance; she would not be able to stomach seeing him laugh with Miss Stratton, too. She slipped out of the room instead, murmuring, "I must get some fresh air."

No one seemed to hear.

She retreated to the stone terrace on the side of the house that overlooked the hedge maze. Though the waxing moon provided enough light to see the heads of marble statues waiting for the intrepid maze explorer to discover them. Amy settled on an iron bench, welcoming its cool touch on her overheated body. Her thoughts were still dancing, and she leaned into the quiet to let them settle.

What did it matter if he were Captain Preston now, lost to her forever? Amy had never expected to see him again, and now she had two new memories with him to cherish. Even if he considered her nothing more than a spinster, why should Amy not enjoy his company, if she could get it? It was not as if she were trying to catch him in marriage. She was not fit to be anyone's wife, much less worthy of being Captain Preston's. She wanted only a few good moments, and here she had them.

Instead of being heartbroken or jealous or sad, Amy resolved to be grateful. And curious. He was Captain Preston because she didn't know him at all anymore. Six years had changed her, and she had remained in the same spot. Meanwhile, Captain Preston had spent those six years embarking on a career, learning how to be an officer, fighting battles in the Great Lakes and the Mediterranean and Africa. He was a stranger not because he was cruel but because he was an entirely new person; Amy would do better to get to know him than to presume she deserved any kind of special treatment from him.

Closing her eyes, she smiled to herself, embalming this feeling as a new resolve to guide her through the rest of his visit.

Which was why she shrieked when suddenly, his voice spoke: "Are you feeling well?"

He stood in front of her, blocking the moonlight so that he was nothing more than a black silhouette.

"I'm sorry, don't be frightened. It's only me."

"Oh." Amy realized her hand was on her heart. She let it drop. "You startled me, that's all."

"I worried you wandered off and fainted again."

Had he really noticed? Or had someone sent him out in search of her? But Amy couldn't think how that would come to be. If Lady Olivia had worried about Amy, she would have sent Fred or Sir Charles or one of the servants. "I wanted some fresh air. I'm quite well, though. Thank you."

"The parlor has grown nearly as stuffy as a ship's hold."

Amy couldn't quite believe that after ignoring her all through supper—not to mention spurning Fred's invitations to the dower house—now Captain Preston was making conversation with her as if they were at a town assembly.

"Do you mind if I sit?" he asked, gesturing to the space beside her on the bench.

Most likely, she should object. But Amy didn't have it in her. She watched him take the seat, her mind completely blank except for astonishment.

"I owe you an apology." He sat forward, elbows on his knees; his words were directed to the stonework beneath their feet. "I spoke cruelly the other day, and I deeply regret any injury my words may have caused."

Her astonishment grew. "I have already forgotten it," she lied, because in this moment she couldn't remember what he had said, could hardly even remember the hurt. She felt only joy that he was beside her. "I'm sure you didn't mean it as it came out. I often speak more sharply than I intend."

Nate—for he must be Nate again, if they were having so personal a conversation—grimaced. He exhaled, and Amy feared he wasn't going to respond.

Yet he did: "I didn't mean the words I said, but I'm afraid I did intend to hurt you. It is an ugly trait of mine. You hurt me, and so I felt I had to hurt you back." He still spoke to the ground. "Most likely I have spent too much time in the wilds and don't deserve to be in polite company."

Her head spun from everything he was saying. "When did I hurt you?"

His chin jerked immediately. His eyes landed on hers, and even in the moonlight, she saw the emotion burning in them. "Surely you don't pretend to have forgotten what transpired between us six years ago."

"Oh. That. Of course I remember." To her horror, tears choked Amy's throat. She swallowed them away. "I thought perhaps you referred to something from this visit. I remember."

"Then you understand what I refer to." He leaned back, his face turning away from her again. With a little desperation, he added, "Why perhaps you owe me an apology, too."

Amy was sure she had apologized in her letter. In her memory, the entire note was an apology, with the ink smudged from all the tears she had shed. "I didn't want to injure you, Nate. If it is any consolation, I broke my own heart in the same moment."

She meant the words tenderly. He scoffed. "Do you think it is consolation to me to know you have been miserable? Do you think I am glad to discover you have spent the last six years becoming your sister's companion and losing your health? I wanted to marry you, Amy. How could I wish misery upon you?"

All night, he had been a blank face. Now, his voice broke with emotion. Amy didn't know what to do with it. "I am not miserable. I am only here helping Mary while she is indisposed, anyhow. Most of my life is still at Swanhill House."

"Where you are companion to your stepmother instead." Nate glared at his shoes. "Everyone has been happy to tell me about what a dutiful daughter you are."

She did not like her situation, yet hearing it from Nate's mouth—discovering the scorn with which he viewed it—lit Amy with a new love for it. "And you want me to apologize for that? How dare I care for my family. How dare I accept the care they give me. Oh, what a monster I am!"

"You were going to be your own person. You were going to run your own household, command your own budget, live life however you saw fit. I thought perhaps you might regret giving that up."

"I was going to be *your* person. Instead of a dutiful daughter or a dutiful sister, I would have been called a dutiful *wife*. You only complain because I am not being dutiful to *you*."

There came that scoff again, but this time, it sounded closer to a sob. Nate jerked to his feet. "Forget I ever asked for an apology. It is clear you would make the same choice over again, even knowing what it would get you."

As he bounded towards the hedge maze, Amy's own words caught up to her heart. And she realized how it had sounded. How she had made it seem as if love had never been a part of the question.

"Nate!" He hadn't gotten far; Amy chased after him; she caught him by the arm, her fingers wrapped around the swell of his bicep. "Nate, wait, please, I didn't mean it like that."

He waited. He even looked at her, his face a storm of emotion.

Amy hated that she was the cause of it. "If the question was whether my heart belonged to you, then my answer was yes. But the question was whether I would leave my family to marry you against their express wishes. If I had run off with you, we would have had a few wonderful weeks together. And then you would have disappeared on a ship, and I would have been alone in Portsmouth, without the help of my family or friends, waiting for your pay and waiting for you to return. With a child on the way, most likely. Knowing life as you know it now, can you really wish that upon me?"

She couldn't keep tears from her eyes. Nate, softening, cupped her elbow in his palm. "Your family might not have forgiven you, but you would not have been without friends or family. You would have had *my* family. You could have lived at Northfield Hall if you didn't want to be alone in Portsmouth."

"Where I wouldn't even be allowed to wear my cotton dresses?"

His face shuttered. "If I hadn't been a Preston, then. If I had been able to promise you some other family connection that wasn't so ridiculous, you would have eloped with me after all?"

It was a question Amy had never asked herself. She clung to him, desperate to keep him close. "I don't know."

He nodded. His fingers rose from her elbow up along the line of her arm and then to cup her chin. Amy knew before it happened that he was leaning in for a kiss; she nudged herself forward, turning her lips to meet his.

It was brief, yet deep. The kiss she had owed him that night six years ago when she hadn't been brave enough to say goodbye in person. Their tongues touched, not so much in a tangle as in a final embrace. Amy had missed this; Amy had missed him; she had missed it all so much.

When Nate ended the kiss, he stroked her cheek one last time with his thumb. Then he let her go. "We will be civil, then, and perhaps even become friends."

"Yes." It was all she could say, her whole body lost in the moment.

"Goodbye, Amy." He disappeared into the hedge, and it was only later that she realized he should have said "Good night."

Chapter Four

Even after all these years, Nate was still learning what it meant to be a Preston.

As a child, it had been his pride and joy. Northfield Hall was his parents' dominion, and everyone on the five hundred acres went out of their way to express their gratitude. Not that Papa and Mama wanted to be lauded; they only wanted to build a community of people who were safe, healthy, and without fear of being turned out in the name of profit. The result was hundreds of tradesmen, laborers, and families who were happy to call Northfield Hall their home. What boy wouldn't love to be praised for having such wonderful parents?

He had always had some vague idea that the rest of the world lived a little differently. Each time a newcomer arrived at Northfield Hall, or a visitor came for a tour, Nate heard them exclaim over how they could never do without their coffee or how they couldn't imagine life without sugar.

Having never had coffee nor sugar nor a fine cotton lawn shirt, Nate had always thought it strange they would prize substances over the fight against evil on earth.

By the time he left Northfield Hall at age eighteen for Portsmouth to take his commission in the navy, Nate knew that people had different beliefs than his family on slavery and colonization and who deserved to enjoy the fruits of hard labor. But he didn't realize how threatening some commentators considered his father. Papa, in the eyes of the establishment, was not a man trying something new in order to break a harmful pattern of behavior. No, he was an instigator, a revolutionary—a voice to be silenced.

Nate thought he had learned that lesson six years ago when Lord Warre rejected his request to marry Amy.

He thought he had learned it as a lieutenant from his officers and men alike, who all profited from the expanding colonial empire. His first captain had sat him down as soon as they were out of the Channel, placed a ewer of coffee on the table, and forced Nate to drink the whole thing in one sitting. "You'll have to be a real Briton, Preston," he had said, in a way that was both threatening and friendly, "or you won't make it at all."

Nate had given up all his family's practices, of course, without much say in the matter. Cotton was everywhere in uniforms, sails, bedding, rope; every port he sailed into existed because European colonizers wanted to extract fortunes from and exert power over people far away; his meals were dictated by the provisions stocked by naval petty officers, the rum-based grog allotted by the Admiralty, and whatever local foods the ship's crew could get its hands on. He acquired a taste for tea, sugar, spices, and coffee, and his favorite piece of clothing was a fine muslin shirt that on a hot summer day near the equator felt almost like wearing nothing.

He never would have expected Amy to live as his family did. But neither had it occurred to him that she wouldn't want to count his family as her own, nor that the very idea of going without a few of life's luxuries would be enough reason for her to reject him.

It seemed he still had a lot to learn about how much the average Briton reviled the very concepts his family held so dear.

Which made it an awkward time for more Prestons to arrive at Selsea Park.

They came in an entourage: Papa on a horse; Caroline, Sophia, and Sophia's husband John in a carriage; and behind them a second carriage with trunks, two maids, and a valet.

Nate watched them coming down the drive with dread swelling in his stomach. When they had sent word a few days before the supper party that they were on their way, Nate had been delighted. It had been a year since he had seen any of them, even longer since he had seen so many members of his family at once.

If only they had arrived in time for the party. Then he would have been swept up in welcoming them, in hearing their stories, in soaking up their company. He would have waltzed with Caroline instead of Amy. He wouldn't have gone looking for Amy in the dark.

And he certainly wouldn't have kissed her.

Instead, Nate watched Papa cantering to the great house and could think only of how Amy would view the visit. Would she cringe each time Papa asked for chamomile tisane instead of tea? Would she cast her eyes away in disdain when Caroline turned down Chef's exquisite sugared pastries? Would she each day think to herself, *Thank God I didn't elope with him?*

Before the supper party, Nate would have told himself he didn't care. Before arriving at Selsea Park, he would have *believed* he didn't care.

Now, with Amy's explanation ringing in his ears and that foolish kiss lingering on his lips, Nate couldn't deceive himself.

He loved his family.

But he cared desperately what Amy thought of them. And she didn't care to think of them at all.

Papa dismounted first, handing his horse's reins to a groom while the carriages pulled along the gravel circle fronting the house. His travel suit was wrinkled and dusty, and he looked so much older than when Nate had last seen him a year and a half ago, just before sailing for West Africa. His hair was whiter, his eyes and mouth lined with heavier wrinkles. Yet when he smiled, he was exactly the same Papa he had always been.

"There you are," he said, taking Nate first by the wrists, then the biceps, and then pulling him into a hug. "There you are."

And Nate realized he *had* been feeling lost.

Caroline came next, practically tumbling out of the carriage and elbowing Sophia out of the way as she did it. Last Nate had seen her,

Caro had been fourteen, more a beast than either child or woman. There was some of that still in how she raced to him, not caring for decorum or even minding the flap of her hems at her ankles, except now she was tall, her blond hair tied away from her face, and her grin laced with new maturity.

Nate realized with a start that she was older than he had been when he had fallen in love with Amy.

"You don't write nearly enough letters, but I forgive you." Caroline beamed at him. "As long as you tell me absolutely everything that has happened since the last moment I saw you."

Nate gave her a solemn bow. "You have my word."

Sophia joined them on the stairs, greeting him with a gentle thwack on the back of his head. "That's what you get for being a terrible correspondent. Now meet my husband, Mr. John Anderson."

They were a striking pair: Sophia's deep yellow gown offset her brown hair and pale white complexion, while John wore a black suit with no adornment, his hair shaven close to his brown skin. He bowed at the neck to greet Nate, then said, "Sophia has told me many stories about you, and if I believed them, I would know you to be the most wicked and also most wonderful brother in all of Britain."

"Just wait until you hear the stories I have about her," Nate replied, shaking his new brother's hand. "You'll consider joining my ship as surgeon just to get away from her."

Sophia and John grinned at each other, the secret exchange of a couple secure in their love for one another. Nate had never expected to see Sophia—who had claimed she wanted nothing but independence, who had been determined to thwart all conventions—like this.

He should have felt glad for her. But instead, he felt envy. She hadn't wanted love, yet she had found it; he had yearned for it and only been spurned.

Nate turned away from the feeling. "I am honored you are visiting me instead of reporting to Parliament," he said to Papa.

"They can go a few weeks without me. I wouldn't dream of being anywhere other than with you just now."

Which reminded Nate that his family had not descended upon Selsea Park simply because he was on leave. They were there because he was waiting for the Admiralty to decide his fate. Waiting for some stuffy old judges who had never seen the inside of a slave ship to decide whether he deserved to be turned out because he'd dared make an independent decision.

This reunion was not simple at all.

Lady Olivia led the chaos of their arrival. After each of his family members had held onto Nate for a sufficient amount of time, they greeted Uncle Graham and their hosts; then Lady Olivia ushered them to their guest rooms. Nate hovered at the landing of the staircase, unsure whether to follow or not. The child within him wanted to cling to Papa's elbow, trail him into his room, and tell him about everything that had gone right and wrong since the last time they had met.

The adult in him didn't have words for such a summary. Nor did he have the stomach to discuss the events of his court-martial, much less hint at the mess he was making at Selsea Park. So he turned back, following Uncle Graham to wait for his family below in the drawing room.

"I told Chef to make up tea without thinking," Lady Olivia said, a little buzz of nerves interrupting her usually calm demeanor. "Will your family eat cold mutton? We had it butchered here on the farm."

"They will enjoy it very much."

Uncle Graham put a pinch of tobacco in his mouth. "You are too considerate, my lady. If I were host, I would say, you're having tea, Marty, or you're not eating at all."

"But then, he is your brother, and one must treat one's siblings with different care." A footman arrived with a tray boasting a beautiful teapot—imported, Nate suspected, from China—and Lady Olivia shooed it away. "Miss Preston will be a welcome addition to our next party, Captain. Has she come out in London yet?"

A question that a good brother might have the answer to. Nate thought back on all the letters he had gotten from home; none of them seemed to have mentioned a Season for Caroline. "I couldn't say, Lady Olivia, but I'm sure she will enjoy whatever entertainment you provide."

"I am thinking of a more formal ball, since the young ladies were so eager to dance the night before last. And you looked very handsome standing up with Miss Stratton."

Nate nodded to acknowledge this, as expected of him. The strategist in him knew he should encourage something with Miss Stratton. Her grandfather would have an awkward time stripping Nate of his naval rank if he were betrothed to his granddaughter. Though Nate would feel bad for Miss Stratton if they did end up together based on so selfish a motivation. She was a pretty woman, excellent at polite conversation, and most likely would be a pleasant life companion.

But Nate had no business flirting with Miss Stratton if he was going to keep following Amy into the shadows.

Which he wasn't going to. He had gotten from Amy all he ever would. An admission that even knowing she would end up like this, she preferred to be the sickly and ill-used sister than to be married to Nate. That she viewed the price of living as a Preston not worth paying in order to sanction their love with marriage.

He wasn't worth the discomfort he would bring to her life, in other words. And how stupid he had been to think that she might feel differently.

In the end, he could only right one wrong. All these years, it had been what he hated most: that their last kiss—by the reflecting lake, hidden from her great-aunt behind a tree—had been their last without his knowing it. So Nate had kissed her in the dark, knowing he would never kiss her again. He had memorized the softness of her lips, the smell of her skin, the way her fingers clung to his hand.

And now he would let her go. He would flirt with Miss Stratton and the other young ladies that crossed his path. He would take what opportunities the future opened up to him. Return to Africa; marry and settle down at Northfield Hall; accept a place in Uncle Graham's company; whatever it might be, Nate knew only it would be without Amy.

"Ah, wonderful!" Lady Olivia cried from where she stood looking out the window. "Fred got my message. I thought the boys might like to meet our company. They have been cooped up in that house with all the rain yesterday."

Nate resisted the urge to stand. He did not need to watch Mr. Bremridge lead his boys across the park. Neither did he need to investigate whether Amy was with them. It was immaterial to him whether she showed up in the drawing room or not. She was nothing more than an acquaintance, and never would be anything more.

Even if she was horrified to meet his family, it meant nothing to Nate. He would not allow himself to care.

His family made it to the drawing room first. Sophia and Caroline claimed the two seats beside Nate, while Papa took a chair by the window. Uncle Graham sat with Sir Charles, and John Anderson took the seat beside Lady Olivia. It was a full and happy party; Nate tried to relax in his chair and enjoy the reunion.

"Where is Eddie Chow?" he teased Caroline. "Last time I was at Northfield Hall, the two of you couldn't be separated. I'm shocked to discover you are miles apart."

"Oh, he is apprenticed in London. I wrote you about that. Didn't you get my letter?" Caro didn't wait for a reply. "He is learning to be a glazier. He'll be done at the end of the summer, and then..." She darted a glance at Papa, who had leaned away for a conversation with Uncle Graham. "He'll return to Northfield Hall."

Sophia twisted her lips in a tease. "To marry Caroline, of course."

Poor Caro blushed. There was an impatience in her that belied her embarrassment; Sophia was speaking her dearest hopes aloud. Nate turned the conversation away to spare her further exposure. "And you, Sophia? I thought you were planning a tour of the continent this year."

"I leave in October. A good thing, too, or I might have missed you. I'm trying to convince Caroline to come with me, but she is eager to return to Northfield Hall."

"Depending on how the Admiralty decides my case, perhaps I'll go with you." It was actually an appealing idea; Nate had never traveled for the sake of traveling. "So long as you agree to skip France."

"Oh dear, but I plan to spend at least three months in Paris!"

Then came commotion: the two little boys raced into the room as if Satan were chasing them. Mr. Bremridge called after them, "Slow down! Be polite!"

Lady Olivia collected the little one in her arms and tried to corral the elder, but he sped around her chair before she could catch him. "Calmly now, Charles," she admonished. "Greet our guests like the little gentleman you are."

But, of course, it was only Amy who could get the boy to behave. "Show us that bow you've been practicing, Charles."

She entered the room a few steps behind Mr. Bremridge. Her gown was dusky pink cotton with a matching scarf tied beneath her chin. Today, she didn't look pale or tired; there was a nervous energy as she looked at Nate and then, immediately, away again.

Little Charles executed his bow, then retreated to his aunt, where he clung to her skirt and stared at the strangers. She caught his little hand in her own while Lady Olivia made the introductions.

"Ah, I recall that Lord Warre and his family were particularly hospitable to Nate when he first came to Portsmouth," Papa said when Lady Olivia declared Amy to be Lord Warre's daughter. He bowed. "Thank you for being so good to my son."

Amy blushed. Nate thought he might be blushing, too. He had never told his family about Amy, though she wouldn't know that. Perhaps she thought Papa was speaking with double meaning. "It is easy to do, Lord Preston," she replied. "One could not ask for more pleasant company than Captain Preston. I'm sure Sir Charles and Lady Olivia agree with me."

"Neither more pleasant nor more handsome." Lady Olivia beamed over the head of the grandson in her arms. "I am already planning another neighborhood party so that the young ladies may enjoy ogling Captain Preston a little more before he has to leave us. The night before last, we had informal dancing—even some waltzing! You can imagine how everyone was captivated."

Nate didn't want to remember the feeling of Amy in his arms.

"How delightful," Sophia replied for the family. "We shall look forward to it, and you must let us know how we may assist in preparing for it. And Miss Lamplugh, perhaps you can accompany Caroline and me to Portsmouth for shopping; I'm afraid Caro might not have a gown suitable for a ball."

Somewhere in this dialogue, they all reshuffled: now Lady Olivia sat beside Sir Charles with the two-year-old in her arms; Uncle Graham and Papa were opposite each other at the card table; Sophia joined her husband near the fireplace; Mr. Bremridge led the elder boy to the window; and Nate ended up back in his original seat, only this time, he was sandwiched between Caroline and Amy.

He drew every one of his muscles to attention to keep his knee from knocking against Amy's.

"I would enjoy that very much," Amy was saying. "Although I'm sure between my sister and myself, we have something that Miss Preston could borrow. Most of Mary's gowns are stored away anyhow, since she is currently in the family way."

"Is she? Oh, you must consider Mr. Anderson at your disposal while we are visiting. Mustn't they, my dear?"

John, who had built a reputation as one of England's finest accoucheurs, bowed. "I am at Mrs. Bremridge's beck and call."

The conversation turned to the usual small talk among gentry, all those present trying to discover mutual connections. Nate watched Sophia engage with a little amazement; when he had last seen her, before her marriage, she had been somewhat feral, always snarling or snapping instead of simply letting people have their little inane moments. Now, she could pass for any genteel lady in any genteel drawing room.

Until Sir Charles made the mistake of bringing up Queen Caroline. Six years ago, she had excommunicated herself from Britain, embarking on an extended tour of Italy, Vienna, and even Jerusalem. Now that her husband was king, she had returned to claim her place beside him—and he had declared war, forcing Parliament into holding a trial to determine whether she had committed adultery while abroad. "I'm sure I will meet with no disagreement that it is a blemish upon our country for a marriage to be open for public scrutiny. A royal marriage, no less!"

Sophia's mouth twisted in that way it did right before she made trouble. "I'm afraid I cannot agree, Sir Charles. I think it is a spectacular event for our society. How many of us must now confront our own definitions of matrimony? How many of us must examine why we are willing to forgive the husband for infidelities but not the scorned wife? When our hearts bleed in sympathy for the queen, how many of us must then question why we still want to trap her in the marriage that has caused her so much misery?"

This was the Sophia whom Nate remembered. She wasn't just sharing a contrary opinion; she was baiting the room, waiting to see who would respond, and she was ready to bite off their heads when they did.

He held his breath. Prayed for Papa or John or someone to intervene. Wished his family would be so very much themselves somewhere *else*.

"Do you think many people are having that conversation?" Amy leaned forward to take up the challenge. "It would be very well if they were, but even in the newspapers, the discussion is limited to the reputation of the country. If anything, people who are sympathetic to the queen seem to believe her wish is to remain in the marriage."

Sophia's lips parted to reply. Nate rushed out his own response to stop her from whatever attack she had in mind. "I think what Miss Lamplugh means to suggest is that while it may be common at Northfield Hall to take every opportunity to examine each and every one of our social customs, the rest of the world rather likes having traditions and institutions on which we can rely."

"Actually, Captain Preston, what I meant was that the rest of the world doesn't engage in the conversation. Instead of questioning the purpose of matrimony, we hear only how important it is, and what a shame that the queen did not better please the king. We are not gaining anything by taking our queen to trial." Amy met Nate's gaze plainly. "I would prefer it if we *did* have the discussions that may occur at Northfield Hall."

Before their kiss, he would have been searching her expression for some kind of hidden meaning—or trying to avoid it altogether. Now, he only stared back. He didn't understand what she wanted. She wouldn't marry him because of who his family was, yet here she was, voluntarily taking non-tea with them, expressing her admiration for them.

"But I cannot think what you mean, Mrs. Anderson," Lady Olivia said. "Matrimony is an essential part of our life. You do not mean to suggest that there are people who think to live without it? I mean, people who are not wicked?"

Sophia lit up at the question. "What is so essential about it? Take Miss Lamplugh. She seems to be perfectly happy without the burden of a husband."

Nate swallowed against the feeling *that* comment gave him. From the corner of his eye—for he surely wasn't going to look directly at her—he saw Amy blush bright red again.

"A person must make do with their lot," Lady Olivia replied, "but I am certain that Miss Lamplugh would have been happier had a husband come her way."

The conversation was beyond ridiculous.

Even more ridiculous: the bolt of protective outrage that seized Nate.

And most ridiculous, his reply: "You use the past tense, madam, yet you cannot mean to imply Miss Lamplugh has lost her chance. She still has youth and beauty and wit on her side. Surely matrimony is still in her future, should she choose it."

The whole room stared at him. Except for Amy. When Nate dared look at her, she stared at her own knees. He couldn't quite tell, but there might have been tears brimming in her eyes.

He shot to his feet. "Of course, it would have to be the right gentleman, of the right family and a good profession and a bright future ahead of him. No one she has yet met, I'm sure. Still, you must not discount her so readily."

Everyone kept staring at him. Nate was quite sure he had made an ass of himself. Lady Olivia's mouth was open like that of a fish.

But before anyone could respond, Amy said, "Excuse me," and rushed out of the room.

Amy was happy to keep to the dower house for the rest of that day. She would keep to it for the rest of her life, if it meant never running into Nate's family again. How stupid she had been to go up for tea!

She didn't know what she had been thinking. Fred had come back from wherever the day had taken him with news that the Preston family was that very moment arriving at Selsea Park, and Amy's body had moved without waiting for permission from her brain. They were characters who had loomed large on the stage of her mind for years: Lord Preston from the newspapers; Sophia Preston as the wild sister whom Nate had dozens of stories about, which he usually pulled out when he wanted either to impress Amy or make her laugh; Caroline Preston as the baby of the family, his cherished littlest sibling for whom he had an obvious love. Of course Amy was going to help Fred take the children up for an introduction; how could she let such an opportunity slip away?

She had been dying to see Nate again, too. Their honest conversation had only made the forest between them thicker and more confusing; the kiss had lit it on fire. Amy wanted to lay eyes on him again and see how he reacted. She wanted to smell the honey scent of his skin. She wanted to have a polite conversation and discover whether they could be friends even after everything.

An idiot. A fool. A simpleton. That was all she was. To think that after a conversation like *that* there was any hope of friendship. What existed between her and Nate were shattered plans. He didn't want to hear from her. He thought her a woman who rejected him and his family out of hand. He couldn't see the nuance of what it was to consider leaving one's home without permission, of what her life would have been if she had eloped with him.

She shouldn't have run out of the room. Crying, to make it worse. The last thing Amy had wanted was to draw attention to herself. Yet she was sure they all had watched her go, wondering what on earth was the matter with her.

Then again, perhaps they all knew. Perhaps Nate had told his whole family about Miss Amy Lamplugh who had thrown off his marriage offer, and he gave that speech only to remind them that she was the one who had broken his heart.

At this very moment, the Preston family might be lighting torches to burn her at the stake.

So Amy hid at the dower house. Fred returned with the boys, and after he recovered from the tax of fathering, he found her in the drawing room with a concerned frown on his brow. "Are you quite all right, sister?"

"Quite." Amy put down her embroidery to prove herself with a smile. "I felt one of my spells coming over me and didn't want to faint in front of all that company, but I am fresh as a daisy now."

He hovered a moment longer, as if he didn't believe her, before being called away by Mary. Later, at supper, he asked once more: "Was it what Mother said about your marriageability that upset you so, Amy? She can't handle that kind of drawing room debate, you know, and I'm sure she spoke without thinking."

Mary, of course, had to know what he referred to, and Fred retold the whole scene from his perspective: Mrs. Anderson had instigated an argument by suggesting matrimony was unnecessary; Lady Olivia claimed that Amy would have been happier had she ever married; and Nate had taken umbrage at that and insisted Amy was still marriageable.

"He still pines for you, then," Mary said, eyes falling shrewdly on Amy. "I thought he might, from the way he looked at you during that waltz."

Amy shook her head; if only that were enough to end the conversation. "We are friends, nothing more. Besides, Lady Olivia is right. My marriageable days are behind me. If not because of my age, then because of my..."

She touched her goiter, which felt as if it were peeking out from beneath the cotton scarf around her neck.

Mary looked down at her food. She was happy enough to deny Amy's condition when Amy had any physical complaints, but even she admitted that Amy had the same disease their mother had. They both remembered the growth on their mother's neck, which had gotten bigger and bigger until the day she died when Amy was seven and Mary five. As far as neighbors were concerned, she had died in childbirth; the accoucheur had told the family that it was her palpitations and goiter that made the birth so dangerous.

"I was not upset, Fred," Amy insisted. "I didn't want to faint in front of company again. That's all."

But even at bedtime, the afternoon still vibrated in her bones. She shouldn't have tried to debate with Mrs. Anderson. What she had *wanted* to say was that all the talk of the royal divorce only instigated people to speak even more casually of the importance of marriage, without remembering there were some souls in the room who hadn't married. If only people did question marriage the way Mrs. Anderson thought they did, Amy might not feel quite so invisible for failing to secure a husband and family of her own.

And then Nate had spoken up the way he did. Seeing her so clearly when everyone else, if they saw her at all, only read her outline and moved on.

She liked being seen by him. She didn't like the rest of the room staring, nor did she want them all to see Nate's heart more clearly. Whatever was between the two of them belonged to them alone. She didn't want his family or Lady Olivia and Sir Charles to start casting their own narratives. If they did, there was no hope for friendship at all.

In bed, Amy fell into a fitful sleep, a nightmare twisting her mind with whispers about her growing louder and louder, until she woke suddenly. Her heart raced, and her body was hot, on fire.

An episode, no doubt because she had used it as an excuse so many times that afternoon.

Amy hated it when she got hot more than when she got cold. At least when her bones felt frozen, she could pile on blankets and drink hot tea while waiting for the shivers to pass.

When heat came to visit, she could take off all her clothes and still need to fan herself.

She rose from bed. There was no point trying to sleep when it felt like the sun itself was pressing down on her. What she wanted to do was pour the ewer on her washstand over her head and let all the cool water rush down her bare skin. But she knew—from a bad experiment at Swanhill House several years ago—that would only result in a puddle on the floor.

Amy moved to the window instead, lifting its sashes to let in the night air. She supposed it was cool; on her skin, it felt like a hot breeze. Still, it was better than the stuffiness of the room. Leaning forward, she eyed the moon, which was almost full. Beneath her, the kitchen garden was bathed in pale silver light.

A garden wouldn't be hurt by a puddle of water.

And the moon was high, near the middle of the sky, which meant it was late enough that no one else in the dower house should be awake. Cook and Iris wouldn't yet be up to start the day's bread.

No one would see her.

She fanned herself with her palm for one moment more, contemplating. Then, lifting the ewer from its place, she tiptoed downstairs. In the corridor, she heard Fred's snore and smiled.

This was the best idea she had ever had.

The night air enveloped her as she slipped out the side door. It certainly was cooler outside than in the house, but still her skin burned. Amy picked her way—barefoot—down the paths around the herb plants. A hedge protected the garden from the open field leading back to the great house. She rounded its other side for extra privacy, just in case someone in the dower house woke and looked out the window.

Then, not hesitating a moment longer, she raised the ewer over her head and let the water run. Cool, refreshing sluices spilled down her hair, her neck, her nightgown. Sweet relief dampened her breasts and swept away the sweat pooling at the cusp of her buttocks.

It was perfect. It was necessary.

It was shocking when a voice interrupted her.

CHAPTER FIVE

Nate hadn't meant to walk towards the dower house. Awake with the moon shining as bright as if it were the full sun, he had been too full of energy to stay in bed. He had too many thoughts—about Amy, about the court-martial, about the ills of the world—that needed silencing. Yet he didn't want to wake the household by pacing the corridors like a ghost.

He slipped out a side door and onto a grassy part of the lawn he hadn't yet explored. It was a field with a slight downward slope; in the darkness, he could make out the trees to his right that marked the woodlands and the main drive winding somewhere on his left. He didn't pay his environs much mind, to tell the truth, for he was walking with the intention of clearing all thought from his consciousness. He wanted to feel only the burn of his muscles and the chill of night air filling his lungs.

Then he got to the crest of the lawn, from which the grasses stretched right down to the edge of a stone ha-ha barrier before dropping three feet to the rougher sod below. From the ha-ha, the hill sloped more dramatically, giving him a view of the dower house as if it were nestled in the bosom of a valley. It looked pale and sickly in the moonlight, and with its side exposed to him, more like a decrepit old house than a grand family home.

He intended to turn around. Instead, his feet propelled him from the edge of the ha-ha to the ground beneath it. He landed in a squat, as if he had been jumping down from climbing a mast.

Perhaps it was that old feeling—of good, purposeful energy surging through his blood—that kept him going forward. The dower house held no interest for him, especially not at nighttime when he couldn't pay a call to apologize to Amy, and yet he strode towards it. He decided he would turn around when he reached the box hedges that protected the house from downhill winds. By then his legs would be satisfied, his body tired, and he could return to his bed ready for sleep.

He was still a ship's length away when Amy rounded the hedge. A pale figure on a black backdrop. The white hem of her nightgown blew up and through her legs in the breeze.

A gentleman would turn around.

Nate's feet kept moving forward. Even as she lifted that pitcher and tilted it over her head. Even as the water sluiced down her hair, her face, her neck. It pasted her nightgown to her body: breasts, nipples, hips, thighs. It pooled at her feet. None of it made Nate turn around. Especially not the grin on her face, careless and free, as she turned her face upward, eyes closed, towards the moon.

A gentleman would have turned around, but Nate walked right up to her.

"What are you doing?"

Her eyes flew open, and her chin jerked inward. She raised the pitcher as her only weapon. "What are *you* doing?"

At the moment, he was doing his very best not to ogle the breasts that were so nicely outlined against her wet nightgown. "Out for a walk. I couldn't sleep."

Amy lowered the ewer. "Ah."

He could not look down, not even for a second, because then he would never be able to peel his eyes away. And he didn't *want* to be ogling Amy. He didn't want the real image of her nipples in his head. He was supposed to be putting her in his past once and for all.

Nate looked instead at her nose. But that was too close to her eyes—which he wasn't sure he wanted to meet, knowing as he did that she was so close to being naked—and her lips, which would definitely be the wrong articles to consider. His gaze dropped to her chin.

Which was when he noticed the lump just beneath it. *Lump* was perhaps too small a word, in fact. It conjured up a bump on the head, or a little hill beneath a bedsheet. Not the globular mass on Amy's neck that could easily span the width of his palm.

This explained the scarves, then. She wore them not as an eccentric fashion choice but to hide herself from curious eyes.

Her hand slapped over the mass after he had looked at it a moment too long.

"How ill are you?" Nate heard himself ask. A bumbling question, one that he immediately wished he could take back. But his brain wasn't going fast enough to keep hold of his tongue.

"It's a goiter," she replied, as if that answered the question. "And you really shouldn't be here."

He had seen goiters before. There had been a sailor on his ship HMS *Relation* in the Mediterranean, when they had gone after the Barbary slavers, who had one larger than his own neck.

Nate couldn't remember if the man had died or if he had simply ended up on some other crew.

"Is there any cure?"

Amy looked away, shifting her weight. The wet nightgown swayed in Nate's lower peripheral vision; the ewer moved to her side.

She was irritated with him, but she wasn't sending him off.

"I take seaweed to keep it from growing too fast. The physician thinks it is the reason for my palpitations, as well as my temperature fluctuations. I get too cold or too hot, you see. When everyone else says it is perfectly temperate and when I don't have a fever. At the moment, I feel as if I were locked in a stuffy attic in the height of summer with the sun baking through the window."

"Hence the water." Nate looked her in the eye now. There was defiance in her gaze, as well as a softness that he could only imagine was fear.

A droplet of water fell from the hair at her brow to the tip of her nose.

Nate wanted to lick it off.

"I thought it would help," Amy said.

"Did it?"

She only looked at him. The defiance was waning away.

Nate had never really known this soft Amy. When he had courted her, they had always been flirting and laughing. Oh, they had shared stories of losing their mothers and feeling misunderstood by their fathers and the strange mixture of love and hate they felt for their siblings. But in hindsight, even those admissions had been safe. Wrapped in the wool insulation of common experience.

Nothing like standing almost naked in front of a man, waiting for him to judge you for being ill.

He opened his mouth to comfort her. What came out was: "All I want to do is kiss you."

Even he didn't know if he meant that as reassurance—*the only thing I want to do right now is kiss you, not judge you*—or a confession—*even after everything, all I can do is think about kissing you.*

Amy's tongue darted between her lips. The pitcher in her hand twitched. Then it fell to the ground, and she stepped forward. Her wet body pressed against him. "So kiss me."

Nate didn't need a second invitation.

This could all be a dream, if she wanted it to be. When she woke up in the morning, no one would know about it except her and Nate, and they could both pretend it was unreal. Two souls intertwining in the land of sleep, instead of two tongues intertwining in the here and now.

They had kissed like this before. Lips open, eyes shut, hips pressing against each other. So much of that summer six years ago had been spent running away from Great-Aunt Hilaria and stealing kisses like this. Amy had been shameless then, thinking that within a few months she would marry this man.

She was shameless now, even without the hope of marriage on the horizon. Her body had started hot and now it was hotter, like molten iron, and Nate the blacksmith who could hammer her into shape. She took his hands, which were cupping the nape of her neck as if she were the most precious porcelain in the world, and dragged them to her bottom. He squeezed, a groan escaping his mouth as their lips parted for just a second, and Amy felt the sensation of his fingerprints in every nerve of her body.

How many nights had she dreamed of this?

Still, it wasn't enough. She rose onto her tiptoes until Nate took the hint and lifted her into his arms. Amy coiled her legs around his waist. She wasn't quite long enough for her hips to match with his. Her breath caught anyhow on the feel of his cotton shirt and muscled torso against the hot space between her thighs.

This was around the point when they would stop, before. Nate had always vaulted himself away, a rueful grin on his lips as he promised they would go further once they had the proper permissions. "I do not want to disrespect you in any way," he would say.

He didn't stop this time. One palm still on her bum, the other flat on her back for support, he staggered a few steps here, a few steps there. Then he pulled his mouth away long enough to ask, "Where do you want to go?"

Amy didn't dare think. She pointed to the woods, where the little path she always walked with her nephews could provide some privacy. She dipped her lips into Nate's neck as he followed her direction, taking his earlobe between her teeth and circling her tongue around its soft flesh.

He missed a couple of steps. "Keep doing that, love, but once we've made safe landing."

Love. How Amy wanted to believe he still felt that. She nuzzled his skin instead and squeezed her legs tighter around him. "Be quick about it, then."

His breath escaped him in what might have been a laugh, had he not been laden with desire. The palm on her buttock tightened—a promise.

A promise of what, Amy wasn't sure. The Nate of six years ago wouldn't have carried her into the woods. The Nate of six years ago wouldn't have sought her out in the middle of the night at all. He had wanted to do things right; they stole kisses from each other and nothing else.

Amy didn't regret that. But her heart was beating faster, and not a little because there was a chance that she could steal more tonight. Spinster though she might be, her body was just like anyone else's; it craved whatever happened between man and wife. It dreamed of Nate fully between her legs, his body at her disposal. It yearned for something more than her own fingers bringing it to release.

The Nate of six years ago wouldn't have given it to her. But Captain Nathaniel Preston just might.

They made it into the woods. Nate kept going a few yards, until the path began to curve and the moonlight got lost beyond the leaves. He backed Amy against a tree trunk. Its bark was rough through the thin muslin of her nightgown, but her body was so aroused that it felt like a tease instead of pain. Her weight pinned to the tree, Nate's fingers slid up her legs and under her nightgown so that there was nothing but skin between his hands and her thighs. *That* was a tease, an overwhelming one, and Amy hoped he never stopped touching her. She let her own palms roam down his sides, between their legs, and toward the secret of his trousers.

"I dream of you inside me," she whispered. It was a line she had once heard her best friend, Henriette, say to her husband when they thought no one else was in the corridor.

Nate groaned.

"I want you inside me." Amy's heart was really racing now, her breath going too fast to catch. It had to be from the kissing and the feel of his bulge pressing against her thigh and his hands on her breasts.

Surely, this was what every woman felt when the man she so desperately wanted was about to enter her.

"I need you inside me." This time, her body was so overwhelmed that the words barely came out. She thought it sounded sultry and perfect.

Nate pulled away. "Are you well?"

Without his weight, Amy's feet dropped to the ground. Her bare soles landed painfully on the natural detritus beneath the tree. "Yes, I'm fine. More than fine. I am having the time of my life."

"You look ill." He touched her goiter as he said this. He had done that earlier and it had been marvelous, like a kiss to the most tender part of her body.

Now, it felt like he was a doctor, and she his scientific specimen.

"I am overcome with desire." Batting his hand away, Amy held her arms out to him. "Kiss me again."

"I had better not."

"Why?" But Amy knew. It was in the way he looked at her right now, his gaze no longer cloudy with desire but instead cold and analytical. It was what he had said before in Mary's breakfast room, and how she looked as old as a grandmother.

For a few moments, perhaps, he had been able to pretend she was still the young and beautiful girl he had once loved.

Now, clearly, he couldn't forget that she was a hag.

Amy felt sick in every part of her body. "I hope you do not think me too forward. I am not trying to entrap you, if that is your concern."

Nate stepped back. "No, I know very well that entrapping me in marriage is the last thing you would do."

"I only meant that I have no ill intentions towards you. You said you wanted to kiss me, and I wanted to kiss you, so here we are. You are under no obligation to kiss me again." She didn't mean to sound angry. She wasn't angry. She was desperate to stop this conversation. She was humiliated and ashamed and yearning to disappear into her room never to emerge again. Nate stared at her, and it was too dark for her to read his expression, so Amy added, "Don't kiss me if you don't want to."

"If I don't want to?" His voice was low and dark. "How could you think I don't want to kiss you?"

"We were kissing, and now we are not."

"You sounded as if you were about to faint."

"I *sounded* as if I were in the throes of lust."

"I beg to disagree."

It was as if the years between them had disappeared and they were once again two young lovers who thought they knew each other's hearts like the backs of their hands. Only Amy wasn't the same person at all.

The last time they had kissed with abandon, Amy had been carefree and confident and healthy. She had thought the world was at her feet and life was about to unfurl like a luxury carpet for her to enjoy. She *would* have been in the throes of lust and not at all about to crumple like a dusty relic brought out from the cellar.

How Amy hated that even Nate could see she was no longer that woman.

"You needn't remain here," she said, because she could not stand to be pinned under his gaze any longer. "If you do not want to kiss me, you mustn't stay a second longer."

"Amy, I *want* to kiss you."

"Then kiss me."

And, with a sudden lunge, Nate did exactly that.

CHAPTER SIX

Nate kissed her again to shut her up. He kept it short, mostly tongue and growl and hands. She wanted him to take her against that tree, and it was more than tempting: he had dreamed of this for years, even as he castigated himself for allowing Amy to remain in his fantasies. To have Amy at last in his arms—to even have the invitation to make love to her—was almost beyond what Nate could bear.

But he could hear her losing her breath again. He could feel her pulse pounding through the goiter far too fast. There was something wrong with her, even if she and her family refused to admit it, and Nate would not make her illness worse.

He pulled away again, though it killed him to do it.

"We mustn't go any further." Nate wasn't ready to stop touching her, and he kept his forehead against hers.

"But it is so wonderful."

"It is."

"You make me feel alive." Before he could even reply, the light in Amy's eyes dimmed. She shielded her goiter with her hand again. "I know I'm not pretty like I used to be, of course. Unrecognizable, I'm sure. Still, when you kiss me, I feel as if none of that matters."

"It *doesn't* matter." He was refuting the wrong assertion. Nate tried again: "I didn't mean what I said the other morning, Amy. I was being cruel. I recognized you the instant I saw you, and I felt cursed, because you are just as beautiful as ever."

Amy shut her eyes. "Your words are worth too much to throw them away on flattery."

"I am being honest. I only made that remark because I was angry. You *fainted*, Amy, and your sister acted as if it was below her notice! And then the very next morning, she had you looking after her children. I am angry at how your family pretends you aren't ill at all, and I am angry that you allow them to! That you—" Nate stopped himself before crying out that she had chosen *Mary* over him.

Amy didn't seem to notice his omission. "It is not as though I have consumption. I am perfectly healthy most days, except a little hotter or a little colder than everyone else. Sometimes I get fatigued. It is only when I am overexcited and my heartbeat starts running that I feel *ill*. And even then, it is more...breathless and a little panicked, I suppose."

"Panicked enough to faint?"

"Really, Nate, I hardly ever faint. I should hate to be treated like an invalid simply because there is a slight chance I shall collapse. There is a slight chance *anyone* might collapse at any given moment. Even you, right now."

She was being impossible. Nate stepped back so he could cut his arms through the air to express his frustration. "And if I did collapse right now, would you not then be concerned and wish that those around me, especially my family, would have a care for me?"

"What kind of care should they have for me? The physicians don't know what to do, other than to bleed me, which I have had quite enough of. I take the medicine offered me, and then I take the remedies necessary to recover from the medicine. What is it you think my family is doing so poorly?"

"They should not dismiss your symptoms as a personal failing of yours."

Her eyes flew open with a scoff. "You would give them more credit, Nate, if you had been here all these years. Sometimes I am too hot, sometimes I am too cold, sometimes I have energy bursting out of my skin, sometimes I can barely get out of bed—and when you see how I eat them out of house and home! I daresay you would have even less patience for me than Mary does, if you had been burdened with me this whole time."

In a flash, Nate saw the life they might have had: him returning from his ship to discover Amy, his wife, was ailing.

If he had been her husband, he would have found a way to cure her.

He would, at least, have found a way to love her. If only she had thought him worthy of her life.

Amy, hearing her words, added quickly, "I do not mean—that is—if you had to deal with me for years instead of weeks."

Nate wanted to touch her. It was, in fact, bewildering that only a few moments ago he had been kissing her as if she were his wife.

Now it felt as if the whole world were between them again. He didn't dare so much as lift his hand to touch her cheek.

"You would not be a burden to me, Amy," he whispered. "No matter how many years of illness we shared, you would never be a burden to me."

She pushed off the tree, as if she were about to walk deeper into the woods. The leaves rustled under her bare feet. Speaking away from him, she replied, "That is a lovely thing to believe."

He didn't know how she could cast off his words as if she alone knew whether he meant them or not. "Perhaps you do not want to believe it because that would mean you made the wrong choice."

Amy wrapped her arms around her waist. "Nate, please."

He should let it go. She looked so frail; he was the one preaching that her family should have a care, and now he was carping at her instead of letting her return to bed for the rest she clearly needed.

Except this might be the last chance he had to ask her. In the daytime, he would be too proud to broach the subject. In the moonlight, with their kiss between them, he found he could not leave without saying—his voice a rasp—"Is there no part of you that wishes you had married me?"

With her chin turned away, Nate couldn't see her speak. "I wish we could have married and set up house in a respectable neighborhood as a respectable couple. I wish you had been a solicitor or clergyman or something other than a naval officer who would be away from me for years at a time."

"And here I thought that, in spite of everything, at least you were proud of my career." He had been a fool to ask the question. Like a mad captain sailing his ship directly into a hurricane.

"I am proud of your career." Her reply was as quick as a bolt of lightning. "I can admire you and be proud of you and think the world of you, yet none of that means I would have been happy with you. I would not change you, Nate, but neither could I be the wife of a naval officer."

"You would only have married me, in other words, had I been someone else."

"No, had you been you under different circumstances."

"Then I wouldn't be me. I am a naval officer—and I have always wanted to be. If that were not my career, I would not have even met you, let alone been a man full of energy and zeal. I am a Preston—that I cannot and would not change, and it is the reason I am compassionate and stubborn. I am a second son with no hope for a title—that is what made me eager to prove myself to the world, and especially to you."

"You were eighteen, not even at your majority, and far too young to make a decision such as eloping. You had no savings to support a wife. You did not yet even have a proper patron in the navy to help smooth things over like finding a house or ensuring that I received your pay." Amy finally looked at him again; she looked as fierce and regal as her father did the day he threw Nate from Swanhill House.

"And yet, if I were to ask you today—" His heart beat faster, even though he didn't mean it. This was a hypothetical. She could neither accept nor reject him because it was not an actual proposal. "—you would still not agree to marry me."

Amy blinked. For a moment, the moon lit her face so beautifully that Nate thought he saw joy written across it. Then the shadows returned, and she looked down at her hands. "We are different people now faced with different circumstances."

His were mostly the same: he was still a Preston, still in the navy, still not up to snuff for Lord Warre. And even worse, his career was in jeopardy.

Of course she would not consider marrying him, not even knowing now what refusing him had cost her.

"I loved you with all of my heart, Nate." Amy's voice was soft and tender, but all he noticed was her use of the past tense. "Please believe that."

Perhaps he should reassure her of the same. Nate didn't have the strength to say it, especially not when the truth was that he still loved her, despite himself. "We shouldn't have kissed. It was the old us bursting through for a moment, I suppose, but we shouldn't have indulged it."

Amy took a deep, shaky breath. "I did so enjoy it, though."

Nate didn't dare acknowledge how much he had, too. "We shall go forward as if it had not happened, then. We are nothing but acquaintances—"

"Friends." Amy grabbed his wrist as she interrupted, and Nate looked up to discover an intense hope on her face. "Please, say we are friends. I cannot bear to pretend to be only your acquaintance, with no more claim to sitting beside you than Reverend Platt."

"Friends." It shouldn't mean anything to him. If it did mean something to him, then he shouldn't agree to it. Yet Nate felt both his heart lifting—just a little—and his good judgment slipping away. "We shall go forward as friends."

Chapter Seven

On the next clear day—which was to say, on the next day that it didn't start raining before dawn and the sky was only *mostly* covered in clouds—Lady Olivia organized a picnic for everyone at the park. The servants hauled down chairs and tables to the top of Selsea Park's hill, from which one had a view of the great house, the hedge maze, and a swath of bluebells blooming through the grassy fields.

"It is my favorite prospect in all the world," Lady Olivia was saying to the Preston family, hands clasped to her bosom, as Amy arrived with the boys. Mary and Fred were still halfway up the hill, taking it slowly on account of Mary's tired lungs and swollen ankles.

Nate stood at the peak of the crest, looking out in the direction Lady Olivia pointed as if at the top of a mast surveying the ocean for pirate ships. For a moment, all Amy could do was stare at him: the wave of short dark hair gleaming atop his head, the blue jacket clinging to his arms, the buckskin trousers that contoured every curve of his leg. An officer, a gentleman.

A mystery.

He had been on her mind almost every moment since that night, even though they hadn't seen each other at all for days. Amy was still delirious from the kiss; she could hardly sleep at night for remembering the tree at her back and Nate's lips on her body. His whisper: *Keep doing that, love.* How perfect it had been, at least for a few minutes!

Amy didn't understand how they had slipped from that to arguing. But for the past few days, she had also walked around with unease in her heart, remembering how such a wonderful moment had shattered into bickering. She wished she could go back and change her responses. All Nate had been trying to do was care for her, yet she had been so horribly defensive.

No wonder that he didn't want to kiss her again. That, in fact, he regretted the kissing that had happened. *We shouldn't have indulged it.*

Of course, he *would* feel that way. He had said such lovely things in the drawing room about how she was still a beautiful woman who could find a husband, but noble sentiment was no match for reality. And the reality was that she was a too-thin, too-old, too-ill woman. Kissing her must have been like kissing an Egyptian mummy. No wonder Nate regretted it.

She didn't blame him. But neither would she join him in that regret: their kiss was a memory she would treasure for the rest of her life.

Nate turned as little Charles charged up the hill to him. Amy focused on looking absolutely normal, perhaps even carefree. They had agreed to be friends, but that could mean anything. Nate could see her and turn away, as he had the first night at Selsea Park. He could greet her with the same measured warmth he offered Mary and Fred. He wouldn't rush to her side or kiss her hand or recite poetry to her—and of course she didn't want any of that—but Amy threw the end of her scarf into the air so it might twirl in the breeze like a ballerina's skirt and allowed herself to hope that he might, in some special way, acknowledge her.

When Charles let out a battle cry, Nate finally looked around. His eyes landed on Amy's—and he smiled.

Then Charles barreled into his knees, and Nate had to bend down and focus on her nephew instead.

But still. That smile reassured her. He had meant it; they could be friends.

Lady Olivia organized the group, seating everyone informally around the three tables that the footmen had arranged. Amy ended up between Lord Preston and Mr. Graham Preston, with Miss Caroline opposite her.

Nate sat with Mary and the boys, as well as poor Mr. Anderson. Amy tried not to stare, but her look lasted long enough for Nate to glance over his shoulder and give her another smile.

He might regret the kiss, but at least he didn't seem to regret the entire secret evening.

"I appreciated your opinion on the royal divorce the other day, Miss Lamplugh," Lord Preston said as the footmen laid out trays of food. "What is your feeling on election reform?"

Amy had been surveying the cold legs of mutton, sliced beef, ham salad, and other meats so heavy that the feet of the table were sinking deeper into the soft ground. The question jolted her focus.

No one had ever asked for her opinion on something so weighty. Talk of election reform was batted about at dinner parties, to be sure, but Pater or Sir Charles or Fred always led with their opinions. No one was interested in anything else except witticisms illustrating their points. *The moment the vote goes beyond the landholder, this empire will crumble,* Sir Charles might say, and Amy could reply, *Much like this delicious apple dessert.*

She didn't even know if she *had* an opinion on election reform, now that she was asked about it. "I suppose the government has been functioning well for the last few centuries. I should hate to see changes that might incite a bloody revolution."

Lord Preston watched her speak rather than taking any food for his plate. He must have been above fifty, with silver hair and eyebrows and more than a few wrinkles lining his face. Yet Amy could see that Nate had his nose and sharp cheekbones. Her mind inversed the comparison, and now Lord Preston was a prediction of what Nate would look like when he was old and gray.

And married, she reminded herself, to some lovely woman who could kiss him without fainting.

"I would argue that the risk of *not* making changes is a bloody revolution," said Lord Preston.

"Look at the Peterloo Massacre," chimed in Miss Caroline. "That was sixty thousand people hankering for change, and it got bloody."

"Yes, but..." Amy had read about it in the newspapers. In Lancashire, a historic mob had gathered to call for parliamentary reform, and in response, the militia had attacked, killing eighteen people and injuring hundreds more. Still, that had been nearly a year ago. If she had had a grasp on the facts, it was weak and slipping. "They put an end to that, and there hasn't been any trouble since."

Lord Preston still watched her, neither friendly nor unfriendly, though it was true there was some kindness in his eyes. "I wonder, Miss Lamplugh, if you have any beliefs that would propel you onto a field with sixty thousand other people even knowing that the armed cavalry is there to 'keep the peace.'"

Amy, the simpleton, couldn't think of an answer.

"Don't be such a prig," Mr. Preston—the baron's brother and Nate's uncle—chimed in. "Not everyone needs to be a revolutionary. Some of us know how to enjoy life. Eh, Miss Lamplugh?"

She managed a nod. Mr. Preston was taller and wirier than his brother, with unruly auburn hair. He wasn't a big talker, but when he did speak, it was more often to soften interactions than to add points of his own.

"I don't mean to imply judgment one way or another," Lord Preston replied, sounding ever-so-slightly defensive. "I am merely curious about what motivates each human soul."

Mr. Preston was not satisfied. "The problem is that *you* would go to battle for a dozen different causes, so you expect that everyone else must want to go to battle for at least one. The majority of *human souls* only want to make it through the day, not put our necks on the line for some lofty ideal."

"That seems unfair, Uncle Graham," said Miss Caroline. "The distinction is not so extreme as you make it out to be. Some people have the interest and the ability to fight for others. Some have the interest but not the ability."

"Yes, dear Caroline, but most of us who have the *ability* don't have the *interest*. Instead of fighting for others, I'd rather make sure my little corner of the street is tidy, and trust that everyone else will get their due so long as they also take care of their corners."

Amy wasn't sure where she fell on Miss Caroline's matrix. Did she have the ability to fight for others? Some days, it hardly felt like she had any control of her own life, let alone anyone else's. Yet if she could dedicate her time or money towards some cause, would she?

Or was she some sort of invisible segment: those who had neither the ability *nor* the interest to fight for other people's rights? And what kind of moral fiber did she lack, if that was the case?

"You must be very proud of Captain Preston," she said to the baron, "since he quite literally has gone to battle to fight the slave trade."

Lord Preston's smile was a little crooked—just like Nate's. "I am proud of him, for that reason and many others. Contrary to how my brother is trying to paint me, I don't believe service to others is the *only* virtue a person can possess. After all, I am glad to see Graham even though he engages in the very import business I avoid."

"And is angling to get Nate involved, should this court-martial not go his way," Mr. Preston added cheerfully.

Amy took a careful swallow. She did not want to seem overeager as she asked, "Why shouldn't it go his way? Surely it is a formality?"

She was desperate for information. Everyone mentioned the court-martial, but no one explained it. Amy knew that captains were court-martialed as a matter of course when they lost ships in battles or to the weather. Those circumstances were hardly anything to quake at.

Yet the whispers about Nate's court-martial made it sound as if he had been accused of something heinous.

Lord Preston frowned at her question. "I'm afraid the court-martial is hardly about the substance of *what* happened and is instead a display of the Admiralty's loyalty to British interests."

He might as well have asked her to solve a riddle. "Shouldn't the British Admiralty be loyal to British interests?"

Mr. Preston, through a mouthful of meat, said, "It is because you voted against the navy bill, Marty. If you had only said 'More money for our navy!' they wouldn't have had any reason to discover that a Captain Preston who happens to be your son was in need of disciplinary action."

Lord Preston grimaced, which seemed to be his way of agreeing.

Amy tried asking Mr. Preston more directly: "Do you mean to say they invented a reason to court-martial Captain Preston? Something he isn't even guilty of?"

"Oh, no, they caught him right enough," Mr. Preston replied. "Didn't need to be a court-martial, though. Nor does there need to be: Nate could just submit to the charges, say 'Aye, I did that,' and they would let him off with hardly a kick in the...well, with hardly any consequences."

Amy's heart twisted. What had Nate done that he would need to admit his guilt to an Admiralty court?

"But he was following orders! He was seizing an illegal ship, as he was supposed to do!" Miss Caroline protested.

"A French ship, which isn't illegal at all," Mr. Preston said. "Oh, you're right, darling Caro, of course. There is nothing wrong with the *spirit* of what Nate did. Yet it was illegal, and therefore they can prosecute him to their hearts' content. The only question is *why* he is fighting the charges instead of letting them castigate him and getting on with his life."

Amy couldn't make sense of it. The war had ended years ago; Nate didn't have any reason to seize a French ship. And if he *had* disobeyed orders—or broken a law!—why would he try to deny it?

She wished she could march over to Nate's table and ask him directly. In lieu of that, she replied to Mr. Preston, "Perhaps it has to do with that conviction you and I both lack."

She didn't mean it as a quip. Mr. Preston laughed anyway. "My dear Miss Lamplugh, I believe you are correct."

At his table, Nate was aware of overdramatizing every movement. Each time he lifted his fork, each smile he offered to little Charles, each nod of his head in agreement with Mrs. Bremridge's complaints was acted out as if he were on stage and wanted the audience in the very back row to see it.

Amy wasn't quite that far away. But she was behind him, which meant he couldn't see her—unless he deliberately turned his head over his shoulder—and so his only option to ensure she noticed him was to make his movements overly noticeable.

Not that he needed Amy to notice him. They had smiled at each other upon her arrival, and once more when sitting down. That had been enough to establish that their nighttime tryst had *not* been a figment of his imagination. They really had kissed and argued and parted as friends.

He almost wished they hadn't. He had wasted nearly every second of the past few days imagining where Amy was: breakfasting or playing games with the boys or stealing upstairs for a rest.

Or tiptoeing outside at night again to feel the cool rain soak through her transparent nightgown...

It was only fair if Amy spent her picnic noticing him, too.

Mrs. Bremridge was monopolizing the conversation, anyhow, by listing her physical complaints to poor John. She was sick, it seemed, from the moment of conception through to the baby entering the world. Nausea, swollen limbs, stuffed nose, hairs growing in unusual places, backaches, foot aches, stomach cramps, shallow breaths. "The accoucheur visits from Portsmouth, Mr. Anderson, but his remedies only make me feel worse instead of better."

John, who must have been born a saint, took in her monologue with great patience. "It is a terrible curse that the mother must suffer so much in order to bring the joy of new life into the world."

This seemed to satisfy Mrs. Bremridge. She sat up a little straighter in her chair. "You know my mother died in childbirth."

"No, I didn't. I'm sorry to hear that."

Nate remembered the afternoon when he and Amy had discussed losing their mothers. It had been raining, so they were confined to the drawing room at Swanhill House. Mrs. Bremridge—then Miss Mary—had sat practicing at the pianoforte, their great-aunt set up in another corner with a pot of tea and her embroidery hoop. Nate and Amy sat side by side on a chaise longue by the window, facing outwards as if to watch the raindrops falling down the glass.

He had gone first. His mother's death had been chronicled in the papers, first as a rumor in the gossip column that she wasn't accompanying Papa to London for the parliamentary season because of an affair, then as an update that she was within three months of death, and finally as a death announcement two years later.

"We had plenty of time to say goodbye," Nate had confided in Amy. "Yet still, it was a shock when it finally happened. I had run off from our tutor that morning and was building a fort in the woods with a few of the boys my age. Uncle Maulvi was the one who came and found me. Who told me. That while I was having such fun, being so wicked, my mother..."

It had embarrassed him in that moment that tears sprang to his eyes, even more when Amy reached out and wiped one away from his cheek. Now, he wouldn't care. In the navy, it was the sailors who cried at their memories who learned to weather the worst storms and battles and scourges. The ones who couldn't cry were the ones who made trouble.

"I was seven," Amy murmured, her voice so low that only he could hear it. "We were expecting the great event. An heir, my father hoped. When she went into confinement, he ordered champagne to be readied for the celebration. Except only a few hours into confinement, she died. Her heart gave out. Palpitations, I think is the word."

It wasn't as if Amy were the first person Nate had met who had also lost her mother. But there was something in that moment, sitting next to each other but facing the window, hushed and solemn, that had made it feel as if their souls were braided together.

Now the story resonated with him a little differently.

"You didn't mention your heartbeat, Mrs. Bremridge. Is it steady, even throughout all your other symptoms?"

Amy's sister frowned a little at the question. "How kind of you to ask, but thankfully, my heart is one organ I have so far been able to rely upon."

"I am glad to hear it. Miss Lamplugh confided in me that she experiences palpitations, and I was afraid that might be a family affliction."

Now Mrs. Bremridge's eyebrows shot up towards her hairline. She reached out a hand to stop little Charles from launching his entire face into a plate of food, then replied, "How wonderful that my sister has taken you into her confidence, Captain Preston."

The old indignation roared across Nate's heart. He wasn't good enough for the Lamplugh family; that had been made clear six years ago, and she didn't need to drag him through it again.

Except, whereas a few days ago his anger would have spiked at Amy too, Nate was able to distance himself. Amy *did* take him into her confidence. Amy *did* want to be friends.

Amy, in fact, wanted him to fuck her against a tree.

That thought in mind, he managed to smile with his reply. "It was my first evening here, when she fainted and I was obliged to carry her back to the dower house."

"She fainted from palpitations?" Across the table, John frowned in concern.

"It was overexcitement," Mrs. Bremridge said. "The family physician has examined her. I assure you, Captain Preston, it is simply a peculiarity of my sister's and not anything that can be improved by medical intervention."

He wanted to bite back that all of *her* maladies were peculiarities of being with child, and yet she seemed to expect medical intervention.

He settled for replying, "And what does the physician say of her goiter?"

"Another condition for which there is not much to be done."

John's eyes had drifted behind Nate, presumably to where Amy sat sandwiched between Papa and Uncle Graham.

How Nate wanted to turn around and look at her, too. But that would call too much attention to the topic of conversation and might even embarrass her.

Like a pirate ship sensing his hesitation to man the cannons, Mrs. Bremridge picked up on his restrained desire and used it in her own attack. "It is unkind to discuss a person's physical condition without them present. You must show more care with my sister's confidences, Captain Preston."

The fact that she was right made it all the worse.

Nate swallowed his first reply, which was that he wished Mrs. Bremridge would show more care for Amy than for her confidences. It was something a gentleman could not say.

But he didn't stop himself from saying to John, "Quite right. I shall leave it to our surgeon to offer the necessary care and conversation."

And then Nate *did* let himself look over his shoulder, just one more time, to catch Amy's eye.

To his great delight, she met his gaze immediately and even gave him a little wave.

Take that, Mrs. Bremridge, Nate thought, and grinned back at Amy.

By the time they all finished eating—Mr. Preston taking the longest as he kept helping himself to more of the roasted meats—Amy's heart was racing. Fluttering around in her chest like a moth captured in a jar and exhausting her with the effort of it all.

She was glad Nate sat with his back to her. He would notice if she grew pale, and she didn't want him to think of it as more proof of her family's neglect.

Though at the same time, a terribly selfish part of her wanted him to turn around again and, seeing her fatigue, rush over to carry her home.

Lady Olivia had risen from her seat at the table with Mrs. Anderson and Sir Charles; she came over to Amy's wearing the mischievous smile that meant she had been making plans. "We have been discussing a ball to celebrate the king's birthday, Lord Preston. I hope you won't object if we invite a few neighbors for a party. You don't forbid dancing or merriment, do you?"

Amy thought the question could have been phrased more delicately. It sounded as if Lady Olivia believed Lord Preston to be some kind of puritan—and as if having such a guest filled her with horror.

Lord Preston took the accusation with an equanimous smile. "We would enjoy that very much, Lady Olivia. You are too generous a hostess."

"Oh, wonderful!" Clapping her hands together, Lady Olivia leaned backward a little, pitching her voice towards Nate. "And Captain Preston, it won't be awkward for you, will it, if we fill out the numbers with some of the other naval officers in town?"

Nate rose from his seat and walked to their table to reply. "You need not worry about me, Lady Olivia. A ball is no time for disagreements. There will be more waltzing, won't there?"

For a brief moment, his eyes landed on Amy, which made her realize she was staring. Then, when Lady Olivia replied that *of course* there would be waltzing, he shifted his smile to Caroline. "Good, because I mean to see my sister's skills firsthand, since she has been bragging to me she is the best dancer at Northfield Hall."

Caroline blushed. "I never said anything of the kind. Merely that I am always begging for more dances."

Amy was blushing, too. She was thinking of another waltz with Nate. This time in a proper ballroom, wearing a proper ballgown, perhaps with her mother's sapphire earrings dazzling in the candlelight.

She wouldn't mind a ball, if it meant she could steal another moment like that.

They were interrupted by raindrops. Amy caught one on her cheek and—a full half minute later—her wrist. Hardly enough rain to cause alarm. Yet sufficient to make Mary shriek, "It is *raining*!"

The whole party turned towards that table, where poor Mr. Anderson was alone with Mary and Fred and the boys.

Fred, on Mary's urging, threw up a parasol over her head. "I'm sorry to break up the party, but we must get Mary inside before she catches a cold."

They had a point, of course. Even a little rain could be dangerous to a person in a weakened condition such as Mary's. Lady Olivia said as much, urging, "Hurry now, but be careful."

"We should get inside, too," Lord Preston said to Miss Caroline. "You only just recovered from your springtime cold."

She rolled her eyes. "I'm hardly an invalid, Papa." Yet Miss Caroline stood. The rain was coming down in more of a drizzle now, frequent enough to darken strands of her blond hair. "Uncle Graham, you had better rush with me. After all, you're not accustomed to this cold English weather anymore."

Amy looked to Nate, who still stood by the head of their table, watching the party break up without comment. If they waited long enough, they would be the only two guests left at the picnic. Would Nate walk her home? What would happen if they stole a moment alone?

But just as she opened her mouth to ask if he would accompany her, Amy heard Mary say to the boys, "Go hold Aunt Amy's hand. She'll walk you home."

A command? A request? An expectation?

Whatever it was, Amy shouldn't have been surprised. She was only visiting Selsea Park to help, after all. It was bad of her to have forgotten to think about the boys at all.

She took stock of her nephews. Four-year-old Charles was too busy tipping his head up to catch raindrops on his tongue to heed his mother's instruction, while two-year-old Kit understood it well enough to toddle a few steps in Amy's direction before falling to the ground and looking around in confusion.

Upon discovering his mother and father had turned their backs on him to hurry down the hill, he began to cry.

"Oh." Amy tucked away her feelings of ill use to rush over and scoop Kit into her arms. Of course she would see the boys home. Who else would?

The sky spun a little as she straightened, her heart still racing faster than it should. The drizzle was worse now, too, more of a cold, steady rain. Mary had been right to rush; a person could catch a fever if they stayed out too long in this.

"Come on, Charles," she called, holding out her spare hand for her other nephew to take. "Time to go home."

At the same speed as the rain increased, the rest of the party had broken up: Lady Olivia and Sir Charles directing servants, Lord Preston hurrying after Miss Caroline and Mr. Preston, Mr. Anderson finding his wife and wrapping an arm around her as they hurried towards the great house.

Even Nate had turned away, helping the servants tie up dishes into the tablecloths and stack the chairs.

Charles, meanwhile, splayed himself on his back and made rain angels in the grass.

"Charles!" Amy tried to imbue the name with every ounce of command in her body. It was too wet to have to combat a mercurial four-year-old.

Her fatigue must have been catching up with her, though, for Charles only rolled onto his stomach and, catching her eye, giggled.

"If you don't come here this instant, Kit and I are leaving without you." She took a few steps down the hill. Kit wailed in her ear, no doubt upset that he was wet, abandoned by his parents, and now leaving behind his brother.

And yet Charles remained where he was. His white playsuit turned into a terrible painting of mud and wet leaves of grass.

Until Nate stepped beside him. "Heave to, sailor!"

Amy had never heard Nate like that. Firm, a little frightening, with no room for mercy in the vowels of his command.

Charles had never heard the likes of it either, apparently, for he scrambled to his feet.

"Forward march!" Nate ordered, and, taking Charles by the hand, started towards Amy.

Her attention should be on the children. She was their caretaker, entrusted by her sister to make sure the boys got home safely, and if they caught a cold, it would be because of Amy's negligence.

And yet, she couldn't tear her eyes away from Nate. He wore the rain as if it had been tailor-made for him. His wet hair contoured around his forehead, deepening the brown of his eyes. His dark jacket molded around his shoulders, so that there was no question that the shape of his torso came from his muscles and not his clothes. His white cravat hung limp at his neck, the shirt underneath it transparent enough to reveal black coils of hair racing down his chest.

And he kept walking closer to her.

"Would you like me to carry him?" Nate asked, eyes bouncing down to Kit.

A dangerous impulse flooded her from her very core, urging her to abandon the children and take Nate somewhere private and strip him naked.

"I have him," she replied, holding tighter to Kit. "We should get them home before they catch a chill."

"Forward march!" Charles cried.

The hill was slippery, even as they kept to the little dirt path remaining from when it was a cow pasture. Amy had to go slowly to make sure her feet remained under her at all times. Still, she hated to walk in silence. She said, "A fine way to end a picnic, isn't it? I was having such a good time with your family, too."

"Were you?"

"Oh yes. They are very proud of you, you know."

His free hand hovered somewhere near her waist, as if ready to catch her. Amy tried not to pay it any attention, even though she fancied she could feel its heat as surely as if his fingertips were on her bare skin. She listened to his reply instead: "I was afraid they would be torturing you with political theory or questions of philosophy."

"Well." She couldn't deny there was some of that. "I felt out of my depth, but it was hardly torture."

"I apologize on behalf of all of them, and most especially my father. He never realizes how priggish he can sound."

"Your uncle was happy to tell him." Amy dared turn a little, even as she was stepping down the hill, to spy at Nate. "Is it true you might join his import business if the court-martial doesn't go well?"

Her foot landed in the mud. Only, it didn't connect solidly enough, for the next thing she knew, her heel was propelling out from under her.

She and Kit would have landed hard on the ground, except Nate caught her. In his strong, sure arms.

Arms that, when last wrapped around her, had held her as a husband holds a wife.

"Aunt Amy, he caught you!" Charles cried out in amazement.

"Yes, he did." And he hadn't yet let go. His hands splayed firmly around her ribcage.

Her body burned where he touched her.

"Are you unharmed? Your ankle isn't twisted?" Nate breathed into her ear.

"I'm fine. Thank you." Reluctantly, Amy stepped out of his hold. His eyes dropped from her gaze downward, and his cheeks flushed red.

No doubt her dress clung as desperately to her body as his clothes did him.

Was she breathless from her palpitations or from Nate? She could no longer tell.

At least she had a scarf on this time.

Amy decided to return them both to more appropriate conversation. "Are you considering your uncle's offer?"

Nate turned away to resume their walk. "I can't see the point in worrying about it until I know how the court-martial goes."

"But *would* you join an import business? Even though your father avoids all imports?"

"I would be foolish not to consider it. A man must earn money for his bread, after all."

There was something in his tone that, like his command to Charles earlier, Amy had never heard before. This time, it was not the cold steel of an order. It was hotter, more threatening, like a forge fire about to leap beyond its hearth.

His tone was telling her to let the topic go. And yet, it made Amy want to cling to it that much harder.

"No one has told me the charges against you. Something about capturing a French ship?"

Nate glared down at the ground instead of replying. They were approaching the bottom of the hill, and the slope was getting more slippery.

He didn't want to tell her. Amy shouldn't have felt hurt about it. They weren't anything to each other, even with the other night between them. Nate had probably kissed dozens of women in his years on the sea, and he wouldn't tell any of them his private business, either.

Amy tightened her hold on Kit. "I'm prying. I apologize. I should know better than to do that."

"It is complicated," Nate said, his words coming from between his gritted teeth. "Certainly not conversation for children."

As if cued by this comment, Kit let out a wail. Charles bounced in excitement, for they were only a few yards away from the dower house's hedge now, and broke free from Nate to race to the kitchen entrance.

"You could come in for tea," Amy suggested. "We could speak while the boys take their naps."

Nate blinked down at her, rainwater sluicing down his nose and lips. Amy was seized by another urge: to pull him inside and offer him a hot fire, dry clothes, and her body to warm him up.

But he didn't want it. His eyes darted to her goiter, even though it was hidden behind her scarf, as he replied, "I had better not. Mrs. Bremridge wouldn't like it."

Which was true—Mary would be cross with Amy for inviting him in when the household was about to have its naps. More importantly, Fred or Mary would probably insist on chaperoning their conversation.

Still, Amy hated that Nate wouldn't come in. "Of course. I understand."

She turned towards the house because she couldn't really bear to look at him anymore.

Nate reached out. He didn't catch her—he didn't even seem to try—but his fingers brushed against her arm. "I might take a walk at midnight again. I could come down this way."

Amy bit back her grin before she looked over her shoulder to reply: "I shall need to take some air. Perhaps I shall see you."

This time, the smile—the beam!—was on Nate's face. Amy let her own free, and it was only when Kit pulled her hair that she managed to stop standing there, grinning at Nate like an idiot.

CHAPTER EIGHT

Nate didn't know why he had suggested it.

It was one thing to accidentally stumble upon Amy in the middle of the night and share a few inadvisable kisses.

It was another thing entirely to schedule a time to meet in the middle of the night, with the implied activity being more inadvisable kisses.

The former, Nate could blame on fate and wild impulses.

The latter, Nate could blame only on himself. And he didn't want to stir up trouble for himself. He was in enough trouble as it was with his career and reputation literally on trial. He shouldn't risk adding heartbreak to his problems. The wisest part of Nate's brain knew he should do everything he could to protect his heart from Amy.

Unfortunately, the more urgent part of his brain ruled his feet.

Still, he fought it. He spent the evening drying out by the fire with his family. Papa read the latest letter from Benjamin, who was establishing a new life in Ireland with his wife Lydia and had humorous escapades involving sheep to share; Caroline shared recent anecdotes from Northfield Hall, including how solemn old Mr. Chow could spend an entire hour making silly faces at his grandson; Nate even forced himself to share some of the harder stories from the Slave Coast. It was a night that almost felt like childhood, with everyone feeling close and loved and Sophia providing the necessary declaration that they *must* stop discussing politics or never find peace enough to sleep.

Nate bid them all goodnight with every intention of going to sleep. And yet, he lay in bed for no more than five minutes before getting out again.

It was too uncomfortable. He had gotten used to sleeping in hammocks that rocked with the sway of the ship. A mattress was too thick, too still.

That was why he stalked to the window to see if the rain had stopped. And why, when he discovered that it had cleared enough for Orion's Belt to sparkle in the sky, he dressed in boots and buckskin and coat for a walk.

He would limit his interaction with Amy to speech. She wanted to know why he was being court-martialed; as much as he hated the story, he would tell her. He wouldn't kiss her, nor even hold her hand. After all, they had no future: Amy had as good as declined his hypothetical marriage proposal, which he was hardly in a position to offer anyway.

He was meeting with her so they could have a private conversation without the censure of her family. Nothing more.

A lantern sat in her bedroom window like a lighthouse beckoning him into harbor. When he got close to the kitchen garden, the lantern moved; for a minute or so the whole house appeared dark, and then the light reappeared through the windows on the ground floor.

He steeled himself. His first words to her would be: "I do not intend for anything nefarious to pass between us tonight."

Except when she joined him by the hedge, Amy was so pale, she looked like a ghost. "I was afraid I would fall asleep before you came."

That afternoon, Nate had attributed her slow movements and pallor to the chill of the rain. Now he realized it must be the goiter or the palpitations or whatever her illness was. "Perhaps you should have. You look like you need rest."

"Oh, but then I couldn't talk to you." She reached out a hand and braced her weight against his forearm. "Shall we go back to that tree?"

Nate helped her walk to the wooded path, a little alarmed at how shallow her breath was. If she fainted again, he would have to carry her to her bed despite the risk of being discovered.

"You see, aren't you glad you didn't marry me?" Amy said with a little laugh as she leaned against the trunk of the tree where, last time, Nate had nearly ripped off her wet nightgown. "Imagine how frustrating it would be to have to restrict your plans based on whether I happened to have the energy to walk by myself that day or not."

Nate hated that Amy felt so deeply that she was nothing but a burden to the people around her. "It sounds more like anguish to me that I would have to watch you suffer and not be able to help."

She pressed her lips together. "Better, then, that you are spared that worry."

Nate didn't feel spared at all. He worried about her, except now, as her not-husband, he didn't have any right to express it. And when he left Selsea Park, as he would whenever the Admiralty convened his court-martial, he would have to embark on a life of worrying about her without the right to write to her for news.

Even if he dared write her a letter, her sister or father would probably burn it rather than give it to her.

Amy, resting against the tree, folded her arms into her cape. "Now, unless you intend to kiss me senseless, I believe you invited me here to satisfy my curiosity about your court-martial."

Despite everything he had promised himself, Nate couldn't let an invitation like that pass by. Not when she looked so dreamlike and inviting. Leaning in, Nate braced an arm above her head and kissed her lips. It was gentle—sweet. When it ended, he grinned at her. "Senseless?"

"I'm floating on a cloud."

This was why Nate had suggested meeting tonight. Because when he was with her, even when he wasn't kissing her, he lost touch with all facets of reality except Amy.

In his years away, Nate had sometimes wondered if his love for Amy had been simply his love for *women*, fixated onto the first girl he happened upon. He had been only eighteen, after all, and away from home for the very first time. If his eyes had fallen on some other lady, if he'd noticed some other girl laughing in the firelight, would she own his heart now, instead of Amy?

Except his eyes *had* fallen on other ladies. At the very assembly where he met Amy, Nate had danced with a half dozen other young women, all beautiful and witty. When he had called on Amy the next day, it had been at her friend Miss Curry's family residence, and he had gone walking with both of them on Southsea Beach. Even as he had spent the summer riding over to Swanhill House on every spare afternoon, Nate had still been dining at his officer's homes and attending social gatherings in Portsmouth.

What he had forgotten in his years away was how Amy was magic. There was no articulating what it was about her that drew him in or why her conversation made him feel more at ease than anyone else in the world. She was Amy, and he was Nate, and when they were together, everything simply felt right.

How could he not steal moments with her, if he had the chance?

She ventured one hand from the cape and linked it in his. Neither of them wore gloves; he felt how cold and soft her fingers were. "No one will tell me what charges you actually face, and it is driving me mad. So please, won't you tell me?"

A part of him wanted to argue that it was none of her business. Except, Nate remembered all those afternoons of their courtship when he had talked endlessly at her about how important the West African Squadron was—and that was before the Preventive Squadron had been formally created. It was Britain's saving grace, the only vestige of the empire that stood for something good instead of something that made money. All Nate had wanted when he signed up for the navy was to get assigned to the West African Squadron.

And Amy, in those days when they both still believed they would get married, had told him she would be so proud to be the wife of an officer of the squadron. That, even though she was afraid he would catch an African fever and die, she loved him for being so brave as to dedicate his life to fighting the slave trade.

If anyone in the world deserved to hear from Nate what had happened to make him the scourge of the squadron, it was Amy.

Even if his confession ended with her roundly condemning him for throwing away his career.

"They have charged me with two main offenses: disobeying orders, and illegally seizing a neutral ship."

Amy's fingers tightened around his. She kept her gaze steadily away from his as she asked, "And did you do those things?"

"I had orders to return to Freetown, yes. That was a thousand miles from the Bight of Benin—a five-day sail in the best conditions. The whole mission of the squadron is to protect British interests and prevent the slave trade. The understanding—and the practice of every officer and every ship—is that no matter where you are or what your orders, if you see a ship you suspect of slaving, you stop her. I was only a day out from the Gallinas when my watchman spotted the *Viper*. Seizing her was within the larger scope of my orders."

Nate paused. He needed a breath. If he could end the story there, he would.

"Was the *Viper* French?"

"She was flying under a Portuguese flag at first, which would have meant we could stop her within the laws of both Britain and Portugal. As we came up beside her, the crew hauled up the French flag. And we aren't allowed to inspect French ships."

"So which one was true? Who were they really?"

As if it were so simple. "Both. Neither. They were slavers, and therefore they had no allegiance to any nation except the nation of greed and evil."

Amy's hand trembled in his.

"We are sick with slavery, Amy. All of us—the British, the Europeans, the Africans. The abolitionists think that the Preventive Squadron is enough to fight it, or at least a medicine against it. As if it will reduce the fever, and therefore the whole disease will disappear. I used to believe that, too. One only has to spend a few months there to learn differently. The Preventive Squadron isn't turning the tide on the slave trade, and outlawing it hasn't done a damn thing to free the slaves in our colonies. Most days, I don't believe there is a medicine available to bring an end to any of it. But when you sight a slaver..."

Nate shut his eyes, as if that would stop the memories from surfacing. The water had been still that day, both ships stuck in the doldrums. The smell had been so intense, the cries even worse. And the fury he had felt: at the supercargo in his linen suit smirking as a sailor switched the flags; at the sailors for watching with hands at their waists, as if ready to stab Nate's men as soon as they boarded; at the whole charade through which he had to act in order to do what was so obviously right.

"It doesn't matter what flag they flew, or where the crew was from, or who has the right to do what. You don't have to board a slave ship to know that there are slaves on her. As soon as you get close…"

But he wouldn't—*couldn't*—describe it. No human soul should ever have to contemplate the horror of a slave ship, let alone live it.

"There were four hundred and one people stuffed into the hold, Amy. Two dozen children who couldn't have been more than ten, two hundred women, and the rest men. We managed to keep three hundred ninety-seven alive to be liberated in Freetown. I don't *care* if those weren't my express orders. I don't *care* if they take my command away from me. I don't even care if my actions spark another war with France. I did the right thing in taking the *Viper*, and not even God can tell me differently."

Eyes still closed, he could only feel Amy's hand as she held tighter to his, and her lips as she pressed them to his cheek. Her forehead rested against his temple. "*I* care if they take your command away from you. I wouldn't trust any officer as much as I trust you to take the right action in moments like that."

This was why Nate had suggested their tryst. Not to steal a kiss, but for this embrace, and the way her words allowed him to breathe again, as if he hadn't been breathing since the moment he heard about the court-martial.

If only he could bottle up this embrace and take it with him wherever he went next.

"You were fulfilling your mission," Amy whispered, "and you were doing the work of goodness, and they haven't any right to take that away from you."

"My uncle thinks I shouldn't fight the charges. I could admit to doing wrong and plead that it was a mistake and probably keep my rank, if not my ship."

"Do you think it is worth fighting?"

"If I keep my position, I can go back to the squadron. But if I say it was a mistake..." Anger rushed through him, weighing down his voice. "When the Foreign Office next negotiates with France, they shouldn't think *I* made the mistake. They should know it is the French, an entire government propping up slavers, who are in the wrong."

He released Amy for fear of crushing her.

"I will not take the coward's way out."

"No, of course not." Amy smiled at him. "And if you think it is worth fighting for, then I shall help you however I can."

"You have already helped by asking about it." Nate leaned away, looking up to the sky—shrouded though it was by tree branches—to anchor himself in reality and not in Amy's spell. "I hadn't realized how much I needed to hear you tell me that I did nothing wrong."

"In fact, you did everything right." Amy folded herself into her cape again. "However, perhaps there is more that I can do. Lady Olivia is inviting Miss Stratton to the ball. She is Admiral Stratton's granddaughter, you know."

"I do know."

"The admiral might be kinder towards you in his decision if his granddaughter has a tendre towards you."

All the good feelings Nate had been enjoying evaporated. "We are under the stars together, and you are telling me to chase after another woman?"

Amy closed her hand—a chilled palm—over his. "I am telling you to have a care for your future, Nate. It is more precious to me than my feelings."

Leaving it clear as the stars in the sky exactly whether she thought he could fit into her future at all.

Nate had known when he left this evening that all Amy could offer him was heartbreak. Why, then, was he so surprised that she had managed to hurt him once more?

CHAPTER NINE

Lady Olivia arranged for the ball in her usual efficient manner: invitations delivered by messenger to all the neighbors within a day; a pastry chef and extra servants hired without drama; the floors of the ballroom freshly waxed and the windows washed the very morning of the event.

Sophia and Caroline—who now insisted that Amy call them by their Christian names—came down to the dower house a few days before the party to borrow a gown for the latter from Mary. Even Iris had fun that afternoon as, along with a silver tea service, she pulled out the best silk and cotton concoctions from Mary's wardrobe. "I've never worn silk before," Caroline—who wasn't touching the imported tea—said. "I'm not sure if I should."

"This gown has already been purchased, cut, and sewn. It is not as if you are asking anyone to do any fresh labor, except perhaps Iris will take it in for you in a few places." Sophia pinched the sapphire-blue gown more closely around Caroline's bust. "Besides, you look so beautiful in it."

She did. At the age of twenty, Caroline was the picture of an English debutante: willowy, blond, optimism blossoming from every movement of her body. Amy remembered that feeling. The one that promised her future was about to unfurl, and that it had nothing but exciting surprises in store for her.

Now, she didn't think about the future at all. She could only take life one day at a time, or else be caught in a maelstrom that felt terribly like despair.

"Still, I wouldn't like anyone to see me in silk and think that I am declaring my allegiance to the East India Company," Caroline objected.

"This is Damascus silk," Mary clarified, "not from the East Indies at all. I'm sure your family's objection doesn't extend to Syria."

Amy knew it did. The Prestons—with Sophia and Nate as exceptions—didn't partake in *any* imported goods, since so much of British trade with territories beyond Europe relied on exploitation of labor or trading of goods for human slaves. It was why, even when she had imagined marriage to Nate, she had never been able to picture herself at Northfield Hall.

A life of linen and wool after a childhood of cotton and silk seemed too strange to contemplate.

"If the dilemma is to wear silk or to go without, I suppose I had better choose the silk," Caroline declared. In truth, she looked a little excited and even took another look at herself in the cheval glass. "What will you wear, Amy? Will we match?"

Amy couldn't help but get caught up in Caroline's enthusiasm. "I think I do have a similar blue from Mary's betrothal ball." She had brought it without expectation of wearing it; it was simply one of her best dresses, and better to keep it with her than let it gather dust at Swanhill House. Retrieving it from her wardrobe, Amy returned to the drawing room to show it to the company. "It is a little out of fashion now, I'm afraid. Neither a ruffle nor a flounce to be found."

"We've still a few days, miss," Iris volunteered. "I could add some lace ornaments, if you would like me to."

The offer took Amy by surprise. After all, Iris more often than not had to be cajoled out of wherever she hid to do her basic tasks.

For her to volunteer to do extra work on Amy's behalf almost stung Amy's eyes with tears.

Little Charles raced into the room, a wooden sword in hand. "*En garde*! I'm a pirate, and your ship is being attacked!"

"Let Aunt Amy finish with her gown, darling, and then she'll play with you," Mary promised from the settee.

He turned towards Amy. She lifted the dress, trying to keep it from his reach, but he was too fast for her and raced directly onto its hem.

The room filled with the sound of the silk skirt ripping.

"Oh, Charles!" Amy had to bite back a curse.

He sensed it anyhow and immediately dissolved into tears. "I'm sorry, Aunt Amy. I didn't mean to. I'm a bad boy. I'm sorry."

Of course, she had to set aside the gown to comfort him and assure him that it was an accident and that she still loved him. Yet the skirt was ripped; later, she and Iris inspected it to confirm that to fix it and hide the repair, they would have to completely alter the design of the gown. A job that would take far more time than they had.

And so, thanks to little Charles, Amy showed up to Lady Olivia's ball wearing her modest green dinner gown. Between the dress's simple cut and the matching scarf Amy wore instead of a necklace, she felt like a parson's daughter instead of the sophisticated lady she should have liked to have been.

Especially when the other guests started arriving in shimmering silks and delicate cottons, all of the highest fashions, to make Lady Olivia's ballroom look like it was in the center of London.

At least Amy had her mother's earrings and matching bracelet to do right by the Warre title.

She knew most of the guests by sight, if not more intimately, except the naval officers invited in from Portsmouth. Their uniforms—blue jackets, white lace cuffs, and gold braid—dressed them in handsomeness, even if one of them was lacking his front teeth and another smelled as if he had fallen into the latrine.

None of them looked even a quarter as dashing as Nate, though. Amy's eyes kept falling on him: first by the bowl of punch, where he fetched two glasses for his sisters; then by the musicians' stand, laughing over some joke with the violinist; later, by the front entrance, greeting Miss Stratton with a bow.

Amy resolved not to get in his way. He was fighting with everything he had for his honor, and Amy was rooting for his success, no matter how much it hurt to think of him marrying anyone. Especially Miss Stratton, who was, like Caroline, so very young and full of hope.

It was a small comfort to know that contemplating her own future was not the only thing that sent her into a black mood; thinking too much about Nate's could have exactly the same effect. Perhaps it was the future in general that depressed her, and not anything at all specific to do with her.

"At last, I have found you!" This from Amy's friend Henriette, whom Amy had only moments ago watched enter with her husband. She, as usual, looked just shy of glamorous in a scarlet silk gown with her raven hair curled into a quivering mass. Henriette clasped Amy's hand in greeting. "You look absolutely ravishing tonight. How do you feel?"

They had known each other too long—since their school days at Miss Weston's in Portsmouth—for Amy to give Henriette anything but the truth. "Fatigued and a little overheated, but I hope to make it through the bulk of the evening."

"To hear Mr. Farraday tell it, you were on the brink of death last time he was here, so it is a good thing you plan on proving him wrong."

"Fie on him. Where is your Daniel?" Amy asked. "I saw you on his arm."

"Oh, he went off to find the card room. He hates dancing unless it is with me, which is so unfashionable." Henriette grinned a little at this; hers was a love match, and as much as Amy couldn't comprehend living with Mr. Owens's shy silence, she loved to see her friend glow even these many years after marriage. "Besides, he knows I want to catch up with you while I can. I must know every detail of your visit with the Preston family. Are they as intimidating as I think they are? How is Captain Preston? And you *are* glad you turned him down, aren't you?"

There had been a multitude of voices in Amy's ear when she had decided she could not elope with Nate. Pater's, declaring he would cut her off without a penny if she so much as invited Nate for another afternoon of courting. Mary's, begging Amy to think of how being allied with the Prestons would impact *her* marriage prospects. Great-Aunt Hilaria's, advising Amy that a father always knows best for his family.

And Henriette's, which had taken all those other voices and put them in the context of reality. Without Pater's money, where would Amy live? Without Nate in port, who would care for Amy's safety? With only the Preston family connections, could Amy even stay in Portsmouth, or would she have to move to districts unknown and rely on the kindness of people she had never met?

Amy couldn't admit now that perhaps she and Henriette had been wrong. "I wouldn't have made a very good wife, would I? It is a blessing that my illness fell upon me when only my father and sister must be affected, instead of a husband who hoped for children."

Henriette narrowed her eyes at this. She had dark features to begin with—her mother had been a Spaniard—and skepticism always made her face crowd together like a teacher's inky slash through poor grammar. "That was not my meaning at all."

They were interrupted by Caroline and Sophia, who begged an introduction to Henriette.

Then Nate himself approached.

He was the kind of handsome that begged the eye to linger. His uniform outlined his strong shoulders and chest; his white trousers clung to his legs; even the pomade in his hair made the dark brown of his irises richer. It took every ounce of Amy's self-control to keep from stepping directly into his arms.

He cut a bow to Henriette. "Miss Curry."

"It is Mrs. Owens now, actually." She curtsied in reply. "And it is nice to see you again, Captain Preston, after so much time."

There was something in how Nate drew himself up—a little stiffly—that suggested he did not appreciate her reference to the past. Still, he said pleasantly, "My felicitations on your marriage." Then he turned to Amy. "Have you any waltzes available, Miss Lamplugh?"

She almost laughed; every single one of her dances was so far available. "I do, thank you. Shall I save you the first one?"

"Please." The stiffness faded, replaced by one of his sincere smiles.

Amy basked in it.

"And save one for me, Nate," Caroline said. "I must judge for myself if you are a better dancer than Benny."

They chatted a little longer before their group was naturally broken up: Lady Olivia stole Nate away to introduce him to other eligible young women, Caroline joined the first set of dancing, and Sophia excused herself to rescue Mr. Anderson from Mary.

Henriette waited no longer than she had to before turning on Amy with a hiss. "You are waltzing with Captain Preston?"

Amy unfurled her hand fan and fluttered cool air towards her chin. "Why shouldn't I?"

"I am not the only one in the neighborhood who knows your father rejected him as a suitor for you."

"My father *and* I rejected him. I was of age. I could have married him without Pater's permission."

Henriette opened her arms in the air, as if Amy had just illuminated her point. "Precisely. Why should you want to waltz with him now when you have already rejected him?"

A ball was hardly the place to try to explain everything that had passed between Amy and Nate. Besides, Amy wasn't sure she could explain it even if she tried.

She settled for: "He is a good dancer, and I enjoy a waltz. Now, would you mind sitting down with me? I am feeling overexcited from standing."

It was clear to Amy that Henriette did not consider the topic finished. Nevertheless, she acquiesced; they sat by the doors leading to the stone terrace, where chairs had been provided for chaperones and spinsters and other women like them who preferred to watch the dancing. Henriette moved the topic along, too, filling Amy in on the local gossip from Portsmouth. It was a town of officers' wives and visiting dignitaries, making it rife with petty jealousies that provided amusement from afar. The perfect topic for a ball, where Amy could even watch some of the subjects of the stories as they danced with people who were not their spouses.

Unfortunately, she also had to watch Nate dance with people who were not her. Specifically, with young women who Lady Olivia thought might catch him in the parson's noose. A girl in a pastel pink gown that showed off her generous bosom; a woman in deep blue—like the sapphire color Amy would have worn—who made him laugh as they waited at the end of the minuet line; Miss Stratton for a quadrille that had far too much deep eye contact for Amy's comfort.

When Mr. Owens emerged to collect Henriette for the supper dance, Amy decided it would be better to take a break from watching the dancing. "You'll sit with us at supper?" Henriette said as she followed her husband to the center of the room.

"Of course." Amy wasn't sure if she would abide by her own promise. Everyone would go through to the dining room after this set, where a half dozen tables waited for them, and the dancers would all sit with their partners. They would be red-faced from exertion, full of good cheer, laughing about who stepped on whose toe and flirting with each other across the tops of fluttering fans.

At the start of the evening, that had all sounded like good fun. Just now, the idea of sitting next to Henriette and solemn Mr. Owens and commenting on everyone else lucky enough to have some excitement that night only made Amy feel sad.

And hot. One of her heat waves was upon her, making the room unbearable even with the breeze from the open garden doors behind her. A good enough reason to slip out those doors into the cool of the night.

They were in the country, so the ball had not started at ten, as it would have in London, but before the sun had even set at seven. Now, the sky still glowed a little purple-gray with the remainder of dusk. Without a moon, the stars glittered like diamonds in a jewel case.

Amy wasn't the only person escaping the ballroom. On the terrace, Mary and a trio of other matrons sat on iron chairs, gossiping. Down the steps, a few couples Amy could only see in silhouette walked along the white pea-gravel paths of the ornamental gardens.

Merriment, everywhere she looked. Optimism, everywhere she listened. It seemed cruel, given how little Amy felt of either of those after wasting the evening in a corner, waiting for anyone other than Henriette to deem her worthy of their company.

Anyone besides Henriette and Nate, that was.

Oh, Amy was being self-indulgent and hardly giving anyone credit. Plenty of people had greeted her and asked after her health; if she had really wanted to dance, she could have bullied Fred or Sir Charles into standing up with her; had her goal truly been to forge deeper friendships with her neighbors, she could have gone and made conversation with the others watching the dancing.

What she wanted was a different life. One where she was married; one where a ball was not her singular excitement; one where she didn't have to run out in search of cool air to appease an uncooperative body.

She wanted more than a waltz with Nate. Even though her head knew there were a hundred reasons why she was right to have turned him down, her heart still longed for the life where she was his wife.

She would have been lonely, with him so much on the seas. She would have been worried and scared for him most of the time, too. But when he returned to her, they would have had such wonderful times together. Amy could almost feel him rushing down a dock to see her, catching her in his arms, spinning her through the air as if she were the most precious thing in the whole world. And at a ball like this, they would have playfully ignored each other, only to link arms at the end of the night and gossip on the carriage ride home.

It wouldn't have been easy, and once Amy's illness struck, Nate would probably have stayed on the seas rather than come home to a weakened wife. Still, there was a part of Amy that couldn't help yearning for it.

Her fantasies overwhelmed her. Amy fled the terrace, rushed through the ornamental garden, and kept walking until she was safely ensconced in the hedge maze. It was lit for the party by dim lanterns placed every six feet and decorated with festoons of spring flowers draped along its yew walls. Still, as Amy ventured inside, it seemed empty. Later, after everyone had eaten and drunk more, it might fill with merrymakers, but for the moment, they were all attached to the dance floor.

Amy knew the first two turns to reach the center: left from the entrance, then right. From there, she never could remember the path. Not unlike her life. When she had reached her majority, she had felt so prepared to seize her future. All her childhood, she had trained to wear the appropriate outfits, make amusing conversation, and entertain the best of company. She had known exactly how to launch herself upon Portsmouth society and catch herself some beaux. When Nate started calling in the afternoons and Amy realized she wished him to be her *only* visitor, she had fancied she knew exactly how to walk the thrilling line between courting and compromising herself.

And then, somehow, she had gotten lost.

Much like she was now. After the last right turn, Amy had turned left twice. Now she faced a dead end, ornamented by a statue of a semi-nude woman titled *Helen of Troy*. Amy turned back, took the opposite turn, only to find herself at another dead end and another naked statue. This one was a man; by habit, Amy averted her eyes from the appendage dangling between his legs.

And immediately hated herself for doing it. How ridiculous was she to still worry about *modesty* at the age of twenty-eight? Most women her age had birthed children. They would be giggling about the size of the statue's appendage or making some other knowledgeable comment, not hiding away as if their reputations would be shattered if someone caught them peering too curiously.

Amy didn't want to be a frail, shrinking spinster. She didn't want to be like Great-Aunt Hilaria, who even at the age of fifty had blushed at Shakespeare's reference to the beast with two backs. She wanted to know the world in all its terrible glory. She wanted to die having lived a full life; she didn't want to go to her grave without ever seeing a man's appendage, especially not if her only reason for not looking was because Great-Aunt Hilaria had warned her never to raise her eyes.

Amy didn't want to be a spinster at all.

She looked back at the statue. A lantern hung right above him, as if Lady Olivia and Sir Charles *wanted* their guests to examine him.

He was a quarter of the size of a real man. He stood on a pedestal that lifted him so that Amy was almost face-to-face with him. A plaque at his feet read *Paris of Troy*; the only references to his identity in the statue itself were a sheet—suggesting a toga—thrown over his shoulder and a helmet on his head.

But she wasn't examining him to observe all the classical allusions in his composition. Amy dragged her eyes across his chest—sculpted with more muscles than she suspected a person could have—and down to the thing between his legs.

Things, more like it. Lumps: one slightly large and irregularly shaped, and two hanging below it like rotten eggs.

Was Amy supposed to feel aroused? Titillated? Scandalized?

She felt more as if she were looking at the back of a horse. She wanted to avert her eyes again, but this time because it was simply distasteful to contemplate for too long.

It didn't at all look the way Nate's had felt pressed against her leg. *That* she imagined as long as a forearm and just about as thick, too.

She felt hot all over again, thinking about the appendage between Nate's legs.

Which just went to show how little she knew about life. Why had she spent so much of her energy protecting herself from threats like this statue, when it didn't even resemble the real threats to her virtue?

If Amy could only see the map of the maze of her life, she would take the path that would lead her where she didn't worry about her reputation, where her gown wasn't ruined by an overeager nephew and his mother, where she could tell which risks were worth taking.

For the moment, all she could do was try to find the center of the hedge maze and call that her adventure for the night.

But Amy decided to take one more risk before turning away. Removing her glove one finger at a time, she reached out and took the statue's marble appendage in her palm.

"*Cock*," she whispered to herself.

Only to jump out of her skin when she got a reply: "I see I have a rival for your affections."

A gentleman would have let Amy have her moment without saying anything. Upon discovering her standing immodestly close to the statue with her bare hand on its marble prick, Nate should have backed away and returned with thumping footsteps. Or he could have cleared his throat and looked away, pretending to peer down the warren of hedgerows.

Nate was too amused to be a gentleman. Worse, laughter bubbled up as Amy—with a startled shriek—leapt away from the statue.

"Shall I meet the fellow at dawn with pistols?" A great line ruined by his own chortle.

Amy's palms spread flat above her heart. "It is poor sport to duel with a man who has no arms."

Indeed, the statue was shorn of everything below its bulging biceps. "I shall tie my own behind my back to wrestle him."

She grinned. How Nate loved her grin, particularly when it emerged in the middle of private moments like these. It was for him, earned by him, and for his enjoyment alone.

Well, his and the statue's.

But her hands remained pressed against her ribcage—on bare skin, he couldn't help noticing, exposed by a low neckline—and her face looked flushed even by the light of the lanterns. Nate remembered why he had followed her into the maze in the first place. "Are you feeling unwell?"

"Oh." From the way Amy's eyes darted around and her fingers twitched against her skin he suspected that the true answer was *yes*, but also that she didn't want to admit it. "I wanted some cooler air before supper, that's all." Then her grin returned. "My heart is racing now, though, no thanks to you."

"Why, because I interrupted your tryst?" Nate couldn't help taking a few steps closer. The dead end was rather small, after all, much smaller than a captain's cabin on a ship, and a few steps brought him within reach of Amy. "Or because of how handsome I look tonight?"

Her lips parted ever so slightly. Enough for Nate to hear a breath escape them. The tip of her tongue darted out and drew a ring around them, as if to prepare them for a kiss.

Nate hadn't come out here for that, he reminded himself.

"I daresay Miss Stratton finds you plenty handsome." Amy's voice was hardly louder than a whisper. She looked down to reapply her glove. "And she looks very beautiful tonight. Her gown flatters her figure just the way it is meant to."

She took it far, commenting on the cut of the gown. Of course Nate had noticed how the girl's gown—while adhering to fashion and modesty—showcased her plump breasts and how, when it swayed, it suggested mesmerizing hips.

He didn't need a gown to make him notice Amy's breasts or hips or legs or lips. He thought enough about those without prompting.

But of course, Amy brought up Miss Stratton for that exact purpose. To shift his thoughts away from everything that lay beneath *her* silks and onto the debutante. Because, she claimed, she cared about *his* future.

Nate had tried very hard this last week to take that as a compliment. Yet he couldn't remember it without a certain bitterness. No doubt, if he probed, she would say that was the same reason she had refused to elope with him. Because she—and she alone—had some clairvoyance that showed her he would be miserable with Amy and prosperous, if not happy, with Miss Stratton.

He turned towards the hedge corridor. "Did you want to find the center of this maze or were you only after a private moment with dear Paris here?"

Amy hesitated. "I was looking for the center. I've found it before, of course, but now I can't remember the way."

"Lucky you have an intrepid officer here to protect you from further statues' overtures."

Nate offered her his arm. For a moment, she only stared at it. He understood: they shouldn't be alone in the hedges together; they shouldn't walk arm-in-arm through the maze; if they *were* to walk together through the maze, it should be to find its exit, not its center.

If, watching her slip away from the ballroom as the dance was about to begin, Nate had truly been concerned for her welfare, he should have sent Mr. Bremridge or Sir Charles—or even the vicar—into the maze to check on her.

He, a bachelor, should not have followed her, a spinster, into a dark place where they could this very minute be tearing off each other's clothes with almost perfect privacy.

Particularly not if he was serious about earning Miss Stratton's affections.

Amy tucked her hand inside the crook of his elbow. "There is a beautiful gazebo at the center, and Lady Olivia told me she set up champagne for anyone who finds it tonight."

"Then by all means, we must not return until we have discovered it."

They walked in silence at first. Not complete silence. Amy seemed to still be catching her breath, and it sailed through her in short inhales and exhales. Her gown, too, trailed behind them in a soft murmur over the pea-gravel path. An owl hooted somewhere nearby. And from a distance, muffled by the high walls of the maze, came the sounds of the ball: the string quartet, laughter, a general buzz of conversation and excitement.

It was a magical feeling. Nate's favorite kind of feeling, in fact. One he had found before when his ship caught a wind or on a still night in the doldrums when there was nothing but hot air and hazy sky. He was suspended in time with no past and no future. There was just *now*, and *now* was almost perfect.

Amy ruined it. "Do you think Miss Stratton enjoyed your dance?"

It had been a quadrille, which was lively and required partners to focus on keeping in the formation rather than making conversation. Nate *had* made a point of complimenting Miss Stratton and smiling at her, for his brain knew that Amy was right and that Miss Stratton could be valuable in saving his career.

And Nate *did* want to save his career. But at the cost of getting the poor girl's hopes up? At the risk of marrying her, just so that he could keep captaining ships that didn't have enough power to do anything *real* about ending slavery?

The calculus was enough to plunge him into a black mood. All he had ever wanted was to do something that was clearly good for the world, and to have a happy marriage while doing so.

He didn't know why it had to suddenly be so complicated.

"She looked very happy to be your partner," Amy added. "However, she looked just as happy dancing with Mr. Farraday."

"Good. She shouldn't place her hopes on me."

They turned left into a new corridor; luckily, it wasn't an immediate dead end. "Mr. Farraday owns a plantation in Barbados, you know."

Nate had suspected as much. "So does half of Parliament."

"I only thought that might spur you into protecting Miss Stratton from getting entangled with such a cad."

They reached another intersection, this one shaped like a T. Amy started towards the right; Nate, on instinct, tugged her left. That would take them farther towards the edge of the maze, but he suspected it was designed that way to trick a person into going right.

"Why won't you take this seriously?" Amy's voice narrowed into something resembling a hiss, and he knew she wasn't referring to the maze. "You have very few options available to influence the outcome of your court-martial, and earning Miss Stratton's affections is your best one. You should be trying to sit with her at supper, not..."

"I'm walking you to the center of the maze." Nate knew his reply was stubborn and unhelpful and maybe even a little angry. He couldn't help it.

"And what will you do when Admiral Stratton strips you of command? Sell your soul to your uncle in the name of making a fortune?"

Amy was the last person Nate expected to accuse him of selling his soul. It nearly took his breath away. "I don't know. Why should I have to know? I can't plan a battle without first seeing the harbor, nor can I decide my future before I know the outcome of the court-martial."

"This isn't the same as entering a harbor you've never seen before. It's more like you are making a plan for three different harbors. One for if they let you keep your rank, one for if you are stripped of your rank but allowed to keep command, and one for if you are removed from the navy entirely."

A lantern along the hedge corridor flickered out, and for a few steps, they walked by starlight only.

"I'm only trying to help you prepare," Amy said, her voice almost back to normal. "What is it you want? That's what I want for you."

But that question wasn't a comfort. It was a taunt. "What I want is apparently what I can't have. I want to be in command of a ship. I want to find a way to stop slavery, instead of stopping one ship at a time. And I want..."

To be married to you.

His brain stopped his tongue just in time from saying that aloud.

"I don't want to think about the future. I *can't* think about it. And I can't make free with Miss Stratton, either, just for my own benefit. Please, Amy, can't you understand?"

He realized he had been cutting his arms through the air for emphasis; sometime earlier, Amy must have let go of his elbow. She reached up now and took his hands in her own. "Yes. I understand."

Nate's heart thundered in his ears. He wished it were from desire. He stared into Amy's eyes, willing it to be a simple reaction to her body and person.

He didn't want to admit the possibility that it was fear.

Amy gave him a soft smile, made more magical by the flickering lanterns. She returned to her position at his side, one hand tucked into the bend of his elbow. They walked in silence once more.

And made a final turn into the center of the maze.

"Well," Amy sighed, "that was worth it."

CHAPTER TEN

Amy had never seen the gazebo like this. A dozen candles in glass cases lined its perimeter, infusing it with a soft glow. White primroses hung from its roof like pearls. At its center, silver trays showcased sparkling crystal glasses.

It was as if some magical spell had been cast, and now they were in a fairy princess's palace instead of Selsea Park.

A palace intended for someone other than Amy. Lady Olivia had gone to such trouble with the gazebo to impress her guests. Perhaps she had pictured groups of couples discovering it with their chaperones still trailing behind at a wrong turn of the maze. Or she may have hoped it would be a refuge for married couples like Henriette and Daniel, who still wanted beautiful moments together.

It wasn't meant for a spinster and a bachelor who had decided *not* to get married. Nor was it for a couple in a heated argument, who weren't sure they would forgive each other even as they blinked in wonder at the candles and crystal and flowers.

Amy didn't care that she wasn't supposed to discover the gazebo. Here she was, and it was spectacular.

She tugged Nate forward. Her hand slid from his elbow into his palm; he caught her fingers in his own before they could fall away from each other.

"Will you drink some champagne?" She felt anxious to smooth over the tension that had just erupted. He had grown so severe, his arms slicing through the air like rapiers in a duel. Amy hadn't *wanted* to be discussing Miss Stratton anyhow. She wanted Nate to be happy, nothing more.

"If you're having some." Nate still clung to her hand as they climbed the steps and crossed to the bucket of champagne. Only then did he release her to pick up a bottle. "I wish I had my saber to open it."

The table provided a knife to cut the string holding in the cork. Nate opened the bottle with a pop; the air filled with the warm smell of celebration. Amy selected two crystal glasses so delicate that she was afraid of breaking them when she lifted their stems.

Nate was still tense, even as he made a good show of pouring the champagne. Amy held hers in the air; the amber liquid caught the candlelight like a lantern in its own right. "Shall we toast to the future?"

He held back his glass from that toast. "The future can go hang itself. We toast to the present."

The look he gave her was dark and meaningful. It filled her head with unsaid words: *to this gazebo, to being alone with you, to us.*

Her heart was racing again.

"To the present," she agreed, but she could barely say the words for the excitement filling her throat.

Their glasses chimed against each other. The champagne splashed onto her tongue in a cold, dazzling burst.

Nate wouldn't stop looking at her.

He shouldn't think she hoped he would marry Miss Stratton. She hoped the very opposite of that, which was why she forced herself to keep considering it. If she focused on a future for Nate that didn't include her, she wouldn't be heartbroken when it came to fruition.

This moment wasn't for the future. This moment was for the present. And at present, all Amy wanted was to bask in the glory of Nate.

The kiss that came next began from each of them equally. Their lips met in the space between them, the rest of their bodies hovering away, as if to prove this was not a joining of the flesh but an expression of their hearts. Nate's mouth was a little cold, perhaps from the champagne, which made Amy realize how very hot her whole body felt. Immediately, she wanted his mouth on every inch of her skin.

She opened her eyes long enough to spot the silver tray on the table and put down her champagne glass. Then she blacked out the world again; with her eyes shut, she could pretend it really was just her and Nate in the universe. Arms around his neck, she leaned her body into his chest, rising onto her tiptoes to deepen their kiss. All her weight belonged to him. He held her with strong arms, his palms fastening to the seat of her bum even as his tongue touched hers in firm, playful greeting.

Between her thighs, Amy could feel the length of his appendage growing stiffer.

She couldn't keep track of how long they stood like that. She knew Nate's hands never moved, only increased their grip on her bum, once squeezing in such a way that a moan sprang from her throat. He repeated that; she moaned again, and their kiss broke for a moment as they both laughed.

His laugh was breathtaking. How could a man be so handsome that her heart both raced and felt like it would never start again?

Amy kissed him more. She felt greedy, like she had to make this kiss worth the thousands she would never have in years to come. Openmouthed, she claimed what she could of Nate, and he surrendered it with the same energy. They were not two lovers marveling over the miracle of finding each other. They were two souls on the brink of expiring with only this one moment left to enjoy.

A kiss—even one with tongues clashing and groins meeting—could only sustain a soul for so long. Amy's heart was no longer just racing, her skin no longer just hot. She ached for Nate between her legs. She yearned for him to touch her breasts. She envisioned herself naked—and him, too, armless like the statue—on the floor of the gazebo, legs and bodies entwined to such a point that there was neither start nor end between the two of them.

"Take me," she breathed, for surely he knew what that meant. "Take me, please, won't you?"

Nate's lips pressed against hers once more. A close-mouthed peck. "Take you where? With me on my next ship?" Now he stepped to the left—and carried her with him, the toes of her slippers pressing against the tops of his shoes. "To London, for a life of sin?" Another step; they approached the perimeter of the gazebo. "To Gretna Green?"

She loved his teasing, but she couldn't bear it anymore. "Take me the way a man takes a woman. Please, Nate, I can't wait any longer."

For a moment—not even that long—his step faltered. Half of Amy's heart panicked that she had said the wrong thing; the other half delighted that she had said the *right* thing and so aroused him that he couldn't walk properly.

Then she forgot all about it because he was laying her down on the cushions of the gazebo bench. Nate came next, hovering over her on his arms and knees. The candles were above them now. His face was nothing but shadows as he leaned down for another kiss. Except he didn't press his mouth to hers: his lips landed on her neck, above her scarf, and the mere sensation delighted Amy's body, sending a shake of desire down her spine. "Oh, that," she couldn't help saying.

He hesitated, grinning at her from just below her chin. "You are so easy to delight."

And then Nate kissed her on her neck again. More than kissed: unraveling her scarf, his mouth teased the bare skin opposite her goiter, his lips and tongue wet and ticklish and awakening her whole body with mind-numbing pleasure.

So much so that she couldn't even worry about the monstrous lump hovering beside his cheek.

He stayed there until her spine spasmed again. Even her legs jerked into the air, quite outside of her control.

It was one of the best sensations she had ever had in her life.

"There." Nate's voice was gravelly in her ear. "Are you satisfied, my darling?"

"Hardly." Even now, Amy didn't quite have a properly working brain. Yet she knew they were both still clothed, and Nate's appendage was large and full against his trousers. There was much more to be done—and if this was the start, Amy didn't want to miss out on whatever came next.

"Greedy." Nate sat back. He still held her hands, and his legs still straddled hers, but his mouth was so far away now. "How do you feel?"

"Wonderful."

"Your heart is not racing too fast?"

It felt like it would jump out of her throat at any moment. "Not at all."

"You do not feel faint?"

Her body was approaching overexcitement, but Amy didn't care. Desire propelled her, like a trade wind in her sails, and she wouldn't surrender to her body's strange moods now. "I feel only a deep need for you, Nate. Please, won't you show me what comes next?"

He leaned forward again and kissed her deeply, his lips and tongue tangling with hers. In between, somehow, he murmured, "You know we shouldn't."

"Lady Olivia"—Amy jerked forward on another kiss—"set up this gazebo"—here, she grabbed his earlobe between her lips, as she had the other night, and earned a groan of pleasure from Nate—"for trysts like this."

Chuckling, he pulled her into his lap so now she straddled him. "You think Lady Olivia wanted you and me to debauch each other in the middle of her ball?"

Amy slid her hands underneath his coat and waistcoat so that she could feel the smooth linen of his shirt and the firm wall of muscle beneath it. "No, she wanted you to debauch Miss Stratton in the middle of her ball. However, one's best laid plans never work out, do they?"

"Certainly not when they involve you."

He grabbed her bum again—sending a heavenly jolt of pleasure through her—and pulled her close. Amy's center rested against the thick excitement jutting against his trousers. By instinct, she rolled her hips across it; Nate threw his head back, eyes shut, bottom lip caught between his teeth.

Amy had never felt so powerful. Or excited. She leaned in to whisper into his ear: "I have plans for you, Nate."

His body reacted beneath her: arms tightening, breath increasing, and his cock twitching against her thigh. This, she thought, was the moment when they would cross the point of no return.

Nate raised his hips into hers. "Why me?"

The words were a bit of a gasp; Amy thought he was teasing her. "Because you are so handsome," she replied, running her thumb along his jaw.

He caught her hand and brought it down to rest on his chest. "No, why...why are we doing this, Amy?"

Her brain moved too slowly. She had thought they were past conversation, past any verbal faculty except whispering sweet nothings. She didn't have an answer.

"You..." Nate swallowed. His eyes were darting all around instead of meeting her gaze. "This is what lovers do."

Amy's heart knocked against itself. "This is what people do. Animals, too, in fact, when they are properly excited."

She did not want to be thinking of barnyard animals, though.

"So you do not consider us lovers?"

Amy searched Nate's expression because she didn't know what he was asking. Did he want her to confess she loved him?

Of course she did. She had never stopped loving him, not even when she tried with every fiber of her being.

What was the use in saying so? Amy had chosen her path years ago, and she could not change that now. No matter that she wished she had been his wife all this time; now, she was an aged and feeble woman not fit to be any man's partner. And Nate had a big future ahead of him, one that might include a wife like Miss Stratton to forge alliances for him or perhaps even a wife who could voyage with him wherever the navy sent him.

Amy couldn't be any kind of wife except a burden.

"I consider us Nate and Amy," she replied, trying to smile. "Two people who are very fond of each other and have a burning desire to...do what people do."

"Fond." Nate's fingers loosened around hers.

"Yes." From the way he looked at her, Amy had said something drastically wrong. And perhaps she had: perhaps she had been so busy basking in how glad she was to be with him that she had misjudged his feelings for her entirely. After all, if she summed up their interactions the past few weeks, he had avoided her or argued with her more than he had expressed any fondness.

She corrected herself:

"At least, I know I am very fond of you. We loved each other once, and for my part, that has aged into a keen pleasure in spending time with you. I understand, of course, if your feelings are not quite the same. Only, all I was trying to say is, we seem to enjoy spending time together, at least like this, and that is all I need to know to wish you would kiss me again."

Nate leaned forward, almost as if he would do as she said and press his lips to hers. Instead, he framed her face with his hands. "We *did* love each other once, didn't we?"

He looked so desperate. Amy nodded. "Deeply."

"And now you are fond of me."

"Very much so."

Nate let go of her face. There was something in his expression that made Amy think he was going to desert her entirely. But he kissed her instead, a light and sweet touch of the lips that sent delight down her spine.

"I'm fond of you, too."

"Good." Amy shut her eyes. It wasn't because she didn't believe him. It was only that, when he finally said it aloud, she wished it were something else. Something more.

Something that declared that all these years, he had been yearning for her, too. That it wasn't merely a happy accident that he had ended up at Selsea Park while she was there, and that he wasn't kissing her now in the gazebo simply because they happened to be secluded together at the right time.

Amy loved him, even if she couldn't say it, and it turned out she wanted him to love her back.

She would settle for the next best thing.

"Now, will you debauch me, please?"

Amy was fond of him.

Amy had *once* loved him. But now, she was only fond of him.

Nate didn't know why it felt so shocking to hear aloud. His heart twisted painfully in his chest, but why was it a surprise?

It wasn't as if she had thrown herself at him the moment he arrived at Selsea Park to declare that she had made a mistake. Nor, in any of their discussions about the past, had she taken the opportunity to assure him that even now, she loved him with every beat of her heart.

If anything, Amy had made it clear that she would make the same choice over again, could they turn back time.

Moments ago, when she'd begged him to show her what was next, he had been prepared to tell her the truth. But that was before he knew how she felt.

Now, Nate knew his feelings didn't matter.

If he confessed to her now that, in fact, he was not *fond* of her, that he loved her as much as ever, she would not return the sentiment. She would be horrified or flee or—even worse—act with great kindness to try to keep him from being humiliated.

Nate was a naval officer with a pall hanging over his honor and a second son of an embarrassing family. Of course Amy was only *fond* of him. She could hardly love a man who couldn't imagine his own future.

He kissed her, as requested, because he didn't have any right to be heartbroken. Six years ago, he hadn't thought he would survive her rejection, but he had found ways to keep living, and one of them was to plunge himself into whatever task was at hand.

That the task now was to debauch Amy made no difference. If he focused on the feel of her arse in his palm, the taste of her neck, and the gasp of her breath, he would forget everything except the blood pulsing into his cock.

They were still in the gazebo, where they could be discovered at any moment. Nate would abandon his feelings in showing Amy all she had been missing, but he would still have a care for her reputation. Which meant he couldn't tear down the bodice of her dress to free the nipples he could feel puckering beneath her cotton corset. Neither could he lay her down on the bench and plunge inside her the way his cock wanted him to.

Nate flipped her so now she sat on the bench, her back braced against the gazebo railing. Candlelight spilled across her face, making her glow like some kind of wicked angel.

Nate banished the thought from his mind. That was allowing his heart to emerge again, and his whole aim right now was to forget his heart existed.

Her eyes were wide with excitement, and her tongue darted out across her lips. She was a woman who was lonely and who hadn't been properly fucked in all her life. That was all she wanted from him; that was all Nate would give her.

If she happened to fall back in love with him because of how he made her body feel, so be it.

"Are you quite sure you want to be debauched?" he asked, sliding to his knees before her.

"I shall die if you don't debauch me this very instant."

With one last glance over his shoulder to make sure no one had found the center of the maze, Nate flipped up her skirts and scooted under them. He was not perfectly hidden—for that, they would have needed her in the hoops of days of yore—but at least he was not immediately visible. If someone happened upon them, he could claim to be on his knees searching for a dropped earring.

In reality, he was alone with Amy and her legs. He heard her gasp as he looped her knees over his shoulders. Grinning, he nuzzled his lips along her thigh. It was dark under her skirts, with only the faintest candlelight making it through the tent of green cotton, so he let his touch lead him along the soft skin of her legs to her hot center.

When he made it to the nest of hair, he paused, tracing its perimeter with his tongue. Amy's breath was caught on an eternal gasp, and, looking up, he could see her belly and the underside of her corseted breasts catching on a wave of pleasure.

"Are you ready for me to keep going?" he murmured against her inner thigh. He wasn't sure she could hear him, but she replied:

"Oh, don't stop now."

He widened her knees a little, then ran the pad of his thumb along her inner ridges. After everything they had been doing—she had climaxed at least once already, and she was nearly panting with desire—Nate expected it to be as wet as a rainstorm. Instead it was more sticky than moist. Neither did she twitch with pleasure at his touch; instead, she froze, her breath suddenly quiet.

Perhaps it was all the talk of feelings that had made her lust shy. Nate sallied forward, this time licking his tongue up to her peak. It was a little soft, a little hidden, so he stayed there, toying with it until he felt it growing rigid and excited.

Amy was breathing again. He ran his fingers along her legs, teasing her knees and the nerves of her outer thighs, as his tongue remained at her peak. Her heels dug into his shoulder blades. He knew they didn't have forever—could be caught at any moment—and yet he waited, devoting every muscle of his mouth to coaxing an orgasm from her tiny ferocious organ.

When she came, it was violent, a ripple that racked every muscle of her body. Nate was squeezed and kicked and pounded.

His cock loved every moment of it.

Nate took advantage of her excitement and slid his fingers between her folds again. This time, he tested the waters by circling his index finger around and—just the tiniest bit—inside her canal.

Still dry. Even his saliva seemed to have evaporated, leaving nothing but flesh that clung to his fingers instead of helping them slide right inside.

Were they in a proper bedroom, Nate would have a few more ideas for what to do about this. As it was, he found himself at a loss.

"Nate, please," Amy sighed. "I'm not sure how much more I can stand. Take me the way a man takes a woman. I want it so much."

He hesitated. In the safety of her skirts, he didn't have to face her. He could just keep kissing her quim until she cried out that she wouldn't survive another orgasm.

But she wasn't asking for that. Nate forced himself to back away and, flipping her skirts again as quickly as possible, return to the candlelit gazebo.

She reached for him almost as soon as he sat down beside her. "I dream of you inside me."

She had said that once before, and Nate had been idiot enough to take it to mean she really had fantasized about him in his absence.

Now, he wondered if it was simply something she thought a woman ought to say to a man.

"Perhaps you do," he replied, pulling away so there was a little more air between them. "However, your body does not seem to agree."

Amy frowned at him. Her expression was loose from pleasure; Nate wished he could keep it that way. "What do you mean?"

"Your...you are not ready for me to take you."

"Yes, I am." Now she was the one to lean away. "You aren't protecting my modesty, are you, Nate? I assure you, I am ready to do away with it."

Nate shut his eyes. "That is not my meaning. To have...a quim must be wet. It helps things go right. It helps you enjoy it. Despite our best efforts, yours simply is not interested tonight."

She was silent for so long that he had to open his eyes again. Her arms had crossed her chest, making her look cold and small.

Nate cleared his throat. "Do you ever pleasure yourself? Surely you must have noticed times when you were..."

"Wet?" Now Amy tucked her knees up in front of her elbows, as if to shield herself from him. "Yes, I suppose there have been times."

"Then you understand. Perhaps it is to do with your illness."

Her hand slapped to her goiter, and suddenly, she spun to sit primly away from him. "I do apologize."

Nate was eager to move past the topic. "You have no need to."

"You must find me very tiresome."

"I do not."

"You think me a tease."

"A tease?" Nate felt rather like he had been transported to hell. He had intended to lose himself in their lovemaking so that he wouldn't have to think about her or her feelings for the rest of the night. This was the opposite of that. He found himself trying to comfort her: "Even if you changed your mind simply because you no longer wanted to make a scene in a gazebo, I wouldn't think you a tease. I certainly won't hold your illness against you."

"I am useless. To you. To myself. Even to Mary. No one can count on me for anything."

"This has nothing to do with you being *of use*. If we were to do...what we were going to do, it would have nothing to do with being useful. It would be an expression of..." For him, anyway, it would have been an expression of love. He settled on, "...mutual lust. Just as visiting your sister has more to do with love than with being useful. After all, if she really needed a nursemaid, she could hire one."

"And if you really wanted a fuck, you could pay for one."

The word was a little shocking coming from Amy's lips. Perhaps even more so because it seemed wrapped in a hatred Nate didn't understand at all.

A hatred she pointed at herself.

"Amy." Nate reached for her, but she shied away from him, sliding all the way to the far end of the bench. His hand landed empty on his knee. "You have it all wrong. You think you are a burden to everyone, but in fact, you are a delight. To me, anyway.

You are a gift, and I am as happy to sit here talking to you as I would be...fucking you."

She still wouldn't look at him. "I'm not a person. I am a body that is failing. I am a daughter that is not beautiful and a sister that is not amusing and whatever I might be to you—lover, mistress..." Her lips wobbled a little to get out the next word: "...wife—I could not do that, either. Clearly. If I am not overcome by your kissing, then I cannot get wet enough. I am not worth your time or attention, Nate. Please, go back to the ball."

It was a terrible speech. Nate didn't know how to break through to get her to hear him. "You are a person with an illness. You mustn't let it define you."

A tear slid down her cheek. Nate waited for her to acknowledge it, for her to do *something*.

After a minute or so, she murmured, "I am so very tired. Could you go fetch Fred? He can walk me home without causing gossip."

Nate couldn't let the conversation end like that. "Amy, please—"

"I'm sorry I'll have to miss our waltz. I was looking forward to it."

"You needn't be useful to be loved." *I love you*, he almost said.

There went another tear down her cheek. Eyes still shut, Amy leaned against the gazebo post. "Will you get Fred? I need to rest."

The candle nearest them sputtered out in its glass lantern. The gazebo no longer glowed with romance; the champagne no longer beckoned with golden promise.

And Amy was as remote and unreachable as she had been that night six years ago when Henriette had delivered the letter; as when he had been on Lake Erie a thousand leagues away; as when he had declared himself out of love with her on the far side of the Slave Coast.

Nate waited one more moment for Amy to buck up. Then, standing, he went off to honor her request.

Chapter Eleven

Amy stayed in bed for three days. She had an overwhelming fatigue that made moving feel like wading through molasses. Yet her heart kept overbeating, leaving her breathless. There was nausea just behind her tongue.

That was what she told Mary, anyhow. The physician, too, when Fred finally insisted on calling him in for a consultation. From the moment Nate had announced she was not *wet*, all the adrenaline propping her up had disappeared, and now she was paying the price for cavorting around the gazebo like some kind of young, healthy debutante.

She wished she could believe that was the sum of her ailments. That none of this was heartbreak or self-disgust. Those were ailments of the spirit, and this was her body. They couldn't possibly be connected.

"You *must* get up," Mary declared on the fourth morning, after an evening spent recovering from the physician's bloodletting. "Come down to the drawing room, anyhow, and watch the boys play. They have been asking after you endlessly."

That much, Amy had been able to hear from her bed. *Where is Aunt Amy? But why can't she come out of bed? Can't we play with her in there? She wants to see my sailor's hat, I know it.*

If only being a wretch were excuse enough. *I can't play because I am useless to everyone. I don't want to see you because you'll only get upset with me. I'm ill because I had a chance once to marry the man I loved, and instead I chose you.*

Nate—always with some contingent of his family—had called at the dower house each day to see how she fared. Amy didn't know why she couldn't force herself out of bed to see him, at least. So much of her soul longed to sit next to him again, even if all she could do was look at him.

And apparently that *was* all she could do. Amy would never forget the expression on his face when he told her that her body didn't want to go any further. That mixture of kindness and pity and care—it humiliated Amy all over again to think of it!

She knew exactly what he meant about wetness. In their courtship, she used to be wet for hours after he left, even when all they did was flirt. And, as a young woman, she had always been able to work herself to a slick ecstasy in the privacy of her bedroom on a long night. It was true that in recent months—years?—things hadn't been quite as excited down there.

Amy hadn't paid attention to her moisture. Until now, when it seemed like something she should have noticed immediately. Hadn't her quim felt more raw under her fingers? Hadn't the overall act of self-satisfaction felt less pleasurable?

Even if she hadn't noticed anything, Amy should have known better. She had made her choice, and she wasn't allowed to rewrite it, even if it was only as a love affair. She was Pater's daughter, Mary's sister, the boys' aunt, and Henriette's friend. That was all she was destined to be.

She was a fool to have believed she could steal moments of happiness with Nate. And it was cruel of her to pull Nate along in her wake. He had been so kind, trying to make her feel there wasn't anything wrong with her when clearly she couldn't even get aroused like a proper woman.

And when clearly, he had been with enough proper women to know how the act was supposed to go.

That very first moment that she discovered Nate was among Lady Olivia's visitors, Amy should have claimed a headache and remained in the dower house, out of sight. Or that night when he had come upon her drenched in the garden, she should have protected her modesty and fled upstairs instead of throwing herself into his arms.

"Little Charles is afraid you're going to die like the cat did," Mary said as part of her cajoling. "He is worried about whether there is room to bury you under the oak tree. Come out for an hour to set his mind at ease, won't you please?"

"What if I *am* dying?"

Mary set her hands on her hips. "Then I suppose I shall have to explain to Charles that we can't afford new clothes for him because we had to pay to move your corpse for burial at the family plot at Swanhill House."

As if Fred would be the one to pay for that. If Amy died, Pater would swoop in to make sure the burial reflected the family status, no matter that Amy had been nothing but a spinster.

But Amy knew she wasn't dying. Not immediately, anyhow. She was indulging herself, and it was time to put a stop to that. So she allowed Iris to help her into a day dress—a dark mauve cotton—with an India shawl wrapped about her shoulders for warmth.

Going downstairs was a harder job than she had expected. As much as Amy had stayed in bed because of the strange combination of fatigue and a racing heart, she had also convinced herself she was making it up. Yet by the time her feet landed on the ground floor, her body was heaving for breath as if she had swum a mile against the current.

"Steady on," said Fred, who was helping her by clinging to her right elbow. "A few more steps, and then you can have a scone. Orange-glazed. Your favorite, if rumor is to be believed."

They *were* her favorite, and usually only to be found at Swanhill House on special occasions. They required special ingredients, Cook had explained once, including oranges and sugar, and were altogether too rich to make for just the family. As much as Pater cared about appearances, they only mattered when there was company to notice them.

Yet there they were: a collection of fat, diamond-shaped scones drizzled with sugar glaze, tempting her into the drawing room from their gold-rimmed serving plate. Amy latched onto them as her target to drown out the noise of her heart pounding in her ears. She was, in fact, so focused on the plate of scones that it wasn't until she sat down that she noticed the full tea service—including six china cups—beside them. And it was only after *that* that she discovered the drawing room was rather full with Nate and Sophia and John Anderson.

"The Preston family has been quite worried about you," Mary explained from her own chair. "Captain Preston has come to ask after your health every afternoon."

Amy couldn't look at him. If she did, she would see whatever reaction he wore in response to Mary's rather rude observation. And she would have to confront however he looked: exhausted from worry, perfectly handsome from not worrying, angry from being toyed with.

She used her energy to serve herself a scone instead.

"Of course, my theory is that you have had your fill of socializing and wanted some peace and quiet," Sophia said. Her words, as usual, were a joke. "'Why haven't *I* thought of that?' I said to myself."

The truth was that Amy was ravenous. As breathless as she might be, her stomach still craved more food, especially now that Mary had reduced her diet to broth and bread. She replied to Sophia with a smile curved around a huge mouthful of scone. "It is a clever scheme if you can stomach a bloodletting or two."

"Ah, that would put me off. I can't stomach a bloodletting even when I have a raging fever."

Despite herself, Amy stole a glance at Nate. He sat on the settee beside his sister, looking ravishingly handsome as usual. Instead of drinking tea, he held his hat in his hands, and he couldn't seem to stop rotating it in circles.

He did not look at her.

"I hope you don't consider it an intrusion, but I have been doing some reading on your symptoms." This from John Anderson, who had a talent for making a person feel cared for with nothing more than a look. Amy wondered if it had been love at first sight between him and Sophia, or if they had taken an arduous route to find each other.

Certainly, Pater never would have stood for it had Amy announced she intended to marry an accoucheur. Add in Mr. Anderson's Indian heritage, and she might even have been locked in her room for a week for suggesting the idea.

"Have you tried bugleweed before?"

She hadn't heard of that. "I eat dried seaweed every morning. It is the only remedy that seems to lessen some of my symptoms."

John Anderson pulled out a corked glass vial full of a brown, powdery mixture. "I created this based on a text I have. It is a travel journal, really, about some chap's journey down the Indus River, but he describes this as a remedy for a companion suffering from symptoms similar to yours. It is a mixture of bugleweed, gypsywort, and gromwell. Take it with care, for I haven't prescribed it before, but I think the worst it can do is give you a stomachache. At best, it might reduce your symptoms to be barely noticeable."

Amy accepted the vial, though she wasn't sure she would try it. If he could promise it would cure her, then of course she would, but with only a nebulous *It might help*, it hardly seemed worth the risk of getting her hopes up.

"Well, I think that is wonderful," Mary said. "Very kind of you to consider my sister, Mr. Anderson. He has been most attentive to me, Amy, and all of his suggestions have worked, though my back still aches."

John Anderson tilted his head to accept this statement, then said, "If you do give it a try, take only a teaspoon, once a day. And please tell me how it goes."

"Thank you." Amy couldn't help it; she looked at Nate again. This time, he was watching her, his face pulled into a solemn, anxious frown. When their eyes met, he glanced away first.

"I received a letter from the Admiralty. My trial will be in two weeks."

This clearly wasn't news to anyone except Amy. She bit back her initial exclamation—and the fear that surged from her heart at the idea of the court-martial. Nate didn't want or need any of that. She replied, "It will be a blessing for it to finally be over."

"Yes."

The room filled again with a pregnant silence. If they were alone, Amy would have so many things to say—and so many things she *shouldn't* say. She took another scone to keep any words from spilling out. Nate turned his hat in nervous circles. Mary said,

"Perhaps you would be so good as to examine me, Mr. Anderson. As I said, my back does ache..."

At the same time, Sophia rose. "Mr. Bremridge, I wonder if you could show me the garden off to the side? I am most curious about the variety of cabbage you grow here."

Suddenly, everyone was standing; everyone was making an excuse to leave the room; everyone except for Amy and Nate.

It was a conspiracy both obvious and surprising. Clearly, they wanted Amy to have a moment alone with Nate.

What she would do with it, she hadn't the slightest clue.

But even as her mind and heart raced, the plan was foiled. Because before anyone had actually left the room, someone new entered.

Pater.

"Lieutenant Preston. I heard you were back."

This was not Nate's day. Or week. Or year.

First, there was the letter from the Admiralty. Cold words, cold tone, cold news: he was to stand trial on HMS *Capricorn* to answer for his crimes of insubordination in two weeks' time.

Seeing it in writing—*crimes of insubordination*!—made him furious and sick all at once.

Then there was Amy. When she had sent him for Fred at the ball, he had thought she was using her fatigue as an excuse to end their interlude. Yet she had been shut up for three days—and a physician called! Nate wondered if it was his fault. He shouldn't have taken her walking through the maze. He shouldn't have kissed her. He shouldn't have discussed her personal health so frankly.

He didn't know how any of that could make her body collapse, yet she was so clearly ill. Slimmer than ever, her wrist bones nearly poking through her skin. Paler than the white silk scarf tied around her neck. Sagging into the chair, as if she didn't even have the energy to hold herself upright.

It was hard to see her like that. But Nate would have been able to bear it if she had looked at him. Smiled. Done something to acknowledge that just days ago, they had been on the brink of making love.

These past three days, he had paid a daily call at the dower house hoping to see her. The first day, before he knew she was unwell, he thought he might be able to convince her to take a walk and steal a private moment that way.

The second day, he told himself to expect nothing more than a group conversation over tea. He planned to catch Amy's eye and somehow—this part he didn't quite have a plan for—indicate he wanted to speak to her at midnight again. Not for a tryst, but to clear the air.

To say what he couldn't say in front of the Bremridges: that there was nothing to be ashamed of, that there were other ways to make love if only they hadn't been in a gazebo, that she needn't be so cruel to herself.

Perhaps, even, he would tell her he loved her. Not because he expected her to say it back—he knew she wouldn't—but because Nate thought she needed to hear it from someone. If her sister couldn't say it, then he would.

Yet by the third day, it was clear that if he were to see Amy at all, it would be within the confines of the dower house's drawing room and while the sun shone. So he conquered a little bit of fear and asked Mrs. Bremridge for a moment alone with Amy.

Nate wasn't sure what exactly he would have ended up saying, faced as he had been with an Amy who seemed determined to ignore him.

Lord Warre had removed the opportunity from him entirely. Even though the man was shorter than Nate, he had managed to sneer down his nose. "My daughter is clearly ill, Preston. Kindly give us the courtesy of privacy."

His hostility was hardly a surprise. What hurt the most was how Amy and her sister had immediately changed upon their father's appearance. Mrs. Bremridge—who had almost seemed pleased with Nate for getting Amy out of bed—suddenly forgot all backache in order to fawn over her father. *Iris, fetch more tea; Pater, please, sit down; Fred, take the boys away, won't you?*

And Amy had sat straight up in her chair, as if her spine had been nailed onto a board, her eyes fastened to the carpet.

Even when Lord Warre added, while Nate and Sophia were still in the room, "You should know by now to keep better company, Amy."

She hadn't said a thing in his defense.

Leaving Nate with nothing to do except storm up the gravel drive back to the great house. Sophia and John trailed behind; probably not even the devil could keep up with the fury propelling Nate's feet forward. His coat billowed behind him from the wind of his momentum.

"Well, Nate, I don't mean to pry, but when I am delivered an insult like that, I prefer to know why." This from Sophia, a long sentence that she called out between huffs of breath. "What did you ever do to Lord Warre?"

"I?" Nate whirled around. He knew he wasn't angry with Sophia. She happened to be a convenient target, though. "*I* did nothing. It is Papa and his ridiculous notions. Our family's insistence on being better than the rest of the *ton*. Better than the rest of Britain, if you think about it. That's what Lord Warre objects to. Can't say I blame him, to tell you the truth. We are smug with our superiority. It makes me sick."

John, at Sophia's side, slid an arm around her waist as if to protect her from Nate.

She, unfortunately, didn't give Nate any vitriol back. "I'm not fond of it either, but I've still never been thrown out of a drawing room for being a Preston."

Nate turned back to the road. He had no interest in telling that story. He didn't want to revisit the terrible, humiliating moment when Lord Warre had first rejected him. It had been the worst moment of his life until Henriette Curry Owens handed him the letter from Amy.

He preferred to be furious in the here and now than to remember the past.

"Nate." Sophia, somehow, had caught up to him, and now she tugged on his elbow until he slowed. "You wanted a moment alone with Amy. It has led me to draw some conclusions."

"Oh, don't." He could see the pity screwed across their faces, and he didn't have the strength or words to combat it. "Your conclusions are wrong."

"Did Lord Warre reject your suit before? Before you took up your commission?" Sophia was running to keep up with him. "Is that why he was so displeased to see you again?"

"Yes." Nate kicked at the mud just ahead of him. "I'm the sailor son of his political enemy without any kind of fortune to my name. Of course he said no. But Amy was of majority. She didn't need his permission. Not if she actually wanted..."

To marry me.

The words were too hard to say.

Sophia reached out to touch him again. Nate shook her off. He didn't need anything from her. He didn't need anything from anyone, except an answer from the Admiralty as to whether he was still a captain or not.

"Leave me be," he snarled at his sister. Then he raced off the drive onto the fields, going somewhere he didn't know, in search of a peace he was sure he could never find.

Chapter Twelve

Pater didn't like the look of illness—especially Amy's, as it reminded him both of things that couldn't be explained and of his heir and wife, dead in childbirth—so he sent her back upstairs almost the moment the door closed behind Nate. "Take these children, too," he commanded, as if in her current state she was both too weak to behold and strong enough to battle the willpower of two young boys.

Little Charles and Kit obeyed, however. Everyone obeyed Pater, even when they didn't want to. They followed Amy upstairs and into her bed.

"Aunt Amy, are you dying?" Charles asked. Then, without waiting for a reply, "Is Grandpater dying?"

"No one is dying." From somewhere within, she was going to have to summon the energy to entertain the boys. She wasn't sure from where. Lying back on her goose-down pillows was about all she could manage physically at the moment. Emotionally—well, emotionally, she was still stuck in that terrible moment when Pater turned Nate out.

It had been rude beyond measure. Amy couldn't bear to look at Nate to see his reaction. She fancied she had heard it, though, in the snap of his heels as he stood and the swish of his coat as he vacated the room.

She didn't know what he had wanted by stealing a private moment in the drawing room. Now, she was quite sure she would never find out. After all, how could he forgive her for letting Pater speak to him like that again, when he didn't deserve it at all?

Amy realized she had fallen asleep when suddenly she was blinking, the boys still playing quietly across her legs and Mary in the doorway. "Are you well?" Mary asked, for once sounding like she meant it.

"Yes." Unless one counted feeling heartsick. "I didn't know we were expecting Pater."

Mary shut the door and sat in the chair by Amy's window. "Apparently, when he heard that Lord Preston was visiting Selsea Park, he left London immediately. Mother Cora is still there. He hardly even gave the household at Swanhill House notice. He arrived this morning and came directly here."

Amy tried to tell herself this was evidence of a father's love. He wanted to protect her from elements he considered insidious. He was even willing to sacrifice the glory of London and the comfort of planned travel to come to her aid.

She had to admit, though, that it didn't feel much like love.

Carefully—measuring her words, in case they came back to bite her—Amy said, "He was quite rude to Captain Preston."

To her relief, Mary's eyes flashed in agreement. "Beyond rude, especially when one considers that Captain Preston is here at Sir Charles's invitation and this is Sir Charles's property. I told Pater as much after you came upstairs, but he refuses to see it any way except his, of course."

Amy swallowed. Her goiter felt overly large at the moment and in the way of her throat. She wondered how grotesque she had looked in the drawing room.

"Pater intends to take you home today," Mary said, her voice a little softer. "He does not want you to see Captain Preston again."

Tears sprang to Amy's eyes. It was like being told she could never breathe again.

Except she knew it was for the best. Wasn't she resolved to leave Nate in peace?

"I suggested he take you to visit with Henriette instead. That way, Pater needn't open up the house again and can even return to London without delay." Mary paused. "I assured him you were only being polite in receiving Captain Preston and that you would never disobey his wishes."

"Thank you." Shutting her eyes, Amy tried to visualize this new plan: a month or so at Henriette's in the heart of Portsmouth. She would help with the children, though they had a proper nursemaid, and go for walks with Henriette along the ramparts, and stay up at night listening to Henriette read novels to the family. It would be a treat, so much better than being here.

Not at all a punishment.

"Captain Preston asked us for a moment alone with you today." Mary's voice was hushed so that it wouldn't carry beyond the room.

Kit, noticing her tone, said in a toddler's shout, "Shh!"

Just as well to cover the triple beat of Amy's heart. Asking her sister for a moment alone was practically the same as declaring his intentions. Marital intentions.

Except of course Nate didn't mean it like that. He was *fond* of her, but he knew better than anyone that she could not marry him. She could not even have a proper tryst in the gazebo!

More likely, he had wanted the moment alone to try to say something kind without her sister overhearing. Or perhaps he would pick up the argument that her family didn't care properly for her. He had wanted the moment alone to convince her to take the waters in Bath instead of staying at Selsea Park.

Or, given the news about his court-martial, he only wanted to speak to her privately to say goodbye.

Whatever it was Nate had wanted, Amy was quite sure it had nothing to do with marriage.

Amy placed a palm on Kit's back as a protective measure and ruffled her other hand through little Charles's hair. "Did he?"

"It has been fairly obvious that he still has a tendre towards you."

"Hardly. He is a good friend to me, that is all." How humiliating for Nate to have everyone speculating that he was in love with the sickly spinster. He was the handsomest sea captain in Portsmouth, in possession of good connections and a good heart. He should be in love with Miss Stratton or some other beautiful young woman who would turn into a perfect wife, and she was quite sure that was the opinion the neighbors would take, too.

"You needn't obey Pater," Mary said, her whisper turning sharp. "If you want to marry Captain Preston, you have every right to do so. I'm sure his family would help. You wouldn't even need to elope."

Now tears really did flood Amy's eyes. She couldn't look at Mary. "You agreed with Pater that I shouldn't marry him."

"Did I?"

Amy remembered it like yesterday. Of course she did: second to their mother dying, it had been the worst day of her life. She had been waiting right outside Pater's study, expecting Nate to emerge triumphant and kiss her hands and formally ask her to marry him. Instead, he had walked out looking shocked. And small. Pater had been right behind him, glaring, so that Amy couldn't even say anything to Nate. *You are the daughter of a viscount*, Pater had scolded. *You will marry much higher than the second son of a reformer.*

Mary had found her sobbing on her bed. "I don't care what Pater says!" Amy had cried. She hadn't even heard from Nate yet; the idea of eloping came as much from her heart as it did from his. "I love him, Mary. I have to marry him."

"You can't! How will I ever find a husband if you elope with a Preston? I won't even be able to show my face in London!"

Mary's opinion then hadn't changed Amy's mind. That had come later, when she started planning for the reality of an elopement instead of the spirit of it.

Now, Amy was shocked that Mary didn't even remember. "You were afraid that if I ran off with Nate, you wouldn't find a husband."

"I was twenty. I didn't know anything." Mary rose from the chair—it required a bit of effort to lift her whole self to her feet—and came to the bed to take Amy's hand. Her voice was as soft as ever. "If you want me to get a message to Captain Preston, I will."

Amy hadn't thought her sister loved her enough to notice that she still loved Nate, much less do anything about it. It was bewildering to have this whole conversation center around her own problems. Too bewildering. "If I married, I wouldn't be free to visit and care for your children as often."

Mary traced a finger along Amy's hairline with all the tenderness of a mother for her child. "Good. Then Fred and I won't have to pay for all your orange-glazed scones and the endless candles you consume."

Little Charles took up this prompt: "I want another scone!"

Mary ignored him. "Shall I send a message to Captain Preston, then?"

But Amy couldn't even allow herself to envision Nate arriving with a carriage to take her away. It was too tempting. Too impossible. She shut her eyes on it. "Leave him be. I'll go to Henriette's."

Nate settled into an unemotional state. The one that, years ago, had saved him on his first ship when captain and crew both had been determined that he would learn his place. The one that allowed him to board a slave ship and behold the horror of four hundred souls packed on top of each other.

The one in which he would remain for the rest of his life, if he could manage it.

Sophia had clearly told Papa and Caroline about Lord Warre—and likely about Nate's infatuation with Amy—because they both started treating Nate even more carefully than they had before. "Would you like me to sit up and read with you?" Caroline offered that first night, when Nate was staring into the fire instead of retiring with everyone else. He assented but didn't hear a word of the pamphlet on chimney sweeps she read to him.

The next day, Papa asked him to go for a walk. They went in the opposite direction from the dower house, which meant they passed the yew-hedge maze.

Nate was pleased that he didn't feel anything more than a brief, soul-rending pain at the memory of all that had happened there.

"I hope you don't feel that I have put too much pressure on you in regard to what you do next," Papa said. "Whatever you choose...Well, Sophia does what she wants, doesn't she, and I love her just as much. You mustn't feel as if I will stop loving you, or being proud of you, if you take up your uncle's offer."

Still, he managed to make the words *uncle's offer* sound as distasteful as yesterday's fish.

He added, "And you mustn't accept anyone's jesting about marrying. If you do marry, you will do it when you want, to whom you want."

Strange advice coming from a man who was forced into marriage with Mama because of a misunderstanding—and found great happiness from it.

Nate wanted to object, as he had done all along, that he hadn't any intention of deciding what to do until the court-martial was decided. Yet he found himself saying instead, "Perhaps I shall set up a company with Uncle Graham that imports only necessary medicines. John gave Miss Lamplugh a remedy for her affliction based on wisdom from the Indus River. If it works—if it makes her life even slightly more livable—surely it must override our moral calculus against importations."

Papa sighed. "There have always been advantages to exchanging goods. No community can exist on its resources alone. My objection is to the unfair exchange. Our companies have, with great purpose, removed every ounce of power from the people who live along the Indus River so that they have no choice except to sell us their goods for nothing. Then we turn a great profit and call ourselves geniuses. I refuse to participate in that, no matter the benefits that might come from it."

Like saving Amy's life. Nate didn't want to think about her. "*We* refuse," he corrected his father, instead. "You bestowed this philosophy on others as part of your legacy, don't forget."

He hadn't meant it to sound so bitter. For a moment, they walked in silence, and Nate glanced over at Papa to see if he had wounded him. But Papa looked worried more than anything. "I have certainly bestowed it upon anyone living at Northfield Hall," he said at last, "but I would hope that even more than that, I have bestowed upon you the strength of mind to decide for yourself how to balance your conscience against your comfort."

It wasn't always balanced against *comfort*. In the navy, anyhow, Nate had always seemed to be balancing his conscience against reality. The reality of how slow his ship was in a race against a Baltimore clipper, the reality of how many of his men would die of fever before they even sighted a slave ship, the reality of how the coastal kings would keep kidnapping inland people as slaves no matter how many times Nate's squadron stopped the ships.

Even if he were to join Uncle Graham's company with the intention of being a beacon of good behavior in a sea of bad—even if all they ever imported was medicine for diseases like Amy's that couldn't be cured by British materials—Nate suspected he would end up being forced to make compromised decisions in bad circumstances.

Like leaving those 397 souls on the slave ship just because it happened to have a French flag.

"Sometimes, I don't think I have the stomach for the fight. Every time we make any sort of progress, they do something bigger and more terrible."

"Such as punishing you for doing your duty?"

That was only one example of hundreds of ways Nate had seen slavers retaliate. "There seems no hope of us actually succeeding. I am tempted to follow Uncle Graham's model and not worry about anyone but myself."

Papa was silent for a few steps. "It does feel impossible most days. I suppose the way I cope is by not worrying about the outcome. I would rather know that I have fought and failed than not have fought at all."

At the moment, the sentiment sounded exhausting.

"I mean that in terms of fighting against systems such as slavery," Papa added, "and also in personal fights, such as knowing you are worthy of love, even when the woman you love does not return the favor."

Nate was saved from having to reply to such a humiliating comment by the appearance of Fred Bremridge at the bottom of the hill. He was mounted on his horse and accompanied by the land steward, whose name Nate couldn't recall. Bremridge raised his hand to hail them.

"Good morning! Out for a walk, then?"

Nate was surprised by the venom that rose from his heart at the inane question. He shouldn't have anything against Bremridge. The man wasn't half as bad as his wife about ordering Amy to do things as if she were some kind of servant, and he had always been welcoming to Nate.

Perhaps it was only because Bremridge had been in the room the day before when Lord Warre had thrown Nate out like some kind of reprobate, but Nate wanted to tear the man in two.

"Taking the air," Papa replied for the both of them.

"Sorry about old Warre yesterday," Bremridge said to Nate. "He is the worst kind of viscount, if you ask me, but I can't hold it against him too badly since he did raise Mary. Don't take it personally."

A fine thing to say when one wasn't the person twice thrown out of the room by Lord Warre.

"Lord Warre and I have had our differences in Parliament," Papa responded, "but I am sure that can be said of myself and every other member of the House of Lords. Life is long, after all, and everyone must stand by their own opinions."

Nate didn't have the stomach for this kind of talk. He found himself digging a toe into the ground, mud lodging itself on his boots.

Then he heard, in the middle of Bremridge's musings, "It is too bad that Miss Lamplugh had to leave with him."

"Miss Lamplugh left?" Despite himself, Nate turned in the direction of the dower house, as if he would be able to see it all the way on the other side of the hill and discover for himself where exactly Amy was.

Bremridge hesitated. "Lord Warre said the visit was too hard on her and that must be why she took a turn for the worse these last few days."

Nate's heart flipped. He knew Amy didn't care for him as he did her. Still, after everything that had happened between them, he would have thought she would at least send a note to say goodbye. "Is she back at Swanhill House?"

"In Portsmouth. Lord Warre took her to stay with Mrs. Owens." To Papa, Bremridge explained, "They're bosom friends, you see."

"Ah," said Papa. He put a hand on Nate's arm. For comfort? To hold him back from racing towards Portsmouth that very moment?

Nate didn't know what he needed, much less what he wanted.

All he knew was that he had gotten used to the idea that Amy was nearby. Even if she was only fond of him. Even if he could only see her in stolen moments. Even if she still didn't think him worth defending to her father.

She had been close, and now she wasn't, and if he didn't stop feeling emotions that very instant, he might succumb to a fit of heartbreak in front of Fred Bremridge.

Chapter Thirteen

Every time Amy looked out the window, she thought she saw Nate.

It was not altogether impossible. He had to come to Portsmouth at some point in the next fortnight for his court-martial. And he *could* be one of the dozens of gentlemen crossing Henriette's street in dashing officers' uniforms. Even the ones with blond hair or narrow shoulders or short statures—at first glance, they might be Nate.

Not that she wanted to see him. That would be too much. She was feeling better now that she was at Henriette's. Away from the demands of her nephews, away from Pater's discerning eye, away from the exquisite anguish of seeing Nate again, her body had settled down. She was sleeping through the night, her heart still unpredictable but its pace keeping within a comfortable range. With the assistance of a daily dose of Mr. Anderson's powder, she even had the energy to join Henriette on afternoon excursions.

It would be terrible for her health if she were to spot Nate on the street. She would wonder where he was off to and hope that perhaps he had seen her, too. Then, she would find a reason to invite him to call at Henriette's. Next thing she knew, she would be looking into his eyes again, not knowing what to do with the overwhelming need swelling her heart.

Besides, it never *was* him. The man who caught her eye was always too old or too young, too slim or too fat, too dark or too light. In all likelihood, Nate was still at Selsea Park, and Amy was wasting precious energy searching the streets for him.

She was too embarrassed about being at Henriette's anyhow. By the time Iris had packed up Amy's trunks, it was nearly dark, yet Pater had insisted on driving the ten miles to Portsmouth that very night. They had arrived at Henriette's doorstep close to midnight; certainly, the coachman's knocking (for Pater would never knock at a door himself) had woken Henriette, Daniel, and their housekeeper.

"Of course Miss Lamplugh can stay with us," Henriette had said, as perfectly polite in her nightrobe as if they'd been at an assembly. She elbowed Daniel, who agreed quickly.

"We are happy to have Miss Lamplugh with us. Will you stay the night, too, my lord?"

Pater had declined. He would take the hospitality of the Lieutenant Governor instead. He said goodbye to Amy with a perfunctory, "Remember you are my daughter," and then disappeared into the night.

It was all so embarrassing. As if Pater *knew* how shamelessly Amy had thrown herself at Nate. She was quite sure he didn't. Not even Mary seemed to have guessed that much. Yet Amy had to make her apologies, blushing at Henriette's kindness. It wasn't until breakfast that she could find the words for an explanation: "Pater did not approve of my staying in the same neighborhood as Lord Preston."

Daniel, who may not have known Amy's history with Nate, accepted this with an innocent, "I never knew political rivalries ran so deep."

In the midst of serving her four-year-old daughter breakfast, Henriette had twisted her lips with skepticism. She didn't bother Amy about it, though. Amy supposed that Henriette could draw her own conclusions without asking. It was rather obvious, actually: Nate had once courted her, Pater objected, and now Pater objected again to his presence.

Obvious and boring and unfair.

Amy tried to make up for it by being good company. She had always liked visiting Portsmouth, anyhow. Because it was a major naval port, everyone in town always seemed on the cusp of doing something important, even if they were just a maid running out to buy fresh fish from the market. Yet, unlike London, it did not have an overwhelming number of neighborhoods or streets running off in dizzying zigzags. If Amy were to leave the house unaccompanied—which she never did, since she was Lord Warre's unmarried daughter—she was confident she could find her way wherever she wanted to go.

And she loved the smell of Portsmouth: the brine of the sea permeated wherever a person went. Even at Henriette's lovely townhouse, despite the pots of incense that Henriette liked to keep burning in the corners of the room. Underneath their floral scents was the ocean, promising that it hadn't gone anywhere.

For the most part, Amy became Henriette's shadow. The nursemaid looked after the children—seeing them dressed, wiping their faces after eating, putting them down for their naps—yet Henriette liked to stay nearby. She played games with the older children while Amy made faces at the baby, or they made up stories together to keep them entertained, or they tried to teach the four-year-old the alphabet.

In the afternoons, Henriette often went out. Amy accompanied her to a musicale, to call on neighbors and some of the parish ill, and to a committee meeting to raise funds for the families of missing sailors.

Henriette's life, in short, was full, in the way that Amy had always longed for her own to be. It was a joy to pretend she was a part of it, even if she would only stay for a few weeks.

She had been there nearly seven days when Henriette caught her staring out the window and—at last—didn't let her be. "Are you expecting him to come after you? Or just hoping for it?"

They were alone in the sitting room, a fire in the hearth and sewing projects in their laps. Amy's was ornamental; Henriette's was mending for her children. Amy was glad no one else could see the blush that must have furiously leapt into her cheeks with the question. "Neither."

Henriette's hands stilled, and she pierced Amy with a long, unwavering look. The look that, since girlhood, had needed only last ten seconds before Amy gave in to tell her secrets.

For the sake of her own dignity, Amy tried to last at least thirty heartbeats. Lucky her pulse was racing at the moment. Once Amy started speaking, she realized she had been longing to pour this out to Henriette since the moment she arrived in Portsmouth. "I don't want him to come after me, that's the truth. I suppose I just got used to seeing him at Selsea Park. I wish I could get a glimpse of him. Just to..."

Amy hadn't any idea what she would do with that glimpse, other than press it into her memory so she could relive it over and over.

"How often did you see him at Selsea Park?" asked Henriette.

"Oh, every few days or so, I suppose." Now Amy didn't know why she had let it be so infrequent. She should have walked up to the great house every afternoon to bask in Nate's presence while she could. It needn't have looked one way or another; she was a guest of Sir Charles and Lady Olivia just as much as the Prestons were.

"You never told me where you disappeared to at the ball," Henriette said softly. "Mary had to comfort me when I grew anxious about your absence from supper, and you know that comforting is not Mary's strength."

"I didn't mean to worry you."

"Make it up to me by telling me what happened. Mary said Mr. Bremridge took you back to the dower house, but you were gone for a long time before he left. As was Captain Preston."

Amy hoped Henriette, with the eagle eye of a bosom friend, was the only one who had noticed.

"Did he..." Now Henriette blushed. "Did he seduce you? Is that why Lord Warre was so anxious to remove you from Selsea Park?"

Out it all came: in the most convoluted manner, Amy found herself telling Henriette about the hedge maze, about fainting at the dinner table, about Nate finding her in the woods, about that last afternoon when he had asked for a moment alone. She couldn't seem to tell any part of it in a straightforward, chronological way: one detail about Nate carrying her under the light of the moon made her jump to when she had been so hot and sought refuge in moonlight; admitting that she had kissed him led her to rush to assure Henriette that she had not compromised her virtue, which then pivoted her to declaring she wouldn't have minded had she lost it; and it all ended with her reminding herself, "I should never have let any of it happen. Even if he were to offer—which I know he has no intention of doing—I can't marry him. You know that better than anyone."

Henriette raised a single eyebrow. "Do I?"

Amy hadn't held it against Mary when she had forgotten her long-ago comment about why Amy shouldn't marry Nate. But her heart dropped into her stomach at the idea that Henriette would forget her part of the discussions six years ago.

Henriette had been the one to hold her dream against reality. *Where will you live when he sets sail? What neighbors will receive you once your father makes it known you have run off without his permission? Will you be happy in a one-room house at the edge of town because that is all he can afford to lease you before his pay comes in?*

Henriette had been the one who, when Amy had admitted that she was afraid she would elope with Nate after all the moment she saw him, suggested that Amy write a letter breaking it off.

And, after she delivered that letter, Henriette had been the one to hold Amy in her arms and let her sob the whole night through.

"Pater would cut me off if I married Captain Preston." This wasn't even Amy's objection to the idea, yet she found herself echoing back Henriette's fears. "Where would I live? Who would receive me?"

Henriette set aside her mending. "It's a very different situation than last time."

"Is it?"

"Then, he was just starting out as an officer. He hadn't even been on a ship yet. He didn't have the money to set up a family, and he didn't have any reputation of his own. Now, Captain Preston is known in the proper circles. He has caught several prize ships, which means he must have at least a respectable amount of savings to set you up properly. And you aren't in the bloom of youth anymore. People would say how nice it is you found a match, instead of worrying that you could have done better."

Amy had always relied on Henriette for plain speaking like this. Moreover, Henriette understood how the world worked so much better than Amy did. While Henriette's father was the third son of a second son of an earl, her mother had been Spanish, and that had weighted the whole of Henriette's girlhood with whispers. Henriette had always understood the practicalities of life: how much a new ribbon cost, how to remove a stain from her gown, whether it was going to rain and how that would impact their plans. She knew, too, the way that rumors swirled around people. She could always tell Amy exactly how much money another Portsmouth family had. She never traded gossip herself but would warn Amy from an unwise acquaintance, saying "I have heard some things about so-and-so I wouldn't wish to repeat."

It was why Amy had trusted Henriette so much when she said that marriage to Nate was a terrible idea.

Amy's breath felt like it was coming awfully fast. "I can hardly credit how a mere six years changed every point of that calculus."

"I agree that Lord Warre would still disown you," Henriette said, her voice a little sad.

Strangely, it didn't make Amy sad to think of that. There was something like relief in her heart when she pictured a life free of Pater and Cora and their distracted disapproval.

Marrying Nate was not the answer to *that* problem.

"I hardly care what anyone else thinks or whether Captain Preston can afford a family. I'm unsuitable as a wife. My health is too unpredictable. I could barely manage to..." Amy had managed to keep the humiliating details of the end of their interlude in the gazebo to herself, and she limited herself now to saying, "...kiss him without becoming overwhelmed. He deserves a wife who can serve all her duties and provide him children."

Henriette frowned. "If Captain Preston were to arrive here this very moment and beg you to marry him, you would say no because you think there is some better woman for him out there?"

Amy's traitorous heart drummed faster at the idea that Nate might walk in as part of some wonderful, convoluted plan of Henriette's.

He didn't.

"Yes," she answered her friend. "I can hardly be the helpmeet he deserves."

"Do you think yourself noble for showing such restraint?"

The question was so direct that it would have been rude from anyone else. As it was, Amy blushed again. "I wouldn't say it that way. The best way anyone can show their love to another is to put the other's best interests ahead of their own."

"You assume you know what Captain Preston needs better than he does."

It felt like an accusation, as terrible as if Amy had refused to pay tithes to the church or give food to a starving child. A flash of anger overtook Amy. "No more than you assumed to know better than I what would make me happy six years ago."

Henriette met this with another direct gaze. "I gave you advice. I didn't make any decisions for you. You decided with your own free will not to elope with him."

"And now your advice is the complete opposite!" Amy found herself standing, her voice shaking through the room. She wrapped her arms around her ribcage to try to calm down.

"Last I checked, you were a twenty-eight-year-old woman with the same education as me. I wonder, Amy, when you will stop blaming me or Mary or your father for your unhappiness and accept that it is of your own making."

Terrible words that were made worse because Henriette knew Amy's heart so well. How many times had Amy complained to Henriette about the way Mary always assumed she would help with the boys? How often had she written to Henriette in their shorthand code to make fun of Pater and Cora? This whole time, had Henriette been rolling her eyes in exasperation? And what did she expect Amy to do about it?

Henriette rose. Her arms enveloped Amy in a warm hug. She must have learned it as a mother, for it imbued every particle of air around them with love. "Your life has changed since the last time I gave you advice. You are so used to being unhappy, I'm not sure you even know anymore what it would be like to do what you want."

Amy shut her eyes. Tears sprang from them anyhow. "Failing Nate as a wife would not make me happier."

"But what if you did not fail him? What if you are what he wants and deserves, exactly as you are?"

Amy could almost picture this: the two of them seated at a breakfast table, holding hands as they discussed the coming day. Was this on a ship? In a tiny house on Lombard Street? At his family's home?

Her mind blacked out the scene before she had an answer.

"He wouldn't be happy with me."

Henriette squeezed her even tighter. "You were meant to be happy, Amy."

A nice sentiment, if one believed it.

I t was strange to be on a ship again. In the past, after shore leave, relief had always rushed Nate when he returned to the ship. The weathered wood, the crew bustling across the deck, the promise of a journey about to unfold, even the slightly nauseating sway of the ship beneath his feet: it had always felt like returning home.

Stepping onto HMS *Capricorn* filled Nate instead with a sense of dread. No doubt because of the court-martial about to unfold; instead of being greeted by sailors readying the deck, he saw only solemn-faced admirals in white wigs. Neither was she Nate's ship: he didn't know the creaks of her masts by heart, nor did he have the right to stride to her prow and look off into the horizon.

Besides, there wasn't much of a horizon to see. Anchored in Portsmouth Harbor, the ship faced the docks and wharves. Casting his gaze beyond the ship's bow, Nate saw the contemptuous facades of the customs house and naval yard staring back in judgment.

His imagination placed Amy in one of their top floors, looking out the window to watch his fall from grace.

He shut that from his mind. For the next few days, he had to devote every thought to proving himself innocent. Whatever Amy felt for him or about him had nothing to do with whether he was in the wrong for boarding that French ship.

Nate had to assume he would never see her again, and that this court-martial was now the most important determining factor in his future.

They assembled on the foredeck of HMS *Capricorn*. The group was not large: there were three admirals serving as judges, along with Commodore Collier, who oversaw the Preventive Squadron, and two of Nate's lieutenants as witnesses. The audience was of almost equal size, with an official scribe taking minutes as well as two journalists recording the proceedings for the local papers; the Duke of Berkwell, there to represent the African Institution; and Papa, there to support Nate.

Suddenly, it all felt very real. Nate had managed to convince himself this was a formality to appease the French, but as the judges rose to read the list of charges against him—trebled in length by honorifics and legal phrasing—his every muscle seized in panic.

Testimony began with Commodore Collier. The court asked him questions to establish the current laws about seizing slave ships. Nate was gratified that even the commodore couldn't quite keep it all straight; twice, he had to correct himself while stating under which circumstances a Portuguese ship could be stopped (only if it was spotted north of the equator). Still, the commodore produced into evidence the pamphlet that Nate and every naval captain was provided for keeping track of these laws, and the court had him show where it very clearly said that French ships were not to be boarded under any circumstances in times of peace.

Now it was Nate's turn to question the commanding officer. How strange it was to look the man in the eye and contradict him, when every fiber of Nate's being demanded that he accept the commodore's word as law.

Especially because he knew Commodore Collier was, in spirit, sympathetic to the mission of the squadron.

Nate focused on asking the commodore questions about reality, instead of the law. Did he know how many ships were seized that raised one flag and then switched to another when they discovered it was a British naval ship approaching? Did he know how many ships had been seized with false papers, including French papers, so as to avoid the British navy? With regard to his orders to return to Freetown, did the commodore know how long it took a ship on average to sail from the Bight of Benin back to Sierra Leone? Was Nate the only captain who stopped slave ships even while following orders to return to Freetown?

The commodore cooperated with each of Nate's questions. He helpfully volunteered that the French flag looked very like that of the Dutch, whose ships Nate had every right to stop and search per the Anglo-Dutch Treaty of 1818.

Still, Nate felt a little ill as he conceded to the court that he had finished his questions for the commodore.

The court next called Lieutenant Littlefield to answer questions about the sighting of the slave ship. Nate tried to listen to each detail as Littlefield described seeing the clipper catching the wind on the horizon; how, as they approached, they could begin to smell her; that she switched her flag as they drew close enough to board her. But the more Littlefield described the ordeal, the less Nate could pay attention. His mind disengaged even though he needed to listen and needed to find some moment to challenge or probe when he was given the chance to question Littlefield.

He remembered how, when he had told Amy what happened, she had declared he was the only officer she trusted.

What would she think if he was declared guilty? If he found her wherever she was hidden in Portsmouth after this was all over, would she even receive him? And if he was sent to Marshalsea Prison, would she say prayers for his health?

The court granted Nate permission to put his own questions to Littlefield. Nate pushed Amy out of his mind again.

If he couldn't find a way to justify his actions as being *lawful*, then at the very least, he was going to force the Admiralty to have on record exactly what horrors could be found on a slave ship.

He dragged it out: how did Lieutenant Littlefield know there were slaves on board? What did the ship smell like, exactly? How did it sound? When they uncovered the 401 people forced into the hold, did the captain of the ship express remorse? Did the slaver's crew show any humanity towards the people Littlefield helped liberate? How did the liberated people react when offered drinking water?

"I must object, Captain Preston," Admiral Stratton cut in. "Please keep your questions relevant to the charges facing you."

"With all due respect, my lord, this is relevant. It establishes for the court my motivations for boarding the ship, even though it was against orders."

"Boarding the ship was not *against orders*," Admiral Stratton replied. "The charge is that it was *against the law*. If it is true you boarded a ship flying French colors, Captain Preston, you jeopardized the peace and welfare of our entire nation."

Nate was suddenly struck by how ridiculous this was. He was bending over backward to fight within the scope of the Admiralty's rules, all to earn back his right to return to a poorly-provisioned squadron with a poorly-defined mission. What Nate *wanted* was to destroy the entire establishment of slavery once and for all. He had thought the navy was the best place to fight that battle.

What if he instead took the fight somewhere else? What if he freed himself from the constraints of being an officer in order to wage war on the entirety of slavery on some other sea?

Why should he waste his time on this court-martial when its very existence indicated he had, in some ways, already lost?

Nate had never felt a single moment of regret about boarding the *Viper*, and he wouldn't let Admiral Stratton force it on him now.

He took a deep breath. The air tasted like the sea—as it had that day in the doldrums before they encountered the slave ship. It could be the last breath of fresh air Nate took for months; this could be a nail in his coffin, sealing him into a fate of disrepute and odd jobs.

He glanced back at Papa, who watched with a tense frown. He thought of Amy, who would read this news in a paper and, perhaps, spare him a kind thought. Then, filling his words with every ounce of conviction in his body, Nate replied:

"It is true, Admiral. I did board the *Viper* even after seeing her French colors. I did so to free the 401 souls being cruelly and inhumanely detained in its hold, and I would do it again."

Lieutenant Littlefield, who all this time had been standing at attention, stepped back with a groan. Admiral Stratton's face turned beet red; behind Nate, there were multiple outcries from the men listening.

One of them—Papa, most likely—applauded.

The judges huddled together in a fast, furious discussion. Then Admiral Stratton announced in a voice as cold as steel, "The court considers this latest statement to be an admission of guilt. Captain Preston is found to be unworthy of his command and is dismissed from all naval service without honor."

Nate had never expected being a scoundrel to feel so liberating.

CHAPTER FOURTEEN

The house was quiet. With Henriette and the children napping, Amy sat alone in the front drawing room, sentenced to keep company with her own thoughts.

Thoughts she couldn't seem to keep straight. She tried to focus on a future—however short it might be—beginning with her inevitable return to Pater's and Cora's domain at Swanhill House. If Henriette was right and Amy *allowed* her family to make her miserable, then what was it Amy could do to be happy at home?

The trouble was every time she asked herself this question, her heart returned to Nate. She remembered him in the Swanhill drawing room, describing with boyish joy everything he hoped to do as a naval officer. Which led to her wondering if he was in town yet for the court-martial, and then she couldn't help worrying about the outcome.

An unmarried woman was never to write to an unmarried man. Especially one whom her father had forbidden her from having contact with.

But if Amy wrote a letter to Miss Caroline Preston, would her words find their way to Nate? And if they did, what could she possibly say? Perhaps Henriette was right that Amy had a hand in her own unhappiness with Pater and Mary, but she was wrong about any future between Amy and Nate. Amy loved Nate too much to endure him as only a friend, yet she was in no position to suggest herself as a wife.

She was so consumed with the thought that when she heard a man yelling from the street "Captain Preston confesses!" she assumed at first that her mind was conjuring Nate's name out of thin air.

Then she heard it again: "Captain Preston confesses! Order your copy of the minutes! Captain Preston confesses!"

She rushed to the window. The peddler was across the street, about to turn the corner. Amy hauled the window open anyhow and stuck out her head. "Come back! I want to order a copy!"

But her voice was too weak. The man didn't even look back her way before disappearing onto the next block. "Captain Preston confesses!"

It was a rainy afternoon, the kind that firmly suggested a lady stay inside. Add to that, the man was gone down the next street already. If Amy were following logic, she would remain at home and ask Daniel to purchase her the minutes.

But more importantly—Nate's trial was over.

Nate's trial had *just ended*, which meant he was somewhere in Portsmouth, perhaps no more than half a mile from Amy at that very moment.

If she was lucky, she could catch a glimpse of him.

Amy rushed into the street with only a shawl over her shoulders and her house slippers on her feet. In her head, she could hear Mary scolding her, Henriette warning her, and Pater forbidding her.

She dismissed them all and headed for the wharves.

Amy hadn't any idea where Nate would be now—he could even be on his way to Marshalsea Prison with hands bound—yet she knew he had, within a few hours, been on one of the ships. They were as good a place to look as any.

Dimly, she was aware that she was acting without a plan. She wanted to find Nate—to do what? She needed to know his sentence—but to what end?

She pushed away these questions as soon as they popped into her head. For once, she was following her heart, and no one was there to stop her. Amy would find out where it led.

The rain, which was heavier than a drizzle but not quite a downpour, hadn't kept many people from their business. Amy had to dodge a cart full of crates, a horse angrily pawing the mud as he waited for his owner in a store, and lumps of manure every few yards. Not to mention the puddles swamping the cobblestone of the finer part of the street. Her slippers were soaked through almost as soon as she started.

Worse, she kept hearing bits and pieces about the trial, without ever finding out what Nate's sentence had been. "They only went after him because he's a Preston," opined one laborer to another as they carried a great big rug into a building.

As she passed a pub, she heard, "If it were me, I would have captured the Frenchies and silenced them before they could report me for a court-martial."

Closer to the docks, Amy passed a sleek black carriage, from which she heard a genteel lady say to her companion, "It is proof for me that the Preventive Squadron is a folly to begin with. If it doesn't kill our men, it tempts them into bad decisions like..."

The carriage rolled in the opposite direction before Amy could hear the end of the woman's opinion. Not that she cared. All Amy wanted to know was what fate Nate faced now that he had admitted guilt.

She was almost at the wharves when she spotted more carriages. Three in a row this time, and one of them emblazoned with a ducal coat of arms. They were moving slowly because of the mud on the street and the vehicles ahead of them.

Amy felt sure they belonged to witnesses from the trial.

"Pardon me!" she called up to the first coachman. "Do you happen to know the outcome of Captain Preston's trial?"

The man looked down at her with something like shock. Rain dripped from the brim of his hat. "Get on with you!"

His horses neighed at the agitation in his voice. It startled Amy, too; she took a step backward. But he didn't need to be so rude. "Do you know or don't you?"

The coachman spat. It landed on the ground, though it rather seemed to have been aimed at her. "Captain Preston don't want anything to do with the likes of you, moll. Out of my way before the horses decide to go over you."

Amy reared back, outrage climbing her throat. "How dare you! I am no..." She was too well-bred to even get the word *moll* off her lips.

But the coachman made it sound as if he knew Nate personally. Perhaps he even knew where Nate was.

Amy summoned her haughtiest glare, the very one Pater had used on Nate in Mary's drawing room. "Where is Captain Preston?"

"Who are you, then?" This from the driver of the ducal carriage. His greatcoat was trimmed with fine gold braid.

"She's nothing but a moll," the first man shouted backward.

"I am Miss Lamplugh," Amy replied at the same time. "Daughter of Viscount Warre."

"Oh, sure, a viscount," the first coachman sneered. "Who lets his daughter run amok in the streets."

Amy moved towards the liveried coachman, sure he would at least give her directions to find Nate. The rain was pounding now, making it necessary to shout. "I am looking for Captain Preston."

She must have really been a sight, however, for this coachman still hesitated. "What business do you have with him?"

Amy couldn't believe how difficult it was to get an answer. She repeated, "I am Viscount Warre's daughter," since for all her life, those words had unlocked her every material desire.

The coachman remained close-lipped.

"I am a personal friend of Captain Preston. We know each other well. My sister lives at Selsea Park, where he has recently been residing." The words tumbled out now. "Please, you don't have to tell me where he is. If you don't think he will see me...I only want to know his sentence. I need to know his sentence. I love him, you see, and I can't marry him, but I love him with all my heart and I must know what has befallen him. Please, won't you tell me?"

Which was when a third voice shouted through the rain. A lovely voice. The only voice Amy ever needed to hear.

Nate's, as he threw open the carriage door to her. "He is here."

N ate hadn't recognized Amy at first. Glancing out the window to see what had stopped the carriages, he saw only a beggarwoman in wet, bedraggled clothes shouting at their coachman.

It was the goiter on her neck—uncovered by either scarf or shawl—that had made him realize the beggarwoman was Amy.

Amy, wandering the wharves in the middle of a squall, screaming at strangers that she loved Nate with all her heart.

He leapt from the carriage. "Miss Lamplugh, whatever are you doing?" He hardly knew what he said. He bundled her into his arms. She was wet and frail and wonderful.

She loved him with all her heart.

"Are you free, then? Did they show you mercy?" she asked, clinging to him.

"Depends how you define mercy. I am dismissed from my post and barred from serving His Majesty or his heirs in the navy for the rest of my life." A sentence that Nate was struggling to comprehend at the moment, so distracted was he with Amy before him. They stepped out of their embrace—they were on the street, after all, not to mention in full view of Papa and the Duke of Berkwell in the carriage—and Nate took stock of her again.

She wore only a shawl over her day gown, and her slippers were soaked through.

What was she doing walking the streets alone in a rainstorm?

"Have you not been staying with Mrs. Owens? Why do you not have at least an umbrella?"

"Oh, but I was looking for you. I heard that you had confessed, but no one could tell me your sentence."

"So you raced through the rain to the worst part of Portsmouth just to find me?"

Amy looked around a little frantically, as if she were only just now noticing their surroundings and her state of dress. Then she looked up at him again, and she beamed like the sun parting clouds. "Yes."

If she hadn't already shouted for all to hear that *she loved him with all her heart*, Nate might have begun to suspect it this very moment.

Behind them, Papa called out, "Miss Lamplugh, won't you come in before you catch your death?"

So prompted, Nate led them both back to the carriage. He held onto Amy's hand the whole time—for what if she slipped on the muddy cobblestones?—and added a palm to her waist to help her into the carriage. She slid onto the bench he had been sitting on, leaving him no choice but to sit beside her.

It took all his willpower not to wrap an arm across her shoulders and hug her tight to him.

Amy loved him, after all!

Papa introduced Amy to the Duke of Berkwell, in whose carriage they were riding. "Miss Lamplugh has been visiting a friend in Portsmouth while Lord Warre has been in London, I believe." Papa said this in such reasonable tones that it made it sound like an explanation for why a lady of the realm would go tearing through the streets as Amy had.

"Ah," the duke said, lifting his quizzing glass as if to see Amy better. "Now that I recollect, I believe we have met in London once or twice, Miss Lamplugh."

"Certainly at my father's wedding," she agreed. There was color in her cheeks now, perhaps from embarrassment, or perhaps her body was just warming up from the rain. Nate was all too aware of her wet clothes, which clung to her skin. If not for her shawl, made heavier and droopier by the water, she might have been too indecent to even be introduced to a duke.

Thankfully, his grace was being a perfect gentleman. He rapped on the coach roof, stuck his head out the window, and ordered the driver to take them at the greatest hurry to the address Amy provided. Then, settling back in his seat, he raised his quizzing glass again. "I gather you want to hear all the details of the trial."

"Oh, please." Now the color rushing up her neck and cheeks and ears was definitely a blush. Her chin jerked towards Nate, as if she were going to look at him, but her face remained stubbornly forward.

Nate wished he could see her eyes properly. He wished they were alone and that he could ask her all the questions that had been circling his heart for weeks.

The duke described the ship, the judges, and the witnesses. "A surprising number of reporters were on board, too. You might be shocked, Miss Lamplugh, at how many people in this country are watching Captain Preston's case with a keen eye."

"I am heartened by it," she said, and then blushed again.

Papa cut in now to describe the evidence laid out by the court and the testimony of Commodore Collier. His version of the story got bogged down by explaining details no one needed on how a court-martial functioned. The duke took over again to say, "The crux of the matter, Miss Lamplugh, is that at a certain point while questioning a witness, Captain Preston did away with all pretense and said, 'Of course I boarded that ship, and I would do it again, if it meant I could save those people!'"

Finally, Amy looked at him. She wasn't exactly smiling: her eyes shone with unshed tears, and the corners of her lips trembled upward. "That does sound like Captain Preston."

It was Nate's turn to blush, and not from modesty. He had wasted so much of the last few months trying desperately to keep his commission that it made him ill to be celebrated now for speaking the truth. If he had insisted from the first hint of a court-martial that he was, indeed, guilty; if he had demanded to be locked in Marshalsea Prison in protest of the terrible laws keeping him from freeing people who clearly needed freeing; if he had done *anything* brave—then perhaps Amy's admiration might feel appropriate.

As it was, Nate felt he had chosen to fight the wrong battle for far too long.

As he had done with Amy. He had been so quick to assume that she had chosen to follow her father's orders and that she had been avoiding him after the ball. Yet here she was, putting her own personal safety at risk to wander through Portsmouth in search of *news* of him, much less in hope of finding him.

Nate had thought there was no battle to fight with Amy. He had thought her *fond* of him, and so he had not dared be brave and tell her how he really felt.

If he had only told her in the gazebo that he loved her—that he had always loved her, despite his best attempts to forget her—they might have confronted their obstacles before Lord Warre had returned, and they could have stood up to him instead of letting him drive them apart once again.

The carriage came to a stop in front of a modest townhouse with tulips in flower boxes at the windows. Nate helped Amy down from the carriage—they hadn't stopped touching all this time—and Papa and the duke followed as the townhouse door opened. Mrs. Owens rushed onto the front step.

"Amy! Where have you been? We have been frantic!"

And, much as Nate hated to give Mrs. Owens credit, she really did look panicked, with hair askew and a spencer on inside-out. Her children followed her outside, clinging to her skirts.

Unfortunately, it was cue enough for Amy to remove herself from Nate. "Oh, Henriette, I'm sorry. I rushed out without thinking."

Mrs. Owens wrapped a protective arm around Amy before taking stock of the rest of them. Nate had to stop himself from objecting: he was the one who should be protecting Amy, or at the very least, Amy didn't need any protecting from him.

The duke bowed with a flourish. "Robert Hathorne, Duke of Berkwell, at your service, madam. It was our privilege to see Miss Lamplugh to safety."

Mrs. Owens blanched at his title and dropped into a curtsy of her own. "Please, won't you come in and have some tea to warm up?"

Nate didn't need any further invitation to follow Amy into the house. He and Papa had been planning to return to their rooms at the King George Inn, and he hadn't any idea where the duke intended to go, but they would have to adapt their plans to an early evening tea at Mrs. Owens's. Luckily, Papa and the duke followed him in without objection.

The townhouse was modest, and Nate was a little surprised that Lord Warre considered it worthy of Amy's notice, seeing how the walls were painted instead of papered and the furniture was decidedly out of fashion. Mrs. Owens directed them into a front sitting room, where painful-looking mahogany Tudor chairs and a silk sofa awaited. Yet even as Nate followed Amy in, Mrs. Owens said to the duke, "Would you like a tour of my porcelain collection? It is just in the other room."

He acquiesced, and Papa said, "I'll join you, if you don't mind."

Leaving Nate and Amy alone in the sitting room.

Amy sat on the chair closest to the fire. Someone had taken her shawl upon entering the house, and now she was shivering in her green poplin dress, though she had a fresh white scarf around her neck. She smiled at him. "I'm sorry for causing such a fuss. I wasn't thinking. There was a man on the street calling out the news, and I just had to find out what happened to you."

She had said as much in the rain. Then, it had made Nate feel like the most important man in the world.

Now, it made him almost tender with joy. His hand flew unironically to his heart, for it felt like it might burst from his chest.

Kneeling, he took Amy's hand. She was so beautiful with the fire casting light upon her face and the scarf making her chin look dainty and kissable. Nate could gaze upon her for hours.

"I heard what you said to John Coachman, you know. That you love me with all your heart. Did you mean it?"

She blushed. "Isn't it obvious? Everyone seems to have guessed."

"Not I." Nate yearned to hear her say it again. "At the ball, in the gazebo, you told me our love had faded and that you were merely fond of me."

Amy's gaze dropped away. "Because I understand that must be how you feel, and I did not want you to say something you did not mean to protect my sensibilities. After all, I hurt you when I did not elope with you. I never expected your love for me would remain. I—"

How foolish they were. Two people in love, yet too frightened to hope there was a point in saying anything. Nate had wasted so much energy convincing himself that he was wrong, that every signal Amy sent him did not reciprocate love, because he had been too afraid to speak his heart.

That ended now.

"Amy," Nate interrupted her. "I love you. My heart has been constant to you, no matter how much I have tried to force it to forget you. You are my love, my one and only."

She was the one to interrupt him this time, her arms clinging to his neck and her lips to his mouth. Tears made her kiss taste like the sea; Nate wasn't sure which one of them was crying with happiness, but it might have been him.

Mrs. Owens and Papa and the duke hadn't given them the room for them to kiss. Nate broke away, taking Amy's palms in his. This question had been swelling his tongue for days—weeks—months—years. "Amy, please, will you marry me?"

Even after all the times she had pushed him away, the look on her face—the one of dismay and imminent rejection—still took him by surprise.

Chapter Fifteen

Their kiss was still on her lips. Amy touched her mouth, wishing she could trap it and keep it as a memento.

He shouldn't have asked her to marry him.

"You know I can't, Nate."

Tears lurched to Amy's throat as she said the words. She had to shut her mouth and bite her tongue to keep them from reaching her eyes. A lady shouldn't cry while turning down an offer of marriage. Especially not Nate's.

He still knelt before her. A moment ago, he'd been the picture of hope, with rosy cheeks and shining eyes. One wouldn't have thought his career had just been smashed to pieces. One would have thought the whole world and all its fortunes awaited him.

Now, he looked pale—gray, even—and small. His hand loosened around hers until it slipped away, bracing instead on the carpet as if to keep him upright.

"How can you love me and yet not want to marry me?"

The question came out in such a frail, young voice that Amy imagined it was the Nate of six years ago come out from wherever he was buried. The Nate she had turned away by letter because she hadn't the courage to do it in person.

She owed him this conversation, as hard as it might be. "I do want to marry you, but I can't."

"Because I am a Preston and your father wouldn't approve?"

Now tears really did sting her eyes. "No, not that. Not this time."

"Why, then? Is it because I have lost my career today?"

"No."

He didn't give her a chance to reassure him that he would have a bright future—as Amy knew he would. Nate balled his hands into fists against the rug. "Must you marry a man with a title and rank? Is that why?"

"No!" Amy's arms shot out of their own accord and braced his shoulders. She couldn't take this litany of reasons why he thought he was not worthy.

He was entirely worthy. So worthy that she didn't even deserve to have been asked the question.

"It is because of *me*, Nate. I cannot marry you. I cannot marry anyone."

His palms landed on her elbows, keeping her in place. "Why not?"

First Mary. Then Henriette. Now even Nate needed a reminder of how unseaworthy she was? "Don't you remember what happened in the gazebo?"

His eyes darkened. "Yes. We shared intimacies that would have any good chaperone marching us to a wedding chapel."

"Yet we did not share *all* of the intimacies we wanted to, and it was because of me." At his frown, Amy added, "And before that, when you went for your midnight walk, you stopped kissing me because you didn't think I could stand it."

"You are ill." Said as if it excused all her body's behavior instead of explaining precisely why she couldn't marry him.

Amy tried to pull away, but he held her arms tightly in his hands. "I am too ill to be a wife. My body would not withstand marital relations, much less bearing any child that might result from them."

"Is that all?" Nate lurched forward, his fingers rushing up to cup her cheeks. "Amy, I do not care. I love you with all my heart. All I want is to be with you every day that I can, no matter what state you are in."

He was too much. Amy stood and pushed away every part of him. "I would be an albatross around your neck when you deserve a wife who is the wings at your back. And children, Nate—you must have children, and you cannot do it with me."

"Must I?" Nate rose to his feet, too. "I have recently been relieved of my duties, Amy, so I am under no one's orders except my own. And I am aware of no requirement that I *must* have children."

A hint of anger steeled his voice. Amy told herself she welcomed it.

Anger would help him leave her.

"All this time, I thought there was something standing in our way. Our past, your family...I even believed it was because I, with my uncertain future, am not worthy of you." He paused, swallowing. "I see now that nothing stands between us except you. Perhaps six years ago, it wasn't your family's censure that turned you away from me—perhaps even then, you were too afraid to take the chance."

The same accusation Henriette had levied at her.

Maybe it was true that Amy had chosen to be unhappy with Pater and Mary. But she wasn't choosing heartbreak now because she was afraid of being happy with Nate.

She was choosing it to keep him from being unhappy. "It is not my heart I am protecting. Marriage to you would bring me great happiness. I am trying to save you from the burden of being my husband."

"You would not be a burden." Nate took up his hat from where it had landed on the sofa. "It has been a long afternoon. I have asked, and you have given me your answer. Therefore, I shall take my leave of you. But know this: I love you, Amy, and even if our marriage contains no intimacies, I still want it. I still have faith that life with you would be superior to any other life I could find. If you do not have that same faith—if perhaps you do not love me as much as I do you—then I must accept your refusal.

"If, however, you are willing to consider that we may be able to piece together a happy marriage, then I ask for one more audience with you. If no is not your final answer, leave a lantern on your windowsill at midnight tonight."

He swept out of the room before Amy could reply.

She knew her refusal *should* be her final answer. Yet she couldn't bear the thought that this was the last time she would see him.

She couldn't stand the idea of Nate walking below her window and not seeing a lantern waiting for him.

She didn't know what he could say that would change her mind, but she knew she would be ready for him at midnight.

There were a few flaws in Nate's plan.

First, he didn't know which room of the Owens's townhouse belonged to Amy. He guessed it was in the back, to prevent the noise of the street from disrupting their guest's sleep, and on an upper story, but for all he knew, he was watching the wrong side of the house entirely.

Second, he didn't have a way of accessing her room, should she light a lantern for him. He could hardly knock on the front door claiming he was there for a tryst. If Amy *did* want him to visit, then he would have to climb to her.

And of course, there was the fatal flaw: Amy might not leave a lantern for him at all.

He had tried not to dwell on this possibility all afternoon. Not when Papa's eyes—and the Duke of Berkwell's whole face!—had filled with pity as he declared Miss Lamplugh needed to rest. Not when everyone at the King George Inn had gone silent on his entrance. Nor when he had retired early, begging exhaustion, to keep from getting in his cups before midnight.

Amy had said no that afternoon, but only because she didn't believe he could love her for her, instead of her body.

She wouldn't say no to him tonight.

At a half hour to midnight, Nate arrived at the townhouse. At quarter to midnight, he vaulted over the back garden wall and crouched behind a bush.

And to his great relief, at ten minutes to midnight, a lantern appeared in the far-left window of the third story.

He hurried across the yard, minding his feet so he didn't accidentally knock anything over and wake the household. Then there was nothing for it but to leap up to the protruding windowsill above his head and begin to climb.

Everything was slippery from the rain. If he didn't judge the climb right, he would plunge to the stone courtyard below—and probably break his neck. Nate knew better than to consider that possibility. He had climbed the foremast of a frigate in the middle of a hurricane; he could survive a Portsmouth townhouse.

With a final haul, he made it onto the window ledge of the lanterned room. The glass was too old and warped for him to see anything more than some dark shapes beyond the panes. Balancing precariously on the six-inch bricks serving as a ledge, Nate rapped a knuckle against the glass.

The wait was no more than thirty seconds, yet it felt like eternity. A shape inside approached the window and—with hardly any rush—pushed open the pane farthest from Nate.

Amy.

She greeted him with a hard look. "You could have died climbing up like that."

"Did you think I would knock at the front door instead?" He swung his legs into the room, then pulled the window shut behind him. In that small space of time, Amy retreated to her bed. She sat primly: back stiff, arms wrapped around her bent knees, feet tucked under the quilt, and chin parallel to the mattress.

Her posture did not invite him to join her.

"I thought you would write me a note and arrange a sensible time for a sensible conversation."

As if any part of their most recent courtship had been sensible. Nate smirked to remind her of all they had already shared. "You did not."

This, at least, earned him a little smile. "No, I did not. But if I had known you were going to climb the side of the building, I would have hung out a rope or something." She tightened her hold on her own legs. "You won't change my mind. I thought we should have a proper goodbye, that is all."

"Ah." Nate forced himself to take in her words. To consider the possibility that she meant them.

Then he discarded them. He had not climbed three stories to be defeated.

"And what is a proper goodbye?" He crept a little closer to the bed until he leaned against one of its posts. "Shall I kiss the air above your hand and receive pretty words of best wishes and felicitations?"

Again, she smiled at his joke. Then, growing earnest, she said into her knee, "I didn't mean for you to hear me say that I love you, you know."

"That was cruel of you. I thought I languished alone in devotion to you."

"What would be cruel of me would be to accept your offer simply because it would make *me* happy. You would end up desperately unhappy with me, Nate, and all the more so because once you loved me. And if I had to watch you stop loving me...I don't think I could survive that."

"You think very little of me if you think I would stop loving you because of your health."

"Because of what my health would require of you. I am undependable. I would need your patience and forbearance for even the most quotidian of matters. And as for the intimacies a man and wife share...you were the one who informed me my body could not withstand it."

"In that moment. Without any interventions available to us." Nate dared sit on the mattress beside her. "You are hardly the only woman who has ever experienced such difficulties."

Amy's gaze—dark, as the room was lit only by the lantern in the window—flitted frantically across his face. "But if I were to get overwhelmed each time we kissed, or if I were to experience those difficulties every time you tried to take me to bed, can you deny that would make you unhappy? The whole reason a man takes a wife is to have those intimacies. *You* deserve to have those intimacies."

Nate rubbed a knuckle along the slim bone defining her cheek. "I am very fond of this face." He dropped his finger to trail along her arm. "And these shoulders. Your legs, too. I quite like your quim. And though I haven't seen them properly yet, I have a strong fixation on your breasts." His body stirred at this line of thinking, but Nate ignored his own response. He brought his fingers to rest in hers. "Yet what I love is *you*. So long as you are alive—so long as I can tell you about my day and you tell me about yours—I will be happy."

Amy's eyes shone in the dark. She licked her lips. "Is that your plan, then? To change my mind by *not* seducing me?"

"Something along those lines." Nate didn't have much of a plan. He had his feelings, his courage, and a bottle of clove oil to facilitate any seduction that might occur.

Beyond that, he had only foolish hope.

"Is it working?" he asked.

"You shouldn't want to marry me."

"But I do."

Amy looked down at their joined hands. Nate could feel another argument rising to her lips.

He would catch every argument she threw at him. He would face every dragon she summoned to protect herself. He had enough conviction to defend himself to the Admiralty, and he had even more to withstand a war for Amy's heart.

So long as she remembered that she loved him.

He squeezed her fingers to pause her next words. "Have a care, Amy. You alone can break my heart."

She shut her eyes. Her fingers clung even tighter to his. "I have long since tried to convince myself that knowing we loved each other once was enough. My heart need not be broken, even though I did not marry you, because I knew you loved me then."

"Yet I thought you did not love me." The memory scraped the dearest, darkest part of Nate's heart. He had to look away because he could not face her as he said, "I wasn't even worth a proper goodbye. I thought you rejected me, that you rejected even our wonderful afternoons together, that every moment between us—which had been the best moments of my life—were only tokens to you. I loved you, and to you, I was a nuisance."

"But none of that is true!" Amy scrambled forward on her knees to hold fast to his forearm.

"What else was I to believe?"

"That I loved you." She paused, her breath coming too fast. "I *love* you. It was never a question of my heart. I was stupid then. I listened to my fears and to the people around me instead of having faith that life with you would bring so much more happiness to me than misery. My love is true."

"And yet, if you make the same choice now, what conclusion am I to draw? Either you do not consider me worthy of your heart, or you do not love me with as much fervor and constancy as I do you."

Amy gripped his cheeks, forcing him to look at her. She was pale and fierce. "Do not doubt my constancy, and do not doubt your own worth. The question of marriage is entirely separate from the question of love—or worth. I love you, and you are worthy of me. That is my whole point: you are worthy of so much more than me."

He believed it. He knew in his heart that this time, even if he could not change her mind, it was not because of who he was.

This was entirely about Amy.

He cupped her palms so they would never leave his cheeks. "I am the second son of a family without a fortune. I am a sailor dishonorably discharged from the navy with a black mark to my name. I have no prospects, only a little savings, and a very small number of connections to anyone of quality. If I can be all of that and still be worthy of you, Amy, then you can be ill and still be worthy of me."

Tears shone in her eyes. She shut them, leaning forward, and touched her forehead to his. Nate couldn't breathe: if she refuted this, if she still insisted she would not marry him, he wasn't sure what else to say. What else to do.

All he knew was giving up would break his heart.

Thank God Amy said next: "I think you had better seduce me."

Amy had not changed her mind that afternoon when Nate had taken his leave. Not even when she'd had time to soak in the feeling that he loved her, too.

Love was no reason to get married.

Neither had Amy changed her mind when she put the lantern in the window. Last time, she had turned Nate away without any chance of speaking. This time, though it broke her heart to have to face him, she wanted Nate to say everything he intended before they had to part forever.

She hadn't changed her mind now, either. It was very hard to remember why she knew she shouldn't marry him, however, when he was right there in front of her spouting lovely things.

Even more so when Amy knew Nate wasn't *spouting* things simply because they sounded nice. He meant them with his whole heart. His wonderful, huge heart. It made Amy want to believe him that he could, indeed, be happy with her as a wife.

Which was why she needed to kiss him now. Kiss him—and whatever else came next.

It would be something humiliating. Something that brought their lovemaking to an end before it even began.

It would be evidence that she didn't belong in his marital bed.

And yet, his words rang in her ears: *You are still worthy of me.*

She kissed him as if she would never have the chance to again. Kneeling beside him, with him seated on the bed, Amy's face was at about an equal height to his, and she could lace her fingers through his hair. His hands responded to her touch almost immediately, wrapping up around her back, holding her close and still, so that there was nothing between them except that kiss.

He smelled like rain. He tasted like home. He was everything she wanted, everything that would make her happy, and Amy wished desperately she could believe in a future with him.

Nate backed away from the kiss, just enough to rest his forehead against hers. "Are you feeling well?"

She hated the question. "You shouldn't have to ask me that."

"Why not? You would have me swive a woman without ensuring she is in good health?"

"You don't have to ask other women if they are in good health. Not in the middle of kissing them."

Nate nipped at her nose. "You don't know that as a fact. You are inventing it because you are afraid of how wonderful we could be together."

Amy didn't think of it as fear. She loved Nate, so how could she condemn him to a half-lived life with a half-healthy wife?

But perhaps he was right. She was afraid: of losing his love. Of marrying him and having paradise in her fingertips, only to watch him grow impatient and bored and burdened by her.

"Have faith in me, Amy," he whispered, almost as if he could hear her thoughts, and pecked her lips. "Have faith in us."

She kissed him again. He propelled himself backward on the mattress so they no longer had to twist into each other; now Amy straddled him, her hips pressing into his torso, and one of his palms wandered down to cup the flesh of her bum.

Pleasure spiraled for an instant through her body. Pleasure—and something more overwhelming, more akin to overexcitement.

Amy pushed that observation away. Nate was flesh and blood beneath her, and she intended to steal every moment of it that she could. She traced his jaw and pinched his earlobe between her fingertips, making him gasp against her mouth.

At least for as long as she lived, she would have this secret that Nate Preston could be undone by his earlobes.

Nate's other hand crept up her back and unknotted the silk scarf around her neck. His thumb brushed across the girth of her goiter.

Amy was the one to rock her forehead to his this time. "Don't touch it."

His fingers dropped away immediately. "Does it hurt?"

"No." His touch felt lovely, in fact, far too lovely for Amy to comprehend. "It is monstrous."

"Nothing about you is monstrous," Nate replied, as if she had offended his very honor.

"Don't be kind to me."

"I'm not. I am being honest." Nate glared at her until Amy couldn't take it any longer and shut her eyes. He asked, "It doesn't hurt to be touched?"

She shook her head.

The next thing she knew, he kissed it. Light kisses, like butterflies flitting softly across her skin. Amy's mind fluttered with pleasure. A sigh slipped from her mouth.

When she remembered her embarrassment, she asked, "Oh, how can you stand it?"

"There is nothing to stand. It is your flesh and blood. I hate that it is the cause of so much chaos for you, but it is as attractive to me as every other part of your body." Nate's mouth quirked with mischief, and suddenly he lunged upward, his tongue licking the very underside of her nose. "Even your nostrils." Then he flipped her onto the mattress and seized her ankles in his two hands. "And your heels." He kissed the soles of her feet. Her nightgown rose up to her hips, leaving her legs bare to the room. Nate ducked under her ankles and kissed the soft skin behind her knees. "And whatever this is called."

Amy was all sensation and no reason. Her naked legs felt more thrilling than anything ever had in her life, and she wanted to tear off her nightgown to expose her whole body to Nate. At the same time, she never wanted him to stop touching her. And more than anything, she wanted him to do what he had done in the gazebo: bring her to white hot bliss.

But Nate let go of her. Kneeling above her—but so far away—he stretched out his arms. "And what about me? What do you find monstrous about me?"

Amy scrambled to her own knees. "Nothing." She wrapped her arms around his neck again. "Certainly not your face—" and she kissed his lips.

"What of my left foot, which is slightly larger than my right?"

How Amy yearned to know such details about him. "Charming."

"What about my spirit? Do you find it hideous that I say cruel things when I feel hurt?"

"No." She kissed him, remembering his comment at Mary's breakfast table and all that had come since. "That's not hideous at all."

Nate broke away from her lips sooner than she liked. "I follow my own judgment instead of listening to others. I wouldn't listen to you this afternoon."

"You are intrepid. You are courageous. You are everything I wish I could be."

"Do you really mean it?"

This time, when Amy paused their kiss, she looked in his eyes, and she saw there a dark, shining fear. The same one that had her tying scarves around her goiter, even when all she wore was a nightgown.

Nate truly didn't believe that she loved him.

And why should he, when all she had done was reject him?

All of tonight, he had been the one offering her assurances, when he was the one who was being hurt.

For once, Amy wanted to take care of him instead.

"I mean it." She kissed his lips as sweetly as she could. "I mean it with all my heart. You are the person I most admire and trust and love in the world. If I could marry anyone, it would be you, Nate."

"Then marry me."

Amy brushed her cheek against his, inhaling him, memorizing him. Then she smirked at him. "The only part of you I might find monstrous is the part of you I haven't seen yet. It might offend my delicate sensibilities."

"You were hardly offended by Paris's cock." Yet Nate preened, thrusting forth his hips.

There was nothing for it but to undress him. He had already removed his coat; now Amy untied his cravat—fingers trembling—and unbuttoned his waistcoat and pulled off his shirt. She paused at his bare chest, discovering the thick muscles peaked by dark nipples and the whorls of coarse hair that tickled her lips as she pressed a hundred kisses across his skin.

She got as low as the band of his trousers. Then, remembering her purpose, she returned her hands to the task.

Nate removed something from his pocket as she undid the six buttons keeping his trousers up. Then, as she slid the buckskin down his thighs, he sighed, a sound of pleasure that Amy wanted never to forget.

She didn't have much room to notice the rest of his reactions, however, because all of her attention landed on the cock springing towards her face. It was much larger than Paris of Troy's—darker, too, and on a slight curve, and, when she wrapped her hand around it, much warmer.

"Is it monstrous?" Nate asked, his voice low and husky.

"Not at all."

"Would you like it to join us in play?"

Amy swallowed, for her mouth had gone dry with desire. "Yes."

He lay her back down across the mattress. Now he was the one straddling her, one knee on either side of her hips, and his head dipped down to kiss her goiter again. This time, Amy didn't even allow shame to flicker across her mind; she gave in to the sensation of his lips on her skin.

Nate worked his way down her body, kisses pressing through her thin nightgown on her breasts, her ribs, her belly, until he reached her quim. Here he lingered, inching her nightgown up her legs, his fingers stroking the outsides of her thighs as they had in the gazebo. Then, after teasing her to distraction, he licked his tongue across her peak.

Heaven, for a moment. Amy forgot that it did not involve his cock, that it wasn't proper marital relations, and tilted her hips so that he would do it again.

He obliged. This time, he remained, his tongue constant.

When he had done this in the gazebo, Amy had resigned herself that physical pleasure was all that he had to offer her. Now, she imagined it was one of a thousand times. She pretended they had been doing this together for six years already. She pictured Nate doing this when he was seventy, his elbows creaking as he braced himself beneath her knees.

She allowed the full force of his love into her heart as his tongue pulsed in perfect flicks against her quim, and she broke into a body-shaking, mind-shattering, soul-revealing orgasm.

Shallow, superficial, or stupid as it was, that was the moment when she changed her mind.

It was also the moment she realized she felt ill.

She noticed it first because her fingers trembled even after the orgasm had left her body. Then she felt her heart galloping irregularly—not with excitement, but as a presage to feeling lightheaded and panicked.

And her breath, well, she couldn't quite catch it.

Nate stretched out on his side next to her. His cock was so alive; it rested against her thigh as he ran a flat palm across her stomach. "How do you feel?"

Amy still hated the question. "That was lovely."

"But now you need some rest."

She might need it, but she didn't want it. Amy caught his cock in her hand. "We haven't played with this properly." Even as she said it, though, she got winded.

Nate closed his fist around hers and guided her hand in a fast pump. "It doesn't require much."

"I want..." Amy had to close her eyes to concentrate on what she was trying to say. "If you were to marry me, I would want to do it properly."

Nate curved against her, his lips burying in her hair. "Properly?"

"The way man and wife do it." Amy smoothed her thumb over the tip of his cock, and he gasped.

Then he replied, "But we don't want to get you with child."

"I want to be a proper wife to you."

"The way we..." He paused, whether to find the right word or because Amy still toyed with his cock, she couldn't say. "The way we play has nothing to do with it being a proper marriage or not." He kissed her forehead, then her lips, then reared back as she slid her fist down to the base of his shaft. "So long as we both enjoy it..."

Amy tried to increase the speed of her hand because it was so clearly pleasing to him. But after one or two pumps, her heart nearly jumped out of her ribcage from beating too fast, and she had to let go entirely. "Won't you just take me, please? If I lie still and you are over me, it shouldn't..." Just saying the words overtaxed her, though.

Nate took her hand in his again. This time, he guided it to her quim. His free hand coaxing her left knee to open wide, he led her fingers to glide down the walls of her quim and ring around her entrance.

Glide was not quite the right verb, though, for instead of being slick with all the desire Amy felt in her heart, her quim had just the barest moisture to keep her skin from rubbing raw.

"We might need some assistance," Nate murmured into her ear.

In the gazebo, when he had informed her she was far too dry, great and terrible emotions had immediately overwhelmed Amy. Humiliation that he should discover her to be so defective. Despair that she was so unable to live like a normal woman. Anger, too—anger that her body should betray her so.

Now, with Nate cradling her head and his lips brushing against her skin, Amy felt primarily the anger and a little despair.

Somehow, magically, the humiliation had disappeared.

"What kind of assistance?"

He rolled away for a moment, leaving her body cold and bare, then returned with his right fingers covered in a viscous oil.

"Is that honey?" Amy asked as he lowered his hand toward her quim.

"Clove oil. It adds moisture when the body needs a little help."

And it felt divine as his fingers slid down along her quim again. He toyed with her peak, which was quick to return to attention, and found a deep pleasure channel leading down to her entrance.

Amy lost her breath again. She couldn't tell if she was going to faint or orgasm.

Then Nate's fingers—still slick with the oil—dipped inside her canal. Amy had done this herself hundreds of times on quiet nights and knew well what it should feel like: delicious, exciting, one more level of sensation to push her closer to the edge.

But Nate's fingers felt too large. Even though the clove oil made it easy for them to enter, they forged a trail of something that was not quite discomfort but was not pleasure.

Amy stilled, waiting for her desire to kick in.

Nate, circling his fingers around her entrance, asked, "How does this feel?"

She didn't have words for it. "How can I be so frigid when you have already driven me to pleasure once and my heart so desperately wants you to take me?"

"You are not frigid." He lifted his hand away from her quim, the clove oil dripping across her stomach as he gripped her rib cage instead, and pulled her into a deep, wonderful kiss. "There, I have taken you."

"That's not what I meant." She wrapped her arms around his neck and held him close. "You should have a wife who can welcome you in every way."

"I should have a wife I love."

"And you love me even though I cannot properly take you in bed?"

He grew still in her arms. "Yes, I do."

"Even though I have been so insistent that you should forget me?"

"Very much so."

He shouldn't forgive her so quickly. Amy reminded him: "Do you love me even though I let my father behave awfully to you?"

"Yes."

If they married, Pater would say even worse things. And Pater was hardly the one who had hurt Nate the most. "Do you love me even though I did not have enough faith in you six years ago and sent you away?"

Nate pressed his forehead against hers. "Despite my best attempts not to, yes, I still love you."

He was a fool, an idiot. Her fool and idiot. Amy still didn't understand why he was willing to forgive her for all her transgressions. She didn't fully believe him when he promised he would love her forever. But she had already changed her mind.

Nate was worth the risk.

Now, it was only a question of doing things properly. Amy took a breath and looked directly in his eyes. His perfect, beautiful, inscrutable eyes. "Then, Nate—" Her heart raced, and she had to pause to will it out of her throat. "Will you marry me?"

He sagged against her. Then he grinned. Then he turned his head into the pillow and whooped—almost loud enough to wake the whole house. "Oh, Amy. I thought you would never ask."

"I have put you through too much," Amy objected, laughing, as he hauled her into his arms. She lay across him, bare skin to bare skin, and they talked through kisses. "You really ought to reject me."

"Never."

"You climbed three stories just to prove how much you love me, and I have said no to you at every turn."

Nate nipped at her lips. "Say you love me."

"I love you."

"Say you have always loved me."

"I *have* always loved you. My heart has been yours, and it always will be."

He rolled them both onto their sides now. One arm braced her close against his chest. The other took up his cock. "Ask me again."

Amy was so distracted by his pumping that she didn't know at first what he meant. "Will you marry me, even though you shouldn't?"

"Yes." This on a raw breath. His chin dug into her neck. The tip of his cock slipped between her legs, so that it bounced between her thighs as Nate worked it faster and faster. "Ask me again."

"Will you marry me, Nate? Will you make a life with me?"

"Yes." He gasped. "Again."

Amy touched her tongue to his earlobe. "Will you be my husband? Will you look at no other woman? Will you spend every moment of every day with me?"

With a cry—again, almost loud enough to wake the whole house—Nate spilled onto her legs. He laughed—or sobbed—into her hair. He shook in a great paroxysm as she held him very tight and very close.

"Yes, Amy," he replied at last, his voice reduced to a rasp. "Yes, I will."

And suddenly, it didn't matter that Amy still wasn't sure it was enough. They couldn't make love the way they should; they didn't have a plan for where they would live or how they would afford it; they didn't even know how long they would have together, for no doctor knew how long Amy could live with her condition.

Amy hadn't changed her mind about any of that. But as they held each other, none of it mattered.

Life would not be easy, but Amy had Nate's love.

She didn't need anything else to be happy.

CHAPTER SIXTEEN

The clock at Swanhill House—freshly wound at eight every morning—counted off each second precisely, the sound echoing through the marble hall. The portraits of Amy's ancestors sneered at her without even trying to conceal judgment. In the drawing room just beyond, Pater and Cora and Mary and Fred drank their tea with conversation as delicate as the imported china in their hands.

Amy had the strangest sense that she had lived this moment before.

Except six years ago, Lady Cora and Fred hadn't been a part of her family. Amy had been in the drawing room with Mary, trying very hard to sip tea while waiting for Pater to emerge from his study. And it hadn't even occurred to her to sneer back at her ancestors, who had no right to judge her when *they* had earned their spots on the wall by advising Queen Elizabeth on creating the East India Company and forming early shipping partnerships to enslave people for colonial plantations.

She found Lord Thomas, second earl of Warre, hanging in a prized location above the stairs and stuck her tongue out at him. Let him—let anyone at all—cast the first stone; Amy would be happy knowing she had for once made the right decision for herself.

The butler approached, his heels clipping against the waxed floor. He extended a card to her. "Mr. Preston would like to see you, Miss Lamplugh."

At last. Although he wasn't late at all. They had agreed he would arrive at half past two, which was when Pater preferred to take tea in the back drawing room with its afternoon light. The clock behind her struck half past as she instructed their butler to show Nate in.

It only felt like forever because Amy hadn't seen Nate for almost a week. After that night at Henriette's, he had left it up to her: should they elope, or should they seek Lord Warre's permission one last time?

Amy knew Pater would be unreasonable about it. She wouldn't let him stop her from marrying Nate, no matter what. But she still yearned for his approval. She couldn't bear for him to find out about her marriage from a letter sent from Gretna Green—or worse, a gossip column spreading news about a misbehaving Preston.

Even more, she didn't want to hide her life with Nate. It was an honor that Nate still wanted to marry her, and she planned to wear that fact proudly. Even in front of Pater.

So they had come up with a plan: she would write to Pater and ask him to reopen Swanhill House. Once he did, Nate would come calling.

In the meantime, Nate had gone home to Northfield Hall with his family. "To see everyone who couldn't travel," he told her, a smile lighting his face, and he counted them off: the Chow family (and especially Spencer), the blacksmith Killian who used to let him try out the anvil, the Shayler family (most particularly William, who had always been a ready playmate), the land steward he called Uncle Maulvi and his common-law wife Aunt Croft.

By the time he trailed off, declaring he couldn't possibly name everyone he was excited to see, Amy had felt jealous—and not proud of it. She had mumbled something like, "I hope you will still return for me once you rediscover this large and happy family."

They had been in Henriette's drawing room with the children and nurse present, which meant Nate could not draw her into his arms as she wished he would. Still, he had taken her hand and held it to his heart. "I will always return to you, Amy."

And now, at last, he had. He strode down the corridor looking so thunderously handsome that Amy placed her palm on her chest to keep her heart from leaping out of it. It wasn't just the perfectly crisp suit without a speck of dust on either the jacket or his boots—which meant he had followed her advice and hired a closed carriage for the errand. Nor was it the cut of his hair, which he was growing out so that it curled over his forehead.

It was the way he looked at her, as if she were the only thing that existed in the world.

Amy was tempted to fling off all propriety and elope with him right then and there.

"Are you ready?" she asked him instead.

Nate was close enough now that Amy could see apprehension flicker across his eyes. "I have faced fiercer foes than your father." He took a steadying breath. "Still, I am glad to go in with you by my side."

Amy touched his hand for the briefest of moments. Then she led him into the drawing room.

"Look who came to call as I was about to join you! Mother Cora, may I present Mr. Preston?"

Cora reacted as if Amy had shoved a dead mouse beneath her nose, though she had enough inbred manners that the disgust disappeared after a second or two.

Pater, meanwhile, stood in outrage. "I do not believe I extended you an invitation, Mr. Preston."

For the whole of Amy's life, Pater had objected to people, objects, or behaviors. Amy had always reacted by either rushing to eliminate the offense from his view or by turning away, pretending not to see the fury purpling his face.

It took every ounce of her courage to reply, "I invited him, Pater."

Nate stepped forward. He was a former naval officer and a gentleman; he would not allow Amy to fight this battle alone. "I do not wish to ruin your tea, Lord Warre. I come to honor you as the father of Miss Lamplugh and to beg your blessing for our forthcoming marriage."

Yet even as he spoke, Pater looked only at Amy. Nate may have been the artillery, but Amy was the sloop of war remaining still under her father's scrutiny, holding her shoulders high and not so much as flinching as betrayal filled his eyes.

"You may not have it," Pater spat. "If Miss Lamplugh is foolish enough to run off with you, it will be the shame of this family—not to mention the ruin of her."

It was no worse than what Amy had told herself to expect. Still, it felt like a knife through her heart. Tears stung her eyes, and she had to look away.

From her seat at the tea table, Mary said, "Ruined, Pater? You are being unreasonable."

She made it sound as simple as a scold, as if Pater were being as out of hand as little Kit. Yet Amy knew it took courage for Mary, too, to say anything against their father.

Fred chimed in: "I cannot see how the connection would bring any shame to the family."

Pater pivoted so his glare landed on them. He leaned on a cane whose ivory lion's head glared, too. "You cannot see how marriage to a disgraced naval officer would shame this family, Mr. Bremridge?"

Fred flushed. He had never been one for confrontation, and Amy had always known him to bow to Pater's opinions. He surprised her by replying, "If you read any paper other than the *Times*, you would discover that most of the country approves of Mr. Preston's conduct."

That was perhaps an exaggeration. Cora's own father had just written to a local Hampshire newspaper with his opinion that

Nate's trial underscored how the West African Squadron wasted the crown's money.

Mary added, "Amy has waited long enough for the 'better connection' you promised her, Pater. Let her have some happiness."

"Happiness?" Pater spit out the word as if he had never heard of it before.

Amy threaded her fingers between Nate's. They both wore gloves—his from the carriage, hers the thin lace Pater considered appropriate for teatime—but she still felt the connection deep in her core. "We are not asking for your permission, Pater. I will, with great pride and delight, marry Mr. Preston. It is because I love and respect you that I wish to have your blessing and that I hope you will still call me your daughter after my marriage."

Pater was so purple, his eyes so fierce, that Amy was quite sure his next words would be invectives. She braced herself to be thrown out of Swanhill House that very moment.

It was a shock when he capitulated. "If I cannot stop you, then I must at least insist you do it quietly."

"Yes, sir," Nate replied.

Inwardly, Amy sagged with relief. She didn't want to feel such obeisance to her father, but she couldn't help it. It was gift enough for him to not stand in her way.

Outwardly, she mimicked his cold restraint. "Thank you, Pater," she said, instead of flinging her arms around his neck in gratitude. She turned to Nate, who had a little smile on his lips. "We shall not disgrace the family name too badly."

Nate would have been happy to rush into a marriage by special license, but Amy objected to any hint of impropriety. In spite of her father's wishes, she insisted on calling the banns and, to Nate's surprise, announcing the engagement in the London papers, so as many of her set could hear of the wedding as possible. Still, Nate won the debate of where to wait for the wedding: he spirited Amy to Northfield Hall and had the banns called in the Thatcham parish.

Which meant a whole month of *not* being married. Summer was at full blush, the southern fields of the estate blooming with hay and barley, the kitchen maids fetching fresh vegetables from the garden for almost every meal. The hot air practically begged for lazy afternoons in bed—or in the glade—or by the pond—yet Nate had to behave like a perfect gentleman and *not* kiss Amy every second of every day.

There was plenty to enjoy, of course. Showing Amy around Northfield Hall was a gift in itself. She had disembarked from her carriage with a certain wariness that Nate knew came from too many years of reading about the estate in her father's terrible newspapers. The house itself—which had been erected a hundred or so years ago and was not much improved—only tightened her lips as she saw the small, dark rooms and well-worn carpets.

It was the estate that won hearts, and particularly Amy's. Unlike Swanhill House, where every inch of every acre was landscaped to please the eye, Northfield Hall's grounds were entirely practical. There were the stables, which were always well-tended, the horses as healthy as could be. The fields, dotted with wagons and tools and laborers singing as they tended the crops. The trade village, where an assortment of workshops, including the carpentry where Spencer Chow now ruled the roost, faced each other over a shared stone well. And the cottages and lodges and dining hall, where people from all over the empire now lived. Some of them had been there for years, others were only staying until their feet were on the ground again.

Nate knew better than any of its critics that Northfield Hall was no utopia. It was home to hundreds of people, which meant there were petty rivalries and poor decisions and a failure to meet every need.

But there was a joy, too, at Northfield Hall that he hadn't yet encountered anywhere else in the world. He had to believe it came from that great vision of his parents' that each and every person on the estate would reap the benefits of its profits. They shared the crops; they shared the wealth; they shared the burden and privilege of being residents of Northfield Hall.

By the time they got to the lilac trees by the pond, Nate could see that Amy felt it too. Papa, who had been leading the tour, stepped away for a moment to examine a patch of field that needed better drainage, and Amy took Nate's hand. "I feel so foolish. I could have been married to you all this time, living here where everything feels so...well, I suspect that even on a rainy day, it doesn't feel gloomy here, does it?"

"Just wait until you've gone a full day without tea." Nate lifted her fingers to his lips.

They didn't yet have a plan for where they would live or what Nate would do after the wedding. That was another reason they had come to Northfield Hall to wait for the banns: it gave Nate more time to make a decision, without burdening anyone as a houseguest. While Amy and Caroline spent their days arranging the wedding party, he holed up in Papa's study or stalked the fields or otherwise tried to determine what the best course of action was.

Benny wrote from Ireland: *Lydia and I regret deeply we cannot return in time to witness your nuptials. Let me make up for it with an offer. Come live here as my steward and help me turn Athenry House into a new Northfield Hall. I could use the help, not to mention how much I would love to meet Amy and for you to meet Lydia.*

Uncle Graham, who had decided to join them at Northfield Hall, pressed his case at each meal: "You will have full command of the fleet. Hell"—here everyone except Sophia objected to his language—"we can even devote some of the ships to pirating the slavers, if it will make you happy."

The African Institution had offered him a position, too. Multiple positions. Any position he wanted, in fact: he could take up a post in Freetown to write reports on the state of the slave trade; he could represent them in foreign courts as an additional voice pressuring colonial powers to outlaw slavery; he could join their headquarters in London to corral the abolitionist forces in Britain. The ideas all spoke to Nate, yet none of them was obviously the right choice for him.

Caroline, with a certain starry-eyed look that suggested she was thinking of Eddie Chow, sighed to Nate one afternoon, "Whatever you do, don't you want it to keep you close to Amy?"

He did. And yet Nate worried that, if he joined Benny in Ireland or if he took a position in London primarily to spend each day with Amy, he would end up unhappy.

It was the day before their wedding that he finally got Amy to speak on the topic. That whole month, whenever it came up, she would simply say, "You must do whatever you think is best, and I shall be happy to make a home accordingly."

Now they walked alone through the wooded grounds. It was not unlike the path behind Selsea Park's dower house where Amy had led him in the middle of the night. When they were out of sight of the fields, Nate reached over for Amy's hand. "I cannot make this decision on my own. Whatever I choose will dictate your life, too. I wish you would tell me what you really want."

She walked in silence for a few steps. Nate watched her as much as he could while also minding his footing. She had stored away most of her clothes at Swanhill House so that at Northfield Hall she could wear only linen or wool as the rest of them did. Now she was in one of Ellen's old summer gowns, taken in at the waist with a blue sash that matched the blue scarf around her neck.

She was utterly kissable.

"I want you to be happy. If you make a decision based on my preferences, you might end up resenting me for it. This must be the right decision for *you*, and then it will be the right decision for me."

As much as he adored her, Nate wanted to shake some sense into her. "First, you won't marry me because you suppose you know much better than I do about what will make me happy, and now you tell me you haven't any idea what will make me happy and I must make the decision all on my own."

"I am trying to learn from my past mistakes." She angled a mock glare at him. "You might recall that you didn't appreciate it when I presumed to know what would make you happy."

"I even snuck into your bedroom to punish you most wickedly."

Her breast brushed against the side of his arm as they walked a little stupidly, caught in a haze of desire.

But Nate would have a lifetime of teasing her body into pleasure. First he had to make this decision.

He brought his attention to the path ahead of them, which was getting a little bumpy with tree roots. "I should like you to be proud of whatever it is I end up doing."

"I am proud of you no matter your circumstances." Amy added more lightly, "Even when you were an eighteen-year-old without any glory to your name, I was still so very proud of you. And I suspect you will naturally choose a career that makes me even more proud."

"All I know at the moment is that I want to be with you. Everything else..." He almost hedged his words and called it *bewildering*. But this was Amy. Nate wanted to be even more honest with her than he was with himself. "Every other thought of the future frightens me."

Amy's fingers tightened around his hand. "Then I shall try to suppose I know best. I want to wake each morning with you. If you are captain of a ship, I can do that in your cabin as well as anywhere else."

It was true: he could bring her along to command Uncle Graham's fleet of merchantmen. But her health was weak at the best of times, although he liked to think she was looking healthier from John's medicine. Her goiter seemed smaller, more of a lump than a globe protruding from beneath her chin. Still, the coast of Africa killed the healthiest of sailors with yellow fever, malaria, and dysentery.

Nate didn't dare risk Amy's life. He would rather be away from her for three years than watch her catch her death.

"What else do you want?" he pressed. "What if we were to go to the wilds of Ireland with no one but my brother for civilized company?"

She laughed. "You are being dreadfully cruel to Ireland. I'm quite sure everyone there is even better company than we English." Amy stepped closer to him, her free hand sliding up his arm so she now held him at both the palm and the elbow. "If it were up to me, I would live in Portsmouth. Near to Henriette, and only a half-day's ride away from Mary and the boys."

Nate could see it now. A townhouse of their own, one that could be managed by a few day servants who could go home each evening.

Close enough to the harbor that Nate could walk down to the sea each morning and take stock of the ships. He could keep a pleasure boat to take Amy sailing on summer days.

"What else?"

"Well, I don't mind only using honey for my sweets and I can make do without cotton, but I should like to drink tea in my own home."

"Tea—and French wine," Nate agreed.

"And..." Amy trailed off, though her whole face had lifted heavenward with a thought.

Perhaps she had the same fear he did: the life they were imagining was an extended holiday. Good meals, good company, good weather.

It hardly answered the question of what Nate would do with his days, nor of how he would pay for the townhouse and tea and wine.

"And?" he prompted.

"And I should like you to continue the fight against the slave trade. You don't talk about it often, but when you do, I can tell it is almost too important to you to admit." Amy leaned her head against his shoulder. "I don't know how best you could do it, but I think you should find a way, even if it means we can't afford tea and French wine."

Nate slid his arm behind her back. They had to change their pace so they could walk together like that, two bodies in tandem, and soon they would need to turn back to the hall anyhow.

For now, he enjoyed the moment. After all, it was the first time in his life that he could picture his future as a whole.

Amy as his wife.

Portsmouth as his home.

The African Institution as his calling.

"I know how I can make all of this come true," he told Amy.

"Then we must celebrate," she replied, and pulled him against a trunk of a tree.

Nate admitted to himself, as he kissed her in that wonderfully familiar way, that the six years had been worth the wait.

Epilogue

Portsmouth, Hampshire

1844 (Twenty-four years later)

By the time the carriage pulled up to 14 Bath Square, Amy's bones had been so jostled one way and the other that she no longer felt them at all. She had to kick out her feet a few times before there was enough feeling in them to step onto the street.

She gave the coachman a nice tip anyhow. It wasn't his fault she had been traveling for two months straight and was now chomping at the bit to get home. He was only the last person she had to encounter before she could cross the threshold back into her own home.

She had been apart from Nate for too long.

As the man-of-all-work took her luggage, Amy rushed into the townhouse as fast as her protesting bones would allow. She hadn't sent word ahead of herself, afraid the ferry would be held up in the storm, and so Nate might very well have gone to his club or down to the harbor to swap stories with incoming sailors.

Instinct told her, however, that he was somewhere near. Not in the parlor, which stood empty; not in his study, which didn't even have a fire in its hearth; nor was he upstairs in their bedroom or his dressing room. Amy ended up climbing all the way to the top of the building, through the hatch door, and up onto the widow's walk before she found her husband.

He stood under the little black-roofed cupola that looked towards the harbor. His brass pocket telescope—a gift from his siblings on the occasion of his fortieth birthday—was trained on the horizon. His wool coat flapped in the bitter breeze.

Amy allowed herself one silent moment of joy at the sight of him. The eighteen-year-old version of him had been full of both enthusiasm and insecurity, anxious to prove himself equal to every gentleman he might ever encounter. The twenty-four-year-old Nate had been prouder of what made him different, yet still he never would have admitted to a secret desire of watching the harbor all day.

Amy's heart almost burst with love at seeing her husband so happily himself.

It didn't quite burst, though, and she was impatient to take him in her arms again. "You've been watching the wrong horizon."

Nate swung around. A grin broke out across his cheeks—pink from the wind—almost immediately. "I wasn't expecting you for two days at least!"

But already he grabbed her up so they were nothing but a jumble of two bodies. Hugging him to her heart, feeling the scratch of his cheek against hers, letting his arms squeeze the breath out of her lungs—it was all wonderful.

Not as wonderful as the kiss that came next, though. That made her feel like she was back in Egypt with the sun warming her skin.

When Nate finally pulled away, he kept one hand on her cheek, the other around her back. "You look well."

"I am." She still had heart palpitations now and then, she still got fatigued, and her hair was still desperately thin, but John's medicine had done wonders for her. The goiter had all but disappeared within a year, she had gained back some weight, and most days, she felt just as well as the next person.

Amy turned her scrutiny to Nate. He had earned more wrinkles since she had left, and she saw now the pink in his cheeks was from the sun and not the wind. His hair, too, was far more silver than she had remembered. "Are you well?"

"In body, anyhow. And much better in spirit now that you're back." He kissed her again. Amy relished the smell of him as much as the spark of his lips on hers.

She was the one to pull away this time. She rotated them so that she could lean against his chest while looking at the flat line of the harbor. "What are you watching for?"

"The *Alberta* is supposed to arrive. Supposedly she is trading in cotton and tobacco, but at Sierra Leone, I heard she had flown under an American flag and taken two hundred fifty people to Havana."

On behalf of the African Institution, Nate had visited Sierra Leone to write a report on the current state of the slave trade. His trip had been the instigation for Amy to join Sophia, Ellen, Lydia, and Caroline on an adventure to Egypt.

She had borne his absence slightly better in the company of her sisters-in-law and with new things to see and learn every day.

Still, Amy wasn't eager to part from Nate again anytime soon. "Is the navy going to seize her before she gets to harbor?"

"The Admiralty is going to order an inspection. If they have been idiot enough to leave the supplies on board, we can seize the ship. More likely, they will have refitted in Havana and will return looking like the proper British outfit they claim to be." Pessimism weighed down his voice, and Nate held her even closer in his arms. "Still, I'm sure between the authorities and my more charming friends at the docks, we can find *some* way to harass the ship's company into admitting what they have been up to."

Amy leaned her head against his shoulder. How she had missed *this*: the moments together when they could share each other's burdens. "You do your share in this fight and then some. I love you for that."

He nuzzled his lips against her ear. "But do you still want to be married to me after spending two months with my sisters?"

"We had a lovely time. Though Ellen has far more energy than a person should, and Sophia flirts with every man she meets, and Caroline and Lydia both spent half the time worried about their children. Despite all that, they remain some of my favorite people." Turning in his arms, Amy dotted her nose against his. "Perhaps because they remind me so much of you."

They kissed again. This one lasted even longer. It practically spread her legs with desire. When they separated for a breath, Nate murmured, "Is there any other news we must desperately share with each other?"

"Not that I can think of."

"Then shall we go inside?"

Amy grinned. "I am feeling in need of a lie-down before lunch, and I very much need your attention to make sure I don't fall off the bed."

"I shall make sure the servants are informed." Nate smirked. Then, hand in hand, they headed for the bed that hadn't been properly used for far too long.

Amy wasn't sure exactly what they would end up doing in it that day. Yet she was sure it would leave her with that wonderful, everlasting feeling that she had chosen happiness, once and for all.

AUTHOR'S NOTE

This story has been sitting in my heart for a long time, and it was an absolute dream to finally write.

In the spring of 2021, I started mapping out the Preston family's stories. I knew from the start that Nate would be a naval captain, giving me a perfect opportunity to dive into my favorite Austen novel and write a *Persuasion*-inspired romance. In my version, I wanted to imagine that our heroine did not lose her "bloom of youth" simply because she was the ripe old age of twenty-eight but instead because she actually wasn't physically well.

In my first plot sketch for this book, I wrote as a problem for a future self: *what illness would make her unwell but not be life threatening?*

Then I ended up in the ER with heart palpitations so fast that the intake nurse actually read my heartrate aloud to the other nurses in surprise. That—plus my unintended weight loss (I thought I was just *really* good at eliminating a cookie or two from my day), hair loss, and some other weird things going on in my body—led to a diagnosis of a type of hyperthyroidism called Grave's disease.

(It's named for a doctor, Thomas Grave, and we really need to start a petition for the medical community to change the name.)

Suddenly, I had my disease for Amy.

Elements of her experience are pulled from my own experience, especially before my medicine kicked in, while others are heightened for dramatic effect.

In modern medicine, Grave's disease is very treatable with a variety of interventions. In the Regency period, it wasn't even a named condition in European medicine. They did have treatments for some of the symptoms, and John's concoction of herbs comes from ayurvedic medicine. Untreated, Grave's disease *can* be grave, but I decided to use romance author magic to grant Amy the happily-ever-after a modern patient can expect, which is improved symptoms with the intervention of medicine.

(Next time, I'm going to write to my future self: *how does this character become a millionaire?*)

As for Nate, I went down a very deep research hole about the British Royal Navy's fight against the slave trade, and about 1% of that made it into this book. British abolitionists believed that eliminating the trade of slaves would cause the practice of slavery to die off naturally. From the abolition of the slave trade in 1807 until the 1860s, the British Royal Navy devoted a few ships to patrol the Atlantic to enforce these prohibitions. There were lots of challenges, primarily that the slave trade was an international practice upon which dozens of countries depended economically. At best, the Preventive Squadron made life difficult for slavers. However, even if it didn't bring about an end to slavery on its own, I imagine the people saved by the Preventive Squadron were grateful it fought its unfightable fight.

To learn more about hyperthyroidism in the Regency, the Preventive Squadron, court martials, Portsmouth and all the research fodder that went into this book, please sign up for my newsletter! It is free, and you'll get a password to unlock my Research Deep Dive archives. Here is the link:

https://bit.ly/katherinegrantresearch

Thank you to everyone who helped bring this book to market! Nate and Amy's story would not be the same without developmental edits from Abby at Victory Editing, the moon would have been waxing and waning in the same scene without copy edits from Sara Israel at Thimble Editorial, and I am always grateful for these gorgeous covers from Julia Gerbach. I also want to thank my sister, Sarah, who gave me feedback on an early draft, and my brother, Jim, both because I don't give him enough attention and because I thought of him (a major in the Army Reserves) while trying to get into Nate's head.

As always, thank you to my husband Michael for his general support and also specifically for his support as I live the ups and downs of Grave's disease!

Keep Reading: The Countess Without Conviction

For nine years, Ellen and Max have been happily married at Northfield Hall. Now that Max has inherited his father's title and estate at Montchampion Manor, their marriage – and ideals – are put to the test. Read on to start their new story!

From the sitting room of Montchampion Manor, Ellen could not see Max.

More properly said, from the blue wallpapered room designated as the family's sitting room—only for use when there was absolutely no company expected!—Ellen could see the last quarter mile of the curved driveway, but Max was not to be seen.

Which did not mean he was not currently on the driveway. Even had she been in the front sitting room with its gilded ceiling and expansive windows, she would not have been able to see *more* than the last curve of the driveway, since the entire five-mile drive had been designed to keep visitors from glimpsing the great house until its very last leg, when the trees cleared and one had a direct prospect of the marble monstrosity waiting to intimidate.

And while Max might not be on the last curve of the driveway, that did not mean that he was not at this very moment somewhere along its five miles, galloping forward at full speed to finally return to his family.

In any case, the dowager countess would not hear of them waiting for Max in any room except the blue sitting room. She disapproved of the way Ellen stood with her forehead nearly pressed against the window, but though Ellen could feel and absorb that disapproval, she did not have to change her behavior just because Lady Odette willed it, and so she remained, looking out the window for signs of her husband.

Rosalind, Ellen's eight-year-old, sat with great composure on the sofa with Lady Odette. "We must be ladylike as we wait, Mama," she admonished Ellen, repeating a dictate her grandmother had said when the note arrived two hours ago, announcing that Max was to be expected that afternoon.

"The earl will not get here any sooner if we smear the windows with our anticipation," Lady Odette added, her words a little thick with her French accent.

Even after six months, Ellen was not accustomed to Max being the earl. The Earl of Meretta. Which made her the Countess of Meretta. Those titles belonged to other people, in Ellen's mind; the earl had always been a political adversary to Papa, and even after she married Max, she had cringed if she heard the appellation.

Now when people said the Earl of Meretta, they meant Max. Charming, arrogant, thoughtful, infuriating, wonderful Max. And Ellen got caught between her instinctual cringe and the comforting embrace of love that came with thinking of her husband.

Lady Odette poured peppermint tea into her cup with precision, allowing the tisane to tinkle against the delicate, imported Chinese porcelain. "I daresay the wait *would* be easier if we had tea."

The wait would be easier if they didn't have to do it together. Ellen would have been perfectly happy to greet Max on her own, or to gather up their five children and walk out to meet him, or busy her hands with some task instead of watching the road. Yet Lady Odette had *insisted* that there was a proper way to do this. Banish the four younger children to the nursery – "One does not want to overwhelm the poor man the very minute he walks in with their youthful cries!" – assemble in the blue room – "He will be famished and thirsty and need refreshments immediately" – and wait in near stillness – "What better way to greet the earl than by presenting a perfect tableau?"

And since Ellen *had* eradicated tea and coffee from Montchampion Manor – along with other imports like sugar, cotton, rice, and tobacco – she was trying to accommodate her mother-in-law with these requests to be "ladylike."

It would be easier if Lady Odette would just move into the dower house and live her own life.

Suddenly, Max appeared on the drive. He rode his gray stallion (named Shortcake by Rosalind four years ago) and moved in a canter that he made look as natural as walking. His blond hair peeked out from under his hat, his white skin a little tanner than she remembered, his arms and legs looking just as muscular as when he left.

Ellen had to curl her fingers into fists to keep herself from racing from the room to meet him outside.

She hadn't seen him for four months. He had been in London, where as a member of the House of Lords, he had been required to attend the trial of Queen Caroline or be fined hundreds of pounds. And Ellen had been here, trying to convert Montchampion Manor from the seat of an egotistical aristocrat to another Northfield Hall.

They were accustomed to being apart for Parliamentary seasons. Ellen hated London, but she and Max both wanted him there, first as an elected MP in the House of Commons and now, as an earl, in his birthright seat in the House of Lords.

The difference was that in years prior, Ellen had always been left behind at Northfield Hall. Her family's home, where she knew and trusted just about everyone she came across. Where she had a place in the carpentry workshop whenever she could make it there. Where the whole community tried to live by its best morals by avoiding imports and sharing the profits of the estate.

She always missed Max when he was gone. She had never before *needed* him so desperately.

It was shocking how angry she was at him for leaving her.

Because they were waiting for him in the blue room instead of rushing out to meet him, it was another eternity after Ellen sighted him before Max finally entered. His hat, gloves, and traveling coat had disappeared. He spotted Rosalind first and gathered her up in his arms, swinging her through the air. "You've gotten at least a foot taller!"

Lady Odette extended her hand from where she sat on the sofa. "Welcome back, Meretta."

When he had been viscount – the mere heir to the earldom – his parents had called him by his courtesy title, Berwick. Now, his name had changed, but still, his mother refused to use the Christian name she herself had given him.

Max bowed in front of her dutifully and kissed her hand. "Are you well, Mother?"

"Well enough." She held onto his hand and murmured something in French, too soft and low for Ellen to hear.

Ellen knew she should not feel neglected. A heart had space for a daughter, a mother, *and* a wife.

It was just that the room felt so crowded, and Max hadn't yet greeted her.

She moved from the window. Rosalind, glowing with excitement at Max's arrival, rushed to her side. At last, Max was turning away from his mother. He was looking over his shoulder, and soon his gaze would land on her.

Ellen opened her mouth to say the perfect thing. Yet when finally she was looking directly into his hazel eyes, all that came out was, "I trust it did not rain while you were traveling."

He blinked in surprise. He bowed at the neck, a formal gesture he would offer a stranger. "Thank you, it did not."

For a moment, they stared at each other. Max did not approve of kissing in front his mother, yet Ellen waited, wondering if she could hold out her arms and receive a hug. They hadn't seen each other for four months. They hadn't held each other for four months. And Ellen knew Max was a physical man; when they had first met, he couldn't keep his hands off her even though he should have.

Surely he was yearning for touch as much as she was.

Unless, as Lady Odette kept hinting, he had a mistress in London making sure he had all the touches he required.

Rosalind squirmed out from where Ellen gripped her two shoulders. "Do you want to see my paintings? Grandmama says my watercolors are very good. They are in the nursery. Grandmama says you don't want to go there. May I fetch them and bring them down?"

Max took his daughter's outstretched hand. "I should love to see them, but only if you take me up to them in the nursery. Is that where you have hidden your brothers and sisters, too?"

"Oh yes, only *I* didn't hide them. Grandmama said you weren't to be disturbed by their wailing the very first minute you came home."

"Ah, well, Grandmama doesn't realize how much I have missed their wailing." The two were already halfway into the corridor. Max paused, looking over his shoulder at Ellen again. The good humor he had offered Rosalind seemed to disappear as he asked, "Aren't you coming, too, Mama?"

Ellen didn't know why she said no, but she did.

Someone—Ellen? Mother?—had determined they would celebrate his homecoming with an elegant supper, and so Max ignored his better instincts and reported to the red sitting room in his formal black evening jacket.

His mother had beaten him there. She wore an extravagant silk gown adorned with golden braids that matched the gilded-framed paintings on the wall. As usual, her silver hair towered over her head, and a heavy necklace of dark sapphires sparkled on her neck.

"You look just like Meretta," she said as he bent to kiss her hand. "Your father, I mean."

Max tried to hide his grimace. His relationship with his father had been complicated for most of his life and then, for the last nine years, it had been non-existent. He had chosen to marry Ellen, daughter of the earl's political enemy, and live the questionable lifestyle of

Northfield Hall, where only British goods were consumed and all the estate's profits were shared among every single person who lived and worked there.

He had no choice in assuming his father's place as earl of Meretta. That was predestined by British law, avoidable only by death.

But if he could help it, Max wouldn't be like his father in any other way, shape, or form.

Her eyes adjusting to something behind him, Mother added, "Is he not very handsome, my dear?"

Max turned. Ellen stood close to the door, as if she were already considering making a run for it. She had changed into her version of an evening gown. It was elegant in its simplicity: perfectly tailored dark blue wool with lace trim to define the shape of the bodice. Max knew this gown well, had seen her wear it a hundred times, had missed it while he was in London.

His mother said, "Meretta, you must buy your wife more jewels. She refuses to wear mine, and without them, anyone could mistake her for a governess."

Ellen's cheeks flushed. Max opened his mouth to defend her, but she beat him to it: "There is no one here to mistake me, unless you think *Meretta* has forgotten who I am in his long absence."

Her venom surprised Max. His wife was not a person who laced her words as attacks. She was earnest to a fault; even when Max himself had insulted her family when they first met, she had never returned the vitriol.

Neither did she use his title, unless they were in formal company. Even then, she was more likely to say "my husband." They had never discussed it, yet Max had always known that she did it purposefully, since he had chafed for so long at being defined by his title instead of as a person in his own right.

He didn't like how she wielded it now. Worse was how she didn't even look at Max as she threw out this rebuttal. She drifted instead to a different corner of the room, almost as far from Max and his mother as she could get, and put all her attention on the painting of a joyful family and their faithful servant.

Max knew Ellen was unhappy at Montchampion Manor. Their reunion had been awkward enough to hint that things had only gotten worse instead of better in his absence.

Now Max feared it was *him* she was upset with, and not the circumstances.

"You are unforgettable," he said in reply to her barb, "and the gown needs no adornment when it is worn by a beauty."

Ellen didn't turn from the painting. Of course not. She didn't like manufactured compliments traded in drawing rooms. Max wished he had ended his sentence with "unforgettable."

From her seat, Mother chimed in, "Well said, Meretta. Surely you feel lucky, Ellen, that your husband is so charming."

Which made Max want to expel his mother from the room entirely. What he needed was a moment—or an hour—alone with Ellen to sort out what was going on.

Mother would not stand for such things, not when the china was already laid for supper.

Still, he could say *something* to save both him and Ellen from being forced into false agreement. He put his hand on his mother's to quiet her, and was about to come up with the perfect response, when the butler—who was new and whose name Max did not yet know—announced supper was ready.

"Excellent." Mother rose and tucked her hand into Max's elbow. "You will lead me in, Meretta. A mother misses her son when he is gone for so long."

As did a wife. But Max found himself without an option. He looked back over his shoulder to see how Ellen responded.

She still stood by that painting, her gaze fixed on something small and faraway.

Download The Countess Without Conviction as an ebook to keep reading!

ABOUT THE AUTHOR

Katherine Grant writes award-winning Regency Romance novels for the modern reader. Her writing has been recognized by Foreword INDIES Book of the Year Awards, the Next Generation Indie Book Awards, the National Indie Excellence Awards, the Romance Slam Jam Emma Awards, and the Shelf Unbound Indie Book Awards. If you love ballgowns, secret kisses, and social commentary, a book hangover is coming your way.

Katherine also hosts the Historical Romance Sampler podcast! Find out more at www.katherinegrantromance.com

THANKS FOR READING!

I am so grateful you joined me on this journey back in time. If you enjoyed it, please consider leaving a rating or review with book retailers, Goodreads, or wherever else you talk about books!

Until next time...